WINGS OVER TALERA

WINGS OVER TALERA

BEING

THE SECOND BOOK OF
THE TALERA CYCLE

by

Charles Allen Gramlich

The Borgo Press
An Imprint of Wildside Press

MMVII

Copyright © 2007 by Charles Allen Gramlich

All rights reserved.
No part of this book may be reproduced in any form
without the expressed written consent
of the author and publisher.
Printed in the United States of America

FIRST EDITION

CONTENTS

About the Author 8
What Has Gone Before 9
Introduction...11
Prologue: Ruenn Begins His Story 15

Chapter One: Coming Home..21
Chapter Two: The End of an Idyll 27
Chapter Three: Shot Down in Flames..................................34
Chapter Four: On the River to Timmuzz 41
Chapter Five: Seat of Empire..48
Chapter Six: A Thin Roll of Parchment................................56
Chapter Seven: Betrayer 59
Chapter Eight: At Dungeon's Heart......................................63
Chapter Nine: A Morning of Wings 69
Chapter Ten: City of Outlaws 75
Chapter Eleven: The "Rattling Saber" 80
Chapter Twelve: Kellet's Bay...89
Chapter Thirteen: Demon-Haunted Dark..............................93
Chapter Fourteen: The Rider...98
Chapter Fifteen: A Tale Spun by Night 105
Chapter Sixteen: In the Memory of Ruins 114
Chapter Seventeen: Brother's Keeper..................................121
Chapter Eighteen: Storm Queen 130
Chapter Nineteen: Going Below 140
Chapter Twenty: When Battle Is Joined 149
Chapter Twenty-One: The Black Pyramid...........................155
Chapter Twenty-Two: Oath of Fealty 162
Chapter Twenty-Three: Blood for Blood..............................172
Chapter Twenty-Four: At the Point of Death.......................180

Chapter Twenty-Five: Heart of War 184
Chapter Twenty-Six: Wrath 191
Chapter Twenty-Seven: Vohanna 200
Chapter Twenty-Eight: Wings Over the Jungle 208
Chapter Twenty-Nine: Afterwar 217

Epilogue: "What About Their Eyes?" 221

To My Father

J. V. Gramlich

And To My Son

Joshua Gramlich

ABOUT THE AUTHOR

CHARLES ALLEN GRAMLICH grew up on a farm in Arkansas, near the foothills of the Ozark Mountains, then moved to the New Orleans area in 1986. He's since sold several novels and numerous short stories. His tales, while mostly in the genres of horror, science fiction, and fantasy, have also included westerns, children's stories, mainstream fiction, slipstream works, and experimental pieces. He has also published poetry and nonfiction, the latter ranging from reference works to articles on writing. He refuses to comment, however, on rumors that most of his work is actually written by Ruenn Maclang.

Charles is a member of REHupa (the Robert E. Howard United Press Association), HWA (the Horror Writers Association), and SFPA (the Science Fiction Poetry Association). He produces a regular column on writing for *The Illuminata*, an online magazine, and is the horror moderator at United Sci Fi Forums. His blog can be found at:

http://charlesgramlich.blogspot.com

WHAT HAS GONE BEFORE

In 1914, on a sea voyage to Japan, Ruenn Maclang and his brother Bryce stumbled on a gate to another world—a world named Talera. They were following the trail of some of the vessel's crew—including their cousin Eric Ryall—who had shipped with them but disappeared. The gate exploded, sucking Ruenn and Bryce through it, but separating them. The first book in this trilogy, *Swords of Talera*, was Ruenn's story of what happened to him on the other side of that gate.

Ruenn was cast into the Taleran Sea and rescued by a dwarfish race of humans named the Koro. It wasn't long, however, before the Koro met the Klar—who were reptiles, pirates, and slavers. Captured by the Klar, Ruenn met a lovely human woman named Rannon Jystral. He found himself attracted to her, but they, too, were separated.

Ruenn learned the discipline of the sword. He learned how to kill. He fought his way free of slavery and in time gathered a band of warriors around him and ventured to the Klar homeland in search of Rannon, and in hopes of discovering his brother, his cousin, and his shipmates. There, he led a slave revolt and overthrew a nation, but he could not locate any of those he sought from earth. He *did* find Rannon, and discovered that she was a princess in the distant island kingdom of Nyshphal. But he already loved her, and he told her that. She told him the same.

At the end of *Swords of Talera*, Ruenn returned to Earth to see about the rest of his family. Though not revealed in that book, Ruenn found his immediate family—parents and two sisters—dead, for decades had passed on our world during his one year absence on Talera. He enlisted the aid of a

WINGS OVER TALERA, BY CHARLES ALLEN GRAMLICH

distant relative to see that money was provided for his sisters' descendents, and he gave that relative the manuscript for *Swords of Talera*.

But Talera called. Rannon called. And there was the need in him to find Bryce and Eric, still lost somewhere on that violent yet beautiful new world. This book, *Wings Over Talera*, is the story of what happens when Ruenn goes back.

INTRODUCTION

By One Who Has Met Ruenn Maclang

October is a month of cold rains and of autumn leaves piled high and burning. It is a month of corpse-gray fogs that twine in low places, and of shadows that do not flee the rising moon. It was in October that I first met a man known as Ruenn Maclang, and it was amid the early frosts of that month, in another year, when he returned. I was standing at my cabin window, watching pale Luna hanging over the wind-tossed trees, when a dark figure came from the forest. I knew at once who it must be.

I met him at the door and held out my hand. "Ruenn," I said. "It's good to see you again."

"As it is you, Charles," he said.

"I've been expecting you," I told him.

He looked at me strangely.

"Or at least I've been expecting *something* odd to happen today."

He nodded in agreement. "I too have had that feeling this day."

"Come in," I invited.

He did so, a tall, lean man, with dark brown hair hanging long. He was dressed in black jeans and a t-shirt. A white scar twisting along the left side of his jaw, coupled with eyes that glittered green, made his face seem cold. Yet, his smile was warm when it came.

I motioned him to an old recliner and sat on the worn couch facing him. I had thought often of seeing this man again. There were many things I wanted to ask him. At our first meeting he had handed me a book called *Swords of*

WINGS OVER TALERA, BY CHARLES ALLEN GRAMLICH

Talera. In it, a man bearing the name Ruenn Maclang is transported to an alien world of swords and savage warriors. Separated from his only brother, who has been drawn to the planet with him, Ruenn fights his way across a quarter of that world, finding slavery and escape, finding honor in the bloody heart of war, finding loyal friends and the touch of a beautiful woman.

But *not* finding his brother.

At first, of course, I had taken *Swords of Talera* to be simply an adventure novel. Then a series of strange mysteries created doubts in my mind. According to what records I could find amid the tattered documents of decades past, Ruenn Maclang had been born in 1888 and had disappeared in 1914 on a sea voyage that he captained to Japan. His brother had been with him. Neither had been seen again—dead or alive. And over two years before this night, the man who claimed now to be Maclang had given me gold coins minted by an empire unknown to Earth's history.

It was almost as if they came from another world.

Yes, there was much I wanted to ask this man. But now, seated across from him in my book-cluttered living room, all questions seemed lost to me. It remained quiet between us, the only sounds the crackling of oak logs in the fireplace and the ticking of the mantel clock. It was he who broke the silence.

Ruenn rose and walked over to me. He grasped my shoulder with powerful fingers and drew me to my feet. His eyes seemed to read me.

"There is something you wish," he said. "What is it?"

"I want to know the truth," I blurted.

His lips quirked, and he nodded. "Very well," he said, so quietly that I scarcely heard him.

His hand dropped from my shoulder and he turned to look into the fire. The flames glinted off the sharp planes of his face. Then his back straightened.

"If it is the truth you want then you shall have it," he said. "My name is Ruenn Maclang and I have been to a planet called Talera. There is a woman there that I love. Her name is Rannon Jystral. I have made a place for myself in her world, and now I call it *my* world as well. Is that the truth you wanted, my friend?"

I said nothing for a moment. I had known what his answer must be, had promised myself not to accept it. What he claimed to be truth was impossible. Yet, with him standing there before me I could not think him a liar.

"I believe you," I said.

He sighed, and I realized that he had hoped for and wanted my belief. Perhaps he had needed it. He went and sat down again, seeming heavy with exhaustion. I asked him why.

"To cross the distance to Earth takes something out of one," he said.

"Then why come?"

"There are always old acquaintances to renew," he said. "And, too, I wanted to ask after the money that I left with you on my previous visit."

I nodded. "For your sisters' descendents. They've been well taken care of. Grants. And trust funds, of course."

"Have there been any questions? Inquiries?"

"A few. Nothing serious. The trail is well hidden."

"Good," he said. "I appreciate your efforts on my behalf."

"You're welcome," I said, smiling. "And there is something else as well."

He frowned in question.

I went over to my bookshelf and removed a slim paperback volume with a rather garish cover. I handed it to him and sat down. He looked at the title and then turned to the first page. He read for a moment before looking up and laughing.

"So, the record of my first adventure was published," he said.

"Yes. It sold well. But tell me. What has happened to you since the night we last met, when you left Earth to return to your new world of Talera?"

"Much," he said, leaning forward.

—Charles Allen Gramlich

Prologue

Ruenn Begins His Story

I sat by a small fire, in a clearing within the pine-forested hills of northern Arkansas, waiting for something to happen while I scratched my name idly in the dirt with a stick—Ruenn Maclang. About me, night's face was dark and cold and lovely. Above me, the stars seemed as clear and brittle as icicle teeth. Looking up at those stars, I could see the familiar constellations of my youth, the big and little dipper, and to the north the pole star.

Seeing those brilliant and familiar points reminded me of my father, Kendall, who had taught me the constellations, and of late evenings in the California vineyards of my mother's family where the first star was a joy. But that was youth. There are other heavens that are important to me now. They hold no stars. I waited in this clearing tonight, not to watch the skies of Earth but to be drawn back to a new land under those other skies, the skies of a world called Talera.

I had arrived on Earth sixty days before this night. I had taken care of a need that had to be met. Now I would return the same way I had come. For there was a gate in this clearing. It could not be seen in the blanket of fallen leaves or the thin topsoil. It could not be heard in the late autumn stillness of a chilled night. It could not even be opened from where I sat. But it could be opened—it would be opened—on Talera. And when it was, I would be drawn through it to the place where—with my parents and sisters dead—I called home.

I closed my eyes to better picture that home. There was one image, one face that I most wanted to see. But it did not come at first. Instead, I saw the bright flash of steel and heard the sharp twang of releasing arrows. There had been a battle fought two months before this night, on the very day that I had left Talera for Earth. These scenes had been a part of it.

With my friends—Heril Rolvfshern, Valyan Tiersal, and others—I had been flying slowly north within the borders of the island kingdom of Nyshphal, the home of Rannon Jystral, the woman I loved. Above our open airship rode the winter sun of Talera, and to the north lay the gate that would take me to Earth. And then there had been smoke on the horizon.

That smoke rose from a burning village called Rakii, which lies on the Sahtern River in a wild land where sheep[1] are the only livelihood of a poor people. I had ordered our airship down to investigate, and we surprised dark raiders at their work. They were mounted upon hyr-qualls, saddle lizards that somewhat resemble an iguana of monstrous size, and they were dressed as outlaws. This they were not. Their steel was too good, their armor too well matched. I did not know what they were, though I was to eventually find out.

Despite their formidable appearance, however, the raiders had not been prepared for much resistance to their attack. And they had received little where the villagers were concerned. This changed abruptly when our ship flew down low over their heads and two dozen trained warriors dropped in on them from the sky.

Our pilot brought the ship to man-height and I was first over the side rail, landing lightly on my feet with a naked sword drawn in one fist and a crossbow locked and loaded in the other. The raiders gaped, smoke and heat rippling in the air above them, and I bow-shot the first one who recovered himself, the quarrel catching him high in the throat and blowing him back over his saddle.

---

[1] I used the term "sheep" for the animals that I saw in Rakii because they were clearly descended from Earth ancestors brought to Talera by the Asadhie race that created this artificial world. Many other Earth species can be found on Talera as well: horses, hawks, cattle of various kinds, deer, pigs, and elephants. Among Earth plants transported to Talera are oak and apple trees, rice, wheat, grapes, and onions.—Ruenn Maclang.

Wings Over Talera, by Charles Allen Gramlich

Sheep milled in the dirt street. People ran. Our enemies lowered their lances and came against us. I heard the screams of the villagers for a moment, then nothing to distract me as my mind centered on the task at hand.

There were men around me now. My men from the ship. Other crossbows released. Other enemy saddles were emptied. A red-bearded raider shouted at his fellows to kill us, and by that I knew him for a leader. I charged him even as he moved toward me, his mount snarling and showing its teeth. A hyr-quall is trained to attack anything that is not on its back. To distract this one, I hurled the unloaded crossbow into its face. It shied, and I ducked beneath the lance tip of its master and sliced upward with my blade, nearly severing the man's arm above the elbow.

Blood sprayed. A new scream cut through the old ones. The fellow reeled in his saddle and I got hold of his boot with my hands and hurled him from his seat. The hyr-quall struck at me over its shoulder and I hammered its face with the pommel of my blade to make it behave. Then I mounted. I had ridden a hyr-quall before. Once. I hoped that I remembered what I had learned.

Heril was near me. I saw him axe down a second raider who he had thrown from the saddle. Valyan had taken yet a third hyr-quall for his own and I signaled him to join me. Heril mounted too, and the three of us moved up the street toward the far end of the town where half a dozen of the enemy had begun setting fire to the huts. They seemed more intent on doing damage than on acquiring loot for themselves. This, too, told me that we were dealing with no common marauders.

There were extra lances beneath my right knee and I drew one out and weighed it in my hand. I knew little of mounted spear work—swords were my strength—but I knew enough not to let better lancers close with me. Our foes dropped their torches as we approached and couched their own lances. Our two groups charged at the same time.

The hyr-quall does not run as smoothly as a horse or a tasaber. They are more like drums, and now their feet were pounding and pounding. And the dust was rising around us. I saw the glittering heads of spears, heard the rattle of armor and the creak of leather.

At ten paces from our enemies, I stood in my stirrups and hurled my lance into a dark-clad marauder. The wedge-shaped head of the weapon shattered through the man's face-plate and exploded into splinters. He went backward, hauling convulsively on the reins, and the lizard that he was riding reared up on its hind legs and fell over into its fellows.

Chaos followed. One hyr-quall snapped its teeth into the neck of another. Heril went past the pile-up on the left, his Koro axe shearing through enemy bone and mail. Valyan's mount smashed head on into the imbroglio, but the Nak-scherii warrior had already loosed his feet from the stirrups and he somersaulted over the heap to safety. He left his lance buried in an enemy throat.

We closed on the survivors, our steel hacking. More of my men joined the slaughter, and in a few red moments the battle was over, though it would be long and long before the village would recover completely from its wounds. I left half my crew behind to start that recovery and flew on toward my meeting with a sphere gate. That could not be delayed if I wanted to reach Earth.

In the end, the battle had not delayed my quest. I'd made it to Earth. Now, tonight, I was going back to Talera. There, I would join the woman I intended to marry, and would begin another quest—to locate my brother Bryce, who had been drawn to Talera with me nearly two years before and who had never been found.

But I did not want to go back remembering blood. I opened my eyes from my thoughts and in that moment I saw Rannon's sweet face, Rannon Jystral, the dark-haired Taleran princess who had said she loved me. Her visage seemed to float in the clearing before me and I took it as a sign that the gate was near.

I waited, and there was no sound.

Then there was.

One moment there were the stars and the shadowy trees and the quiet. In the next there came a humming, and a gray, whirling vortex opened in the air a few feet from my fire. I stood up, dashed the flames to blackness, and went forward, carrying nothing with me save a present for Rannon.

WINGS OVER TALERA, BY CHARLES ALLEN GRAMLICH

I stepped into the swirling air and felt something pluck lightly at my body, at my clothes, at my hair. There was an instant of chill and of twisting in my stomach, an instant of pain. And then I stepped out of the same air onto a flat wheel of stone that lay half buried amid drifts of snow. It was morning in this place, the sun rising blue-white, and the breeze that stroked my body was that of Talera.

Of home.

Chapter One

Coming Home

Where before it had been dark, it now was light, the sharp-edged light of the Taleran dawn. I stepped down from the stone upon which I stood, and behind me a whisper died as a door into void closed. The prickling on my skin was gone as well. I was wholly of this world now, wholly of Talera. I breathed deeply, mouth open to taste the sweetness in the chill morning. The first sound of home that I heard was the wakening cry of the kryshawk, the second, the soft crunch of snow beneath a shifting boot.

Four figures stood before me, hooded and cloaked against the cold. All were human, though one bore the yellow eyes and green skin of a Llurn, of that people who call themselves Nakscherii. One was bearded; one was tall; one was broad; one was a woman. It was the last that I watched.

Rannon Jystral came forward across the snow and put herself into my arms. I held her tightly for a moment before kissing her. Valyan Tiersal—the Llurn—joined us, coming up to place a firm hand on my shoulder. I smiled at him as I clasped Rannon's slender form. The broad figure was Kreeg, once a gladiator, a rahnvin slave of the Klar. He nodded, shaved head bobbing once on a bull neck, but did not speak. His presence said enough.

The last of the four, with a face heavy and bearded, was a man named Tovaris. It was he who had opened the gate between Earth and Talera. From the stone wheel where I had stood he took up the toir'in-or, the milky jewel that held the power of the sphere gates inside it. He then turned and left the rest of us alone.

"Heril?" I asked, somewhat worried. I had expected the Koro warrior, perhaps my closest friend on Talera, to be here.

"His father," Valyan replied, knowing my unspoken concerns.

"I am sorry," I said.

"Heril swore he would return when matters were settled. That may not be soon, though. The Rolvfsherns are an important family among the Koro. His father was a leader among them."

"If word can be sent then I would like to send it," I said.

"I will see it done," Rannon said. "Our ships trade with Korosphal regularly now."

"And my brother?" I asked. "Bryce?"

"Nothing has been heard," Rannon answered. "But the word is spread and many are searching. For your cousin, Eric, as well. Or any sign of others from your Earth."

"Good," I said.

"And now we drink, yes?" Kreeg asked.

"And now we drink," I agreed.

It was only a short walk to the hunting lodge of Hurnan Jystral, father of Rannon and Emperor of Nyshphal. Other friends awaited us there, and for refreshments there were wines of Thresh and the Starkayan Islands, cheeses and meats from Pangala and northern Nyshphal, and—as always—rich verhlis tea by the flagon.

I drank and ate heartily. It seemed long that I had been away from decent food after the processed chicken and processed beef of the new Earth. It was good to bite into a terval steak and feel the juices bursting ripe into the mouth. It was good to have wine in brass goblets. And after the food there was good talk of many things, with Rannon always there beside me.

In the evening I forced my muscles to recall the sword while fencing with Valyan. After that I slept, as if that, too, I had been long without. I awoke refreshed in the very early morning, well before the dawn, and dressed myself in the clothes of two worlds. I pulled on the jeans I'd worn from Earth, and gray wool socks that were covered with soft boots of stugah hide. I slid on a shirt of green Starkayan silk that lay open at the throat, and tucked it into the jeans.

A heavy belt of Taleran make went around my waist, and stitched to it were the heavy steel hooks upon which I hung my scabbarded sword, the same sword I'd left behind on Talera so many days before. I drew the blade out and held it to the ceiling where the glassine light of the night lanterns burst along it. The glistening died when again the sword was sheathed.

It was early enough so that only the cook was awake, and he busy at laying a fire for the heating of the morning tea. I nodded to him and went out, striding through the chill and the low drifts of snow that lay on the ground. The sky was graying.

About a hundred tahng from the door of the lodge there ran a majestic gorge through which the morning mists flowed like rivers. I leaned against a boulder there and watched those mists. Dawn birds were just beginning to hunt, wheeling about me in search of early rising insects. There was little wind.

I was still there half a dhaur[2] later when Rannon came up and took my hand. She was dressed in trousers of tanned leather, rust-colored boots, and a white silk shirt beneath a brocaded vest of yellow and green. I loved the heart shape of her face, and the brilliant violet-blue of her eyes against her dark hair, and the clean scent of her skin. The two of us stood quietly for a time, feeling comfortable there together, and at last I turned to her as if to speak. She hushed me with a hand over my mouth.

"Wait a bit," she whispered.

A moment later the rising sun touched the great atmospheric shield that envelops Talera, and jade and purple streamers of light burst outward like wagon spokes from a central rotating core of gold. The display lasted only seconds and was gone. It is called the dawn lights by most cultures

---

[2]The common Taleran measures of distance and time are: Distance—1 Heka = 9.18 in.; 4 Hekas is 1 Tahng = 1.02 yards; 2500 Tahngs is 1 Verlang = 1.449 miles. Time—1 Shri = 2.34 sec.; 100 Shri is 1 Dhorrin = 3.9 min.; 20 Dhorrin is 1 Dhaur = 78 min.—Ruenn Maclang.

and occurs only in northern areas. Rannon had told me of them before, and of the belief in some religions that the lights are a sign of the sky menstruating. Knowing of them was not the same as seeing them, however. I stood in awe of their beauty.

Even after nearly two years on Talera, it was still hard for me to believe that this was an artificial world condensed from the heart of a gas-giant planet. The advanced race who built it—the Asadhie—may have been cruel, but they were skilled at creation.

The atmospheric shield that surrounds the planet protects the living world from the poisonous gases above. And somehow the sun and moons have been placed inside that shield, though I suspect some kind of optical illusion gives those orbs the appearance of rising and setting naturally. Rumors have it that Taleran adventurers have even tried to reach the moons aboard powerful flyers. There are some who claim to have succeeded, though I do not know the truth of such tales.

Only with the ending of the dawn display did Rannon turn and kiss me. She told me that she loved me, and I said the same as I gave her the present I had brought her from Earth. She gasped in surprise, then clapped her hands and laughed as she kissed me again.

She thought it only a clever necklace at first, till I showed her how the hands moved and what they represented. That left her even more enthralled. Hers was the only watch on Talera, though there are timekeeping devices such as sundials and water clocks. I'd had the devil's own time persuading a watchmaker on Earth to make me a chronometer that measured twenty, extra long hours instead of the usual twenty-four. It was worth it to see Rannon smile.

Soon, we heard the cook shout for breakfast and went in to eat among friends. After that we loaded our gear aboard Rannon's airship for a trip to the south, to Timmuzz, the capital of Nyshphal and Rannon's home. The ship we boarded was called the Aestor, named for a quicksilver little beast that haunts high mountain valleys. The Aestor is winged and fox-like, arctic colored. It hunts dangerous prey and its name seemed aptly applied to the swift and white ship

WINGS OVER TALERA, BY CHARLES ALLEN GRAMLICH

of Rannon Jystral.

The airships of Talera are not like the airplanes of Earth. They are slower for one thing, and open to the sky—more like a sea going yacht than a pressurized jet. Their power source comes from the same toir'in-or stones that opened the world gate—the sphere gate—for me. These are mind-amplifying crystals that can be used by adepts to work "sorcery," and by the pilot caste of Talera to guide airships of inanimate wood and metal. Smaller craft, like the Aestor, get both lift and drive from crystalline wands that have been charged from a toir'in-or and attached to rotors that run propellers. Larger ships get only lift and must use sails to move their bulk through the air. Both types of craft need pilots to initiate and manipulate the wands' energy flow, however

The open nature of Taleran airships invites attack and most all are armed. Rannon's ship was no exception. At fore and aft were ballista that could hurl four pound arrows upwards of four hundred yards. Amidships was a trebuchet for throwing stones. Also aboard were two dozen gray-cloaked guards of the Princess's Own Elite, among them the massively thewed figure of Rhandh the Vlih.

Rhandh and I had fought side by side in the lava mines of the Klar and I knew him as a professional, worth as much on his own as any dozen other guards. With steel strapped to both his prehensile tail and to the glistening dark tentacles that writhed below his arms, Rhandh made a formidable opponent. I regretted that I could not count him a great friend of mine, as I did Heril and Valyan, but we did share a mutual respect, not least of which came from our love of Rannon.

It was Rhandh's love for Rannon, for his Jhesana, that kept him by us as we lifted into the blue-white Taleran sky and turned our prow to the south. It was love that kept his huge, dark fist on a sword. And I believe that it was love that sent him away from us when Rannon moved closer under my arm and lifted her face to be kissed.

So much time had passed since we'd seen each other that I wanted the kissing to last forever. But Rannon was too excited by something she had to show me on the way to Timmuzz. As it turned out, I was not to find out that day what she meant. For even as the torpedo shape of the Aestor cut swiftly through the wind, our enemies stalked upon us. And even as I stood there with Rannon and felt a moment of incredible peace, I should have known better. This was, after all, Talera.

Ten verlangs north of the capital, nearly a mile above a river called the Shauval, the reivers struck from out of the sun's glare.

Chapter Two

The End of an Idyll

When the attack came, it marked the end of an idyll. Rannon had gone below, out of the cold, and I was standing at the stern with Kreeg and Valyan, on what would have been called the poop deck on a sailing vessel. The pilot was in his glass enclosed cage amidships, and Rhandh had positioned himself at the hatch leading below to his Jhesana, his princess. At the prow were a few more of Rannon's graycloaks.

The raiders struck first at the prow. They were mounted on vullwings, huge saddle birds the likes of which had never graced the skies of Earth. Before now, I had only seen such creatures on the ground. There was no comparison to when they were in flight. They were savage and beautiful, their eagle-shaped bodies bearing elongated necks and massive wingspreads, the sunlight spilling dark from their indigo feathers. Their riders wore swords and carried short, recurve bows, light metal lances, and multi-bladed throwing knives called wheel-daggers.

The plan was clearly to take the Aestor and those aboard her. They had perhaps fifty men to do it. We had fewer to stop them.

The first wave of attackers came in above the front of the ship and their heavy bows cleared the forecastle of everything living. The second wave consisted of vullwings carrying double, and the spare warriors were soon dropping onto the foredeck with drawn blades. They had to board us. The vullwing is swift but a flyer can outpace it. They must have dived on us to pick up speed, and now they had to rain men onto our decks if they were to hold us. Our job was to throw them back overboard.

Rhandh stood closer to our foes than the rest of us did. He shouted below for more guards, then charged forward, broadsword clutched hard in a black fist. His off hand carried a shield and the two tentacles below his arms were strapped with daggers. Only his prehensile tail bore no weapon. An arrow caromed off his brigandine; another cut flutters from the coarse mane of hair that ran the mid-line of his scalp before falling down his back. Then he was among the enemy, raging.

Valyan, Kreeg, and I were right behind, slowing only long enough to pluck up three of the shields that were commonly lashed to the inside of an airborne flyer. These would be put over the side when the ship was landing so everyone could see the vessel's origins and history from the lacquered designs on their surfaces. They would serve us now against arrows instead. I blocked several such darts as I raced forward.

In my right fist glittered a saber. I did not remember drawing it. It was the same weapon I had used in the lava mines of Andertalen when we had broken the slave chains of the Klar (see *Swords of Talera*). It had served me well there. I hoped it would again.

Rhandh was hard pressed at the prow and the three of us battered a way to him and threw his attackers back. Steel edges shrieked across metal and leather. In almost an instant my saber drank two men's lives; my shield grew new designs, inscribed without artistry by the tips of thrusting swords. The taste of blood fogged my throat.

It wasn't my blood.

Behind us, then! A shout!

I turned to see more of Rannon's guards boiling up from below. Then a third wave of vullwings went over and dropped reivers to the aft. They took out the first of our guards to reach the open air and seized the hatchway to prevent others from following. It looked as if it would be four of us against many—the kind of battle of which songs are written.

WINGS OVER TALERA, BY CHARLES ALLEN GRAMLICH

Kreeg was not one to care for such songs. He merely grunted in angry pleasure as fresh enemies rushed upon us. His sword was knocked aside as a man lunged at him with naked steel. Kreeg avoided the cut to the left, caught the fellow's arm and jerked him forward. He broke the man's wrist, hurled him into a second raider. Both men fell back, and over the Aestor's railing while we were half a verlang in the air. Both screamed. But not for long did we hear them.

Valyan and I went to sword strokes with new foes. I took an arrow in my shield; a cutlass's edge crashed against the bronze boss and rebounded. My own blade licked out, sliced through a throat, then leaped back to parry a thrust, driving an enemy's sword-tip down to scrape the planks of the deck. The vullwings were past us now. They'd not catch the ship again unless the pilot could somehow be taken. He would not be killed unless by accident, for the skills of the pilot caste are rare and are greatly valued on Talera.

That didn't mean he couldn't be threatened.

The absence of bird-riders around us meant no more arrows and for that I was grateful. It made me wish for a parrying dagger rather than the shield. I had never felt comfortable with the heavy things dragging on one arm. I wasn't about to drop this one, though. Not just yet.

Beside me, Rhandh was a devil in iron, his knife-strapped tentacles whipping up under opponents' defenses to slash flesh while his broadsword demanded their attention. Valyan was almost as quick, and with a bit more élan in the way his blade twinkled, and danced, and ripped.

I carved my way through, parrying, thrusting, riposting, but going mainly for the cut and bludgeon. The middle of a melee is no time for refinement. One reiver thought to fence with me. He styled himself a talent. I barreled past his guard, using the shield to ward his tip, and smashed the hilt of my saber savagely into his mouth. He went backward over the railing and his talent didn't keep him from dying.

Rhandh bellowed in frustration beside me as he realized that he'd come too far forward, too far from his Jhesana, who was now trapped below deck. He sought to disengage, to forge a road back to the hatchway—where I wanted him too. But struggling bodies clotted his path. I yelled for Kreeg and

Valyan, and the three of us hacked a space for the huge Vlih to slip through. As Rhandh began to run, I ordered Kreeg to go with him, leaving Valyan and myself to hold at the prow.

Valyan's green skin sheened with perspiration. That only meant he was warmed up. He flashed a quick white grin in my direction as he slipped away from two raiders and left them stabbing empty air. His own attacks didn't miss and both of his foes went down.

I ducked under a sidearm swipe, slashed open an unarmored thigh. A wheel-dagger whirred past my ear. I caught a second one against my shield, hearing the thunk and letting it anger me. A sword clattered along mine. I thrust the enemy weapon aside, forced my steel down the length of the raider's blade, let the tip leap up to take him in the face. He screeched, fell back. I kicked a second warrior in the chest, hurling him from his feet.

Our attackers were a mixture of Humans and other, which meant they were probably mercenaries—verdredi. National armies usually consist of only one race, and even outlaw bands often form along racial lines. Talera has its prejudices. Most of these verdredi were Human, but I saw a few variations among them. I was glad there were no Black Llurns or Nokarra, who are among the deadliest of warriors. There *were* Vhichang, lithe and avian within their covering of feathers, and there were the members of a race called the Ss'Korra, which I had heard of but had not seen before.

Humans sometimes call the Vhichang "birds" and the Ss'Korra "the wolf people."[3] Neither is accurate. The Vhichang resemble birds only in their feathery coats and in the sharp, hooked shapes of their faces, which sport small

---

[3] I once asked a Taleran savant why so many of the planet's races resemble Humans. Like Humans, most of them walk upright, have various numbers of limbs, have something like hands at the end of those limbs, and see with two eyes in the front of Human-type heads. Yet, they are supposed to have developed under far distant suns.

He told me that the intelligent races brought to Talera, including Humans, were probably all guided in their development toward this common pattern. I asked if he thought the Asadhie were responsible for this, and he said that they were themselves likely products of this vast manipulation.—Ruenn Maclang.

beaks. They are not winged and do not have a bird's hollow bones. They do not lay eggs, though they do not suckle their live-born young as mammals do.

The Ss'Korra *are* mammals, though they can only generally be said to resemble wolves. They have fur, except on their bellies, and they do have something that might be construed as a muzzle. But their overall appearance reminds me most of a baboon. They have the same small ears lying close to the head, and the same facial expression. Both races are superb fighters, with the Ss'Korra being the more vicious of the two.

It was an Ss'Korra who came against me next. He was bigger than the average for his race, almost as tall as my six feet, and was given to hacking with the strength of his arm. I caught that arm with a hand. We strained together for a moment—he trying to kick my legs from under me, I trying to block with my knee. He spat the word "Human" in my face. I didn't hold it against him. But when I got my shield past his guard, I hit him hard enough with it to break his jaw and stretch him senseless.

Beneath me, abruptly, the airship faltered. I could see amidships that the pilot was unharmed, but perhaps the frothing savagery around him had broken his concentration on the power wands that drove the ship. For whatever reason, the flyer staggered and slowed. That meant the vullwings would come up to us again. I didn't relish that idea.

Two Vhichang, working in tandem, tried to isolate me from Valyan and cut me down. It didn't work. Valyan and I had fought side by side too many times. I killed one attacker, watched the second one back away with fear in his eyes. In that lull, I saw that Rhandh and Kreeg had freed the Aestor's hatchway. Gray-clad members of the Princess's Own roared up from below, anxious to come to hand strokes with the enemy who had bottled them up.

For an awful moment I had the fear that Rannon would come up with them, a sword in her own slim fist. I should have known that Rhandh would not have allowed it. He shouted one word, "Jhesana," before dropping down the hatch to keep his princess safe below. It felt good to know that Rannon had the Vlih to protect her, that she was all right for now. Unless we lost the war above.

I'd not let that happen.

The reinforcements provided by Rannon's guards were winning the fight for us when the slowing of the ship let the vullwings catch us from behind. Once more the rain of enemy arrows loosed, but this time our people were ready with shields and few of the darts found their mark. Those arrows would slow our attempts to clear the decks, however, and given a chance the reivers would land more of their own to counter our hard won advantage. We had no bows on deck, no way to strike back at them in the air.

Or did we?

I was on the midship riser, the aft ballista sitting below me. I dropped down beside the weapon, Valyan warding my back, then spun it outward from the ship and pulled the lanyard to fire the five side-by-side arrows. Those arrows weighed almost four pounds apiece. They cut the air with a heavy swish, and they scarcely slowed as they went through the feathers and flesh of two vullwings flying close together. I regretted the birds. But not the men on their backs.

A slap of my hand reloaded the weapon and I swiveled the mechanism to the left and fired again. A vullwing was just landing at the stern. Two raiders stood beside it. The ballista load swept the deck clear like a broom, spraying crimson over the railing.

A vullwing was above me then, on its back a lean Human in black leathers. His dark brown hair was braided at the sides and a savage scar writhed palely through the stubble of beard at his chin.

Strange how one notices details at such times. I noticed most the man's crossbow, jaguar-spotted and of an odd design. Its quarrel was triple sized and glittered like the sun. He fired it at me. And Valyan, who was beside me with his emerald skin splashed red with blood, dove in front of me and caught the quarrel in his shield.

The glittering bolt thunked home in the lacquered surface of the buckler and exploded, literally exploded, as if pregnant with gunpowder. I'd thought there was no gunpowder on Talera, though there were the materials to make it. It seemed *someone* had discovered how.

WINGS OVER TALERA, BY CHARLES ALLEN GRAMLICH

Valyan's shield shredded in the explosion, scattering shrapnel on the wind. The heavy boss knocked down a guard nearby and a wood fragment as long as a nail went through the meat of my forearm. Valyan was down, the front of his body porcupined with splinters.

The man in black hung only a few feet above me, the wings of his mount buffeting the deck. He was reloading. I shouted in rage, put one foot on the bracing of the ballista, and leaped upward for his throat. At the top of my arc I swung my sword overhand and down.

The reiver was quick; I'd give him that. He got the crossbow in the way of my saber and the steel blade snapped on the steel heart of the bow. The second bolt released on its own, hissing evilly as it went past my head. I didn't see it strike, though I heard it boom. My hand caught the man's boot on the way down.

The good leather failed to yield and my weight yanked the outlaw from the saddle. There were straps and ties that held him to that saddle, and they didn't yield either. But the combined weight of the two of us dragged the vullwing to one side and crashed it to the deck. Its neck snapped, killing it.

I was on my feet in an instant. Only a stub of blade hung in my hand but it would be enough for this outlaw, whether or not he had murdered Valyan. The fellow was trying to get up, and trying to draw the rapier belted at his left side. I took a step toward him and the deck dropped beneath me, stealing my balance and throwing me to the planks.

I cast a glance toward the pilot's glass chamber and saw it cracked open like an egg. Now I knew where the second explosive bolt had landed. The inside of the chamber was splashed with blood, and fire licked around on the deck beneath.

We were going down in flames. Without a pilot. Toward the snake curve of the Shauval River beneath us.

And Rannon was below decks.

Chapter Three

Shot Down in Flames

We hung half a verlang in the air—three quarters of a mile—in a flyer with no pilot. The only hope we could cling to was that we were sinking rather than falling. The toir'in-or charged wands that provided lift for the flyer seemed to be draining slowly of their power rather than failing all at once. That gave us a sliver's hope of living. A very thin sliver, for we were also on fire.

The few mercenary reivers still on our decks didn't seem to think much of our future. They were busy grabbing the nearest vullwing and abandoning ship. I looked across at the black-clad outlaw whose explosive bolt had killed our pilot and set our ship ablaze. He would not be joining his fellows. I would see to that, and gave him a look that let him know it. He shrugged, then calmly began unhooking the ties that bound him to the dead saddle bird at his side.

My rage at him evaporated as other concerns stabbed at me.

Valyan! The flyer!

The thoughts tortured and I turned under their goad, saw Valyan lying near me painted with his own blood. I dropped to my knees beside him. He was breathing. And I breathed as well, in relief. He seemed more stunned than anything. Though a number of splinters from the shield had been driven into his chest and the lower part of his face, the concave surface of the buckler had directed most of the force of the small explosion around his body. He'd live, and even as I thought it he opened his eyes.

WINGS OVER TALERA, BY CHARLES ALLEN GRAMLICH

"Lie still," I told him. "We've got a problem."

His pupils dilated but I didn't take time to explain. He'd smell the smoke soon enough. Kreeg was nearby with an axe, his broad body scarred, sweat beaded on his hairless head. I told him to watch Valyan and our mercenary guest. There would be questions to ask the latter if we lived. Then I came to my feet to see what might be done about the ship.

The surviving members of Rannon's elite guard, less than half a dozen men, had turned away from the fleeing reivers and were gathering amidships to douse the flames surrounding the pilot's chamber. Hope surged inside me as I saw that those fires would soon be out, and I ran to the hold instead, to find Rannon. She and Rhandh were coming up from below as I arrived at the stairs. Their faces were smoke-smudged, their eyes streaming, and I could see by their expressions that my hope of moments before was dust.

"In the cabin," Rannon shouted. "The curtains caught. By Sevarian I'll never listen to those court fools again about what a princess should have in her flyer."

Seldom had I seen Rannon so angry, and I almost laughed despite the shock of our situation. Or maybe because of it. But Rhandh grabbed my shoulder, jarring me back into control.

"The pilot?" the Vlih demanded.

I shook my head at him. "Dead," I answered.

Just then, Rannon's guards finally got the flames beat out around the pilot's chamber and carried the fellow's body out to lie on the cool wood of the deck. A sliver of glass the size of a man's forearm had been driven through his throat. His flying days were over. And it wasn't like *anyone* could pilot the ship. The power sources for airboats are the toir'in- or charged energy wands controlled by a trained and disciplined mind. Even for those with talent, it takes months of practice just to manage the lift of a flyer. I couldn't do it. Nor any of the others that I knew of. It seemed our choices were to wait until the wands gave out and we crashed to our deaths, or until we burned alive in the air.

"If we could take the ship down faster," I said. "If we could get to the river before the cabin fire catches the decks we might have a chance. Is there *anyone* aboard with pilot training?"

Rannon shook her head. And someone behind us cleared their throat for attention.

"I have a bit of experience," a voice said.

It was the mercenary in black leathers who had spoken. He had risen to his feet, with Kreeg directly behind him, an axe poised while he debated whether to strike. I put up my hand for the ex-slave to hold his blow.

"I can't fly it much," the reiver continued. "But if you keep the flames off me I might be able to land it in the river without killing us all."

"A few minutes ago you were *trying* to kill us all," I said. "Why should we believe your change of attitude now?"

"Because that was for money and I had a saddle bird. Now my mount is dead and my life is worth more than money to me."

"Axe him and throw him over the side," Kreeg said.

"Yes," agreed Rhandh. "Only, let me do it."

"I don't think so," I said. "This one fought like a devil to stay alive when I wanted him dead. I doubt he's changed his mind now."

"Believe it," the man said. "Only, we'd better do something fast or the flames will cook our decision-makers for us."

"No they won't," I said quickly. "I'll get you the time. Have you more exploding quarrels?"

"To what purpose?"

"To fight fire with fire. Now where are they?"

His eyes lit with sudden understanding. "In my bags," he said.

He dropped to one knee beside his dead vullwing, his fingers dipping into a handy leather pocket of his saddle, coming up with a thorn-wood box that opened to show the glittering heads and shafts of three more darts.

"You haven't a crossbow," he said, as he handed me the box.

"They'll explode on impact if I throw them hard enough, won't they?"

"Aye," he nodded. "They should."

"Then that'll have to do."

WINGS OVER TALERA, BY CHARLES ALLEN GRAMLICH

"Wait," said Rannon. "What are you planning?"

I grabbed her shoulders, kissed her. "I'm going below," I said. "I'll use these darts against the fire to slow it. You put this man in the pilot's chamber and have him take the ship down to the river."

"No," Rannon said, but Rhandh was taking her arm and I was pulling away, tucking the case of darts into the belt at my waist.

The mercenary was already running for the pilot's position. I took the axe from the hands of a surprised Kreeg and staved in one of the water kegs that stood against the midship riser. I ripped off my shirt and dunked my upper body. Skin burns more slowly than cloth, wet skin more slowly than dry.

Rannon recovered herself then. She'd been afraid for me. Still was. But she trusted that I knew what I was doing. She tore off the silken sleeve of her garment and wet it before tying it across my nose and mouth. I plucked up a second water keg and stumbled down the stairs into the burning symphony of the cabin below.

At the bottom of the steps I hesitated. Some of the rundal-oil lamps were still alight, but even without them I could have seen well enough. Streamers of fire bloomed across the front of the long cabin in brilliant shades of red and gold, like sunlight come down to earth to play. And it was as frightening as anything I had ever seen. Or hoped to.

The pilot's chamber had stood directly over the forepart of the cabin and the explosion above had driven fiery debris into the room. Curtains had caught. Silk hangings had gone up like tinder. The heavy oak paneling of the walls and ceiling had not yet started to burn. But the temperature was rising. I could feel it in the sweat on my skin. There was no way through to the far end of the room, where the heaviest flames ate the rugs and bed, and gnawed at the floor.

Almost, I turned to go back up the stairs, but the image of Rannon's face held me where I stood. I axed open the keg I carried and splashed the water against what flames I could reach. Then I jerked out the case containing the three explosive bolts and opened it. The swollen heads of the darts gleamed a sullen yellow. They looked evil, though I knew it was my imagination that dressed them so. I drew one out, balanced it in my hand, and threw it at the point on the floor just beneath where the fire ate most furiously.

I understood, as few people on Talera probably did, that an explosion could rob a fire of its fuel. Destroying the material upon which the flames fed, or even scattering that material, would dissipate the heat. And it was the heat that would cause the walls and deck to catch. Until that happened, we had a chance.

For more than one reason, my breath held as the first dart struck. Valyan's shield had nearly blocked the blast of one of these quarrels so I knew their explosive power was weak. They didn't have enough punch to blow holes completely through the ship. I hoped.

A rush of light dazzled; the boom followed like thunder, half deafening me in the echoing space. Ashes and embers swirled upward, thickening the air, and the floor planks buckled beneath the bed, dropping one side of it to hang over the ship's hold below. But the wash of the blaze went quiet where the blast had hit. I coughed, choked, but quickly threw the other two darts, the explosions caving in floor and wall panels but scattering the thickest of the flames. The temperature dropped.

The effect would be temporary. The fire *would* escape the confines of the cabin and the decks would burn. But we needed only moments. Already, I could feel the ship slanting downward under the guiding hand of the mercenary who had claimed a bit of pilot's knowledge. I hoped it was enough.

My coughing had turned to gagging now, as I fought to clear my lungs of smoke and draw in a breath. I tried to yell up the stairs for more water but no words came out. I stumbled for the steps, tripped and went down to a knee. Then sturdy arms grabbed me and I felt myself half carried toward the stairs. Kreeg was beside me, one arm wrapped around my shoulders. Rhandh stood next to him and took the axe from my left hand as Kreeg dragged me past. I heard the sound of shattering wood as the Vlih broke open a barrel of water he'd carried with him.

The blue-white window of the sky seemed far away at the top of the stairs. I wished it closer, and in another moment the wish came true. I staggered out onto the deck where the cool breeze thrust against my body. Rannon was there with a sweet, wet cloth pushed against my face and lips. I hacked up black grit. My ears were still ringing from the blasts.

We were headed downward at a steep angle and I could see the mercenary at the controls with his legs spread and locked. His face made a study in concentration as he channeled his mind into the toir'in-or charged wands that drove us.

Braced against the pull of our descent, I glanced over the side of the flyer. The air looked clear and hard beneath us, and further below surged the verdigrised copper of the Shauval River. Grasslands stretched to either side of the banks, broken by large tracts of dark wood, with here and there the blunt square of a plowed holding.

I looked back at the mercenary, who had said he didn't want to die. No flames roiled through the torn deck by his boots, a sign that my attempts at explosive surgery had been successful for the moment. It was time to get ready for a landing. Or a crashing. We were only a few hundred yards above the river.

I hoped the mercenary had been truthful about what he wanted.

An injured Valyan was carried over to the midship riser and braced between two hitching rails where saddle birds could be tied. Most of the men joined him.

Having dumped the last of his water, Rhandh came up from below to be with us as well. His shoulders steamed smoke as he joined Kreeg, Rannon, and myself. The four of us wedged ourselves into a corner where the riser met the railing. We locked arms, Rannon in the center. My legs were tight about one stanchion, my free arm wrapped around another. The river was coming up hard toward us.

Now, I knew, our makeshift pilot would bring up the nose of the craft so that we would strike the water at a shallower angle, so that we would skip like a stone instead of disintegrating.

Yes. At any instant he would bring up the nose. At any instant!

"Damn!" I muttered, reverting to my native tongue. *Why*

doesn't he bring up the nose?

But then he did. Slightly. And we hit.

The bow slapped the water firmly and we bounced. Then the port railing smashed in as we slewed sideways in the water. A wave of green river sluiced across us. It held a winter cold and took my breath. I clung tightly to my stanchion, and to Rannon. She nestled quiet in my arms, though some of her men shouted in their fear. We slowed and began to settle. We'd float for a bit.

A ragged cheer erupted. We were down; we would live.

I glanced toward the pilot's chamber. Already damaged, it had broken up the rest of the way on impact. Flames were reaching through the deck from below now, but the mercenary in black leathers was not there to be burned amid the debris. I saw him go over the railing, by intent, with a stolen sword at his waist. He would try to escape us, knowing that the best he could hope for would be a dungeon in the capital city of Timmuzz. Worse would be if he were turned over to the pilot's guild for having killed one of their number.

I did not resent the man's attempt to flee—I would have done the same in his place—but I was determined not to let him get away. There was information to be had.

I came to my feet, loosing my hold on Rannon.

"The reiver," I shouted.

The others saw, leaped up as well.

"I'll fetch him," I said. "Rhandh! You and Rannon get everyone ashore." I had no fear for their safety. All of them were excellent swimmers and there was plenty of wood to cling to.

I ran forward, stopping only long enough to borrow a rapier and thrust it into my belt before diving over the side in pursuit of the mercenary.

I wondered if I would have to kill him to stop him.

I wondered if he was better with a sword than I was.

Chapter Four

On the River to Timmuzz

I sliced the water cleanly in my dive, going deep to come up again a dozen feet out from the side of the crashed airship. The shock of the winter river seared my burns, sucked at my air. I fought through it, struck out for shore in the wake of the man ahead of me.

The ship had come down closer to the northern bank than to the southern, and it was to the nearest spit of land that the mercenary headed. That land was perhaps seventy-five tahng away, close to eighty yards, and the outlaw had a good head start on me. He flailed at the water rather than cutting it smoothly, though, and I had no doubt that I could close the gap. It seemed unlikely that I would catch him in the river. In the end, I did not.

He came to shore a few feet ahead of me and should probably have made his stand there where I would be awkward coming out of the water. Instead, he turned and ran inland. I followed, in better shape because I'd burned less energy in my swim.

Fifty tahng from the River Shauval's edge, in a small field at the border of a wild wood, the mercenary turned at bay and drew a rapier that he'd stolen from our decks. I didn't think he'd return it without a fight.

I pulled my own blade and bore in quickly, not wishing to give him a second to recover from his hard swim and the hard run that had followed. We crossed swords and the steel shivered. Beads of water flew. He blocked my rush and dropped into a fencer's stance. I was familiar with such fighting, having learned much of it on Earth. The rapiers we carried were also suited to the work, though far heavier and broader than the fencing blades of my own world. The differences could be adjusted for.

I struck toward his left, in what would be called the high "4" line among Earthly fencers. His parry was ragged; he hadn't yet recovered his breath and control.

I attacked again. A straight thrust. Not giving him time. The swords tapped together behind the tips, locked to each other in that part of the blade called the foible. I twisted my hand, abruptly increasing the lateral pressure against his blade. My steel slid along his, the edge shrieking, the point darting for his belly.

His parry should have been a simple midline movement, but, as I'd hoped, his relative exhaustion made him use too much strength on the block. His weapon swept too far to the left and in that instant I disengaged, dropped my blade beneath his, then followed with a lunge toward his unprotected right flank. My thrust was deliberately low, aimed to wound and not to kill, and the tip of my sword sliced only a half inch into his thigh before I brought it out again and stepped back into the guard position.

The mercenary's eyes went wide. He knew how badly I could have hurt him, wasn't sure why I had not. He would try to be more cautious now, try to feel his way through me. It was not in my best interest to give him time to do so.

I moved forward, tapping his sword lightly with my own, then lunged. He parried, and I immediately transformed the lunge into a fleché, a running attack that carries the fencer past his foe in a flurry of blades. One stroke of a razor-edge slashed away the leather at his left shoulder, leaving behind a pale furrow that rapidly filled with red. The blow could have as easily taken an eye.

And he knew it.

He glanced down, and back up again. I expected to see rage, but instead got a twisted smile. He lowered his guard, then tossed the rapier onto the forest leaves at my feet. He spread his arms.

"I can't match you," he said. "I never imagined you would be so good."

"You were exhausted from the swim," I said. "Else you would have made a better defense."

"But I still would not have won."

"No, probably not."

"What is your name, swordsman?"

"Ruenn Maclang. And yours?"

I was watching him as I spoke and saw him start as if he recognized something about my name. Of course, he might very well have heard of me. Any organized force attacking Nyshphal would have had their spies in the country for a time. And those spies would surely have picked up word of the strange fellow keeping company with the daughter of the Emperor. I knew the tale was muchly about.

"Diken," the mercenary said after a moment. "My name is Diken Graye."

* * * * * * *

Rannon and the others were sitting on the banks of the Shauval when I came out of the fields behind the river with my prisoner. Sticky gray mud covered everyone's hair and clothes but they did not seem much put out by it. I suppose they were happy to be alive. Behind them in the water I could see no sign of the flyer. It had sunk.

Already, the locals had begun to arrive. They came in canoes or on small rafts, occasionally on something bigger. This area was mostly farmland but had a fairly substantial population. An airship going down couldn't have been a very common sight. It had attracted attention.

Even covered with mud, Rannon looked the part of a princess. And the sightseers were soon vying with each other to offer their services. She acknowledged all offers graciously, but finally selected a burly red-headed tradesman with eyes as clear as gin to take us downriver in his firewood barge. He and his men moved quickly to earn their honor, and we were soon loaded and on our way to Timmuzz. Diken Graye went with us, but this time his hands were bound so he wouldn't think of going overboard again.

There were many questions to be asked of the mercenary, and a few to be asked of Rannon. She admitted to me that there had been other attacks against Nyshphal of late, that airships had come up missing and that villages had been burned across the north. The raids had begun around the time I left for Earth, two months before, and I remembered of a sudden a battle fought over a little settlement called Rakii. I recalled how odd the assault had seemed to me then, as if the raiders wanted more to destroy than to loot. I said as much to Rannon.

"Their first strike," she agreed. "There have been others. My father stepped up air patrols but that hasn't stopped them. This is the furthest south they have come, though."

"What about survivors?"

"A few. In the villages. None from an airship before." She shook her head. "Someone is moving against us but we do not know who. Or why. All the raiders that have been seen have been mercenaries."

I tried not to show my concern but the fact that the attacks were still moving south in the face of increased air defenses, worried me. Nyshphal had a very strong air-fleet.

"Have those explosive bolts been used in other attacks?" I asked.

Rannon shrugged, then gestured at our prisoner. "Perhaps this one will know."

Our guest had found a pile of firewood to sit against. He was trying to be inconspicuous and failing.

"Kreeg!" I called loudly. "Would you come here a moment? And bring your axe."

Diken Graye met my gaze and showed me a faint smile. He thought Kreeg an empty threat. He knew I would not have him killed.

I walked over and squatted on my heels before the mercenary. Kreeg was behind me, attempting to look menacing. He was doing an excellent job.

"Who is your master?" I asked into the outlaw's eyes.

"I don't know."

"He lies," Kreeg said.

"Perhaps not," I replied to the ex-fighting slave, though I didn't take my eyes off the black-clad reiver. "Whoever is hiring these men seems not to want us knowing quite yet who it is that tasks us. But there are surely other things this one *does* know.

"Where were you hired?" I asked.

"I see no reason to answer."

I reached out then, and touched a finger lightly to the braid at the left side of Graye's face. It was, perhaps, six inches long, tightly wound. He jerked his head away and his lips tightened to white with anger.

"I prefer not to be touched," he said.

"I am sure."

I stood up. "Kreeg," I called. "Cut off this braid with your axe."

"Nay!" The mercenary who called himself Diken Graye was on his feet. He was prepared to attack me I saw, though he was weaponless and with his hands bound. I held up my own hand to Kreeg, stopping the big man as he started forward.

"You have lied to us," I said to the prisoner. "A crime in my eyes and in yours."

"I have not lied. I do not choose to answer. It is not the same."

"You told me your name was Diken Graye. That is a lie."

The mercenary's eyes narrowed. "Why do you say that?"

"A man new to Talera reads much," I said. "Perhaps he reads of distant peoples who he might one day meet. He reads of history and customs. The war-braids of the Thorn Nomads are widely known. And it is said that Thorn warriors do not lie, on pain of having their hair shorn. By what name are you known among the nomads?"

The mercenary's face would have made stony ground look inviting. His eyes were dark and savage. Only the scar at his chin revealed an emotion, one deeper than anger. It had flushed with blood.

"My name among the people was Chay-el Vayne," he grated out.

"Was?"

"I am no longer that man. You see now that I did not lie to you. My name is Diken Graye. It is one that I have chosen."

WINGS OVER TALERA, BY CHARLES ALLEN GRAMLICH

I would not ask him why. Such things were private and I doubted that he would answer anyway. Instead, I spoke to him of something else.

"This barge that you are on. These people. This river and the sky above. They are my world and you have endangered it. Whether you believe it or not, I know of honor. I would not ask you for anything you cannot give. But the questions I ask are important to me in a way that they cannot be to you. Answering them puts no stain on your service."

Diken Graye, once known as Chay-el Vayne of the Thorn Nomads, considered for a moment. I could see him weighing thoughts of his hire against the request that I had made. Too, I thought from his demeanor, that perhaps he rather liked those of us here aboard this ship. He had seen our easy camaraderie, our willingness to sacrifice ourselves for each other. He must have felt the sense of purpose that animated our actions. These were things that he understood but must have seldom experienced since leaving his people.

"I was hired in Trazull," he said after a moment. "On the Roshjavik Peninsula."

"I have heard of it," I said. "A free port where many such bargains are made. Did you know, when you attacked our airship, that the Princess of Nyshphal was aboard?"

Diken glanced at Rannon. I do not believe he could have pretended to the surprise he showed.

"No," he said, looking back at me. "We were told to attack an airship near the Capital. Yours was the first one we found. Other than military craft there seem to be few vessels about."

"As a result of your kind's predations," Rannon snapped.

Graye shrugged. "Mercenaries are paid to fight," he said. "Most of us are decent men only trying to earn our hire."

I could see from Rannon's face that she did not accept the decency of most mercenaries. Yet, I believed myself that it was true.

"Have there been more of the explosive quarrels used in your attacks?" I asked.

"I heard much talk of magic weapons, but saw none until the quarrels were given to me."

"Why you?" Rhandh asked.

"Because I was the best shot with a crossbow. I was told to use them all. At least that part of my hire was accomplished."

"The vullwings are not long distance fliers," I said. "Where was your attack launched from?"

"That I will not answer. I would not be responsible for a reprisal against any who might still be at the site."

I smiled and shrugged. "All right. I did not think you would tell us but it was worth the attempt."

His answering smile matched mine, though thinner.

"Let me kick it out of him," Kreeg said.

"No," I said. "A beating would get nothing from this one. Watch him, though."

I turned away toward Rannon and heard my name called. "Wait! Ruenn Maclang, wait."

I looked back at Diken Graye, expecting him to ask now about his future. He did not.

"There is one more thing I would tell you," he said. "There is one of your enemies I would name."

I waited, as did we all, and inside of me was something that seemed afraid.

"The man who hired me," he said. "The man who gave me the explosive quarrels. He had a false right hand. His name was Bryce Maclang."

Chapter Five

Seat of Empire

"His name was Bryce Maclang," Diken Graye had said. And those words filled me with both elation and relief. My brother was alive! It seemed to me impossible that Graye could be lying outright, for he had mentioned a false right hand, and only I recalled the revolver that had blown up in Bryce's grip just before we were sucked through the sphere gate to Talera. Even if someone had heard the name Bryce Maclang and urged Diken Graye to use it, that person could not have known of my brother's hand without seeing him.

No! Bryce had to be alive. And this was the first clue I'd had of him.

Yet, mixed with my happiness was a darker emotion. If all that Graye had said was true, Bryce was working with those who had made themselves my enemies, and the enemies of people I cared about. There was no reason, of course, why my brother could not have joined a mercenary band. He would have been alone when he arrived on Talera—like myself—and on a planet such as this who could predict what companions one might be thrown among.

And, I realized suddenly, my brother surely could not know that it was my adopted country his verdredi band was attacking. I just needed to find him and tell him. Then we'd be together again. Perhaps, my thoughts ran, Bryce had even located our cousin Eric. Might not I get them both back at the same time? Or others of my Earth crew?

A faint voice in my head suggested that things wouldn't be so simple, but the warning was easy to ignore as my mind turned toward a search. The first place to look was Trazull, on the Roshjavik Peninsula where Diken Graye had been hired. Bryce had done that hiring. With any luck he would be there still, recruiting others.

Before Trazull, however, I had to see Rannon safely back to her father. This proved easy enough to accomplish. Where our airship had crashed, the Shauval River still ran deep and swift from its upland birth, but soon our borrowed firewood barge carried us down to the vast, cedar-fringed plain of Nyshphal, down to where the Shauval was joined by the blue-green Coulder and the muddy Vehr. And just past that point lifted the rose-colored buildings of Timmuzz, the capital of Nyshphal and the home of Rannon and her family. My home too.

In childhood dreams of exotic cities, I had always pictured them with vastly tall towers and slim jade bridges running like sweet fairy magic between them. Timmuzz has no such towers, no such bridges. She has been built solidly by a practical people, erected on a simple plan with an eye toward both defense and function. And yet, she is lovely.

Few structures in Timmuzz stand more than four stories high, but they are roofed in tiles, and slates, and shingles of many colors. Only government buildings are cut from rock—marble and quartz and massive gray granite. The houses of the citizens are walled with rose-colored stucco that gleams bright and clean in the light. Polished woods and metals add luster to doors and frames and shutters, and to the robust grillwork of balconies and porches. But there is nothing delicate about Timmuzz. She is a wealthy lady and has no need to embellish her charms with false perfumes.

The people of Timmuzz are as pragmatic as their city, and as sturdy. The city is young, as the empire which she governs is young, and most of her citizens are only a generation removed from farmland roots. They have retained the sense of hard work and the openness in dealings that so often mark rural people. They tend to be courteous and friendly, though no civilization is without its predators. I had dwelt in Timmuzz only a brief time but it felt comfortable to me. It was good to see the place again after having been gone for the past two months.

WINGS OVER TALERA, BY CHARLES ALLEN GRAMLICH

"Makes you think of sunrise," Rannon said, looking with me out over the shining expanse of her home.

"Yes," I agreed, then grinned at her. "And of a woman."

She smiled and took my arm as our firewood barge was warped against one of the massive quays that run like a monster spine along the city's river-side. Rannon had been seen and crowds awaited us as we disembarked. It was much warmer here than in the highlands where I'd returned from Earth. There was no snow and laughing throngs escorted us through cobbled streets toward the palace.

On all sides of us the city stood decorated for the Spring Passage, the ten day period when the blue-white sun of winter turns green for the spring. This "Passage" is only one of four such periods. At start of summer the sun bakes to gold, and in the fall its light shifts to a sullen red. In the cold, cold of winter, the sun grows an icy pale blue, such a color as was only just now starting to fade.

The Spring Passage was already a day old and the people were in a festive mood. Perhaps most of them did not yet know of the air attacks that had been occurring along their borders, or perhaps they knew and were ready to release their tension at a carnival.

My own spirit, my "khi" as the Talerans call it, was filled with another kind of tension. I ached to be away in search of my brother. But there were certain conventions to be observed. I well recalled the words Rannon and I had said to each other just before I left for Earth two months earlier.

On that winter day we had walked alone in a glass-enclosed garden of her father's vast palace. Heated fountains had drawn skeins of mist in the air. Miniature trees had bloomed with flowers that thrived in the artificial heat of this private spot. I had stopped her where a vine-covered path of polished stones gave way to an open space alive with butterflies.

"I could never love another," I told her.

"Nor I," she'd replied.

We had spoken, then, of a wedding. And in the speaking I created for myself a position as consort to the Princess of Nyshphal. Neither the lady nor the position were to be taken lightly.

Wings Over Talera, by Charles Allen Gramlich

It was Rannon I cared for, but part of loving a princess is loving her people as well. There were duties that I would be expected to perform during the Spring Passage, parties that I would be expected to attend. With word of Bryce so fresh in my ears, I felt even the thought of such duties as a yoke around my neck. And I feared that yoke would chafe until my impatience exploded in anger.

Rannon would have understood my leaving Timmuzz, even at this time. She would have known that the need to find my brother was no slight on my love for her. Her father was a different matter. Already he had doubts about me, not particularly from personal animosity but just because I was the man who was going to marry his daughter. And he did not think that I, or any man, was quite good enough to do so.

As well, Rannon had told me that there were nobles of the empire, some of whom wished to press their own suits for her hand, who were urging her father to send me away. I imagined he still wavered in his decision, wishing his daughter had chosen another, but not quite willing to put aside her desires. It could only harden his heart against me if I left the city before the festival, if I failed to carry out my first real duties as a future prince of Nyshphal. And yet, of course, Bryce was my brother. I had to find him while the trail remained fresh.

Temporarily, however, thoughts of Bryce were pushed aside amid the excitement of our arrival at the palace. Word had reached Hurnan Jystral, Rannon's father and Emperor of Nyshphal. He greeted us himself, at gray granite steps marking the entrance into an inner courtyard of silver fountains and black marble walkways. The tension that tightened his shoulders beneath the gold and scarlet cloak of his office showed his concern for his daughter. But I had already seen how much he loved her.

In any gathering, Hurnan Jystral would have been branded a leader of men. He was taller than I, several inches over six feet, and broader at shoulders and chest. His eyes were a blazing sapphire blue, set deep within an almost predatory face. His hair was just beginning to gray. He was a powerful man, in more ways than one, and was very aware of his position and its demands. But he loved his daughter.

Wings Over Talera, by Charles Allen Gramlich

I had learned about Hurnan Jystral from Rannon, had learned how he was born to be king in the coastal city-state of Teleur, and of how an invasion from the sea had taken his father's life and driven him and his mother from their homeland. Hurnan had been six at the time. At seventeen he took back his father's lands, and much, much more.

He raised a peasant army from the western uplands, stiffened their ranks with wild clansmen from the southern range of the Katari Mountains, and he rode back into Teleur at the head of thousands. The original invasion had been followed by others. Everyone had wished to carve a piece of the Nyshphalian roast. But Jystral beat them all, fighting on many fronts over half a decade. By the end he held most of the island under his sway, though he had done as much unifying as conquering. Nyshphal was as close to a democratic empire as existed on Talera.

This had all taken place nearly thirty-five years ago, but today—standing tall over his retainers with his eyes darting quickly to his daughter to see if she had been injured—must have been one of the few times in Jystral's life when he had looked so vulnerable. His wife was years dead, and, though he had a son, Rannon remained the most important thing in his world.

"How is it that my daughter leaves home aboard her own flyer and returns on a firewood barge?" Jystral demanded, his voice a harsh contrast with the pale worry of his face.

He was looking at me. But it was Rannon who answered, who explained to him the details of the raid, leaving out only the part about my brother's involvement. Jystral's body reacted with anger, fists and eyes tightening. His words when they came were calmer, though honed, like the edge of a freshly sharpened hunting knife. He grasped the arm of an imperial officer standing nearby. I saw the man wince under that grip.

"Send the air-guard," Jystral said through lips that barely moved. "Find where the attack was launched from. Bring me the bodies."

The officer hurried to obey and Jystral turned his attention to Diken Graye—our prisoner. Copper-helmed soldiers stepped forward at a gesture from the emperor.

"Take this one to interrogation," Jystral ordered, motioning toward the scarred mercenary.

"I don't think that'll help," I said.

Everyone looked at me. I knew that Graye would not be tortured. Not in Nyshphal. But he would be grilled to the point of exhaustion, with no sleep and no respite. Most crack under such pressure. I didn't think Diken Graye would. The whole thing was a waste.

Jystral did not believe that. Clearly. He frowned at me, a speculative light in his eyes.

"And what would *you* wish done?" he asked.

"Free him in my custody," I said.

Of all those there, including myself, the emperor alone did not seem surprised at my words. The others were. Rhandh the Vlih snorted through widened nostrils, his face a study in open disgust. Even Rannon seemed troubled that I would speak on behalf of someone who had tried to kill us. I could not say *why* I defended the man. I only knew what I felt, that we would be better served by treating Diken Graye honorably than by making him a criminal. But my wish was denied.

"No," said Hurnan Jystral. He turned away.

I glanced at Kreeg. Only *he* had not questioned my motives. He never did. Ever since the lava mines of Andertalen he had followed wherever I led, had carried out whatever task I asked of him. I looked at him then, and saw that he was ready to defend me if need be, even against the might of Nyshphal. I hoped that wouldn't be necessary, but I had already reached a decision about what my actions must be. And I did not think Hurnan Jystral or his daughter would be happy about it.

* * * * * * *

It was not until much later that night, though, before I had a chance to speak to anyone about my plan. Rannon had been whisked away soon after our arrival at the palace, and I'd not even seen her the rest of the night—though I wanted so badly to tell her what I must do. Then, at the bell tolling the eighteenth dhaur, I was summoned to the quarters of the Emperor of Nyshphal.

Hurnan Jystral awaited me there, in a room far more spare than one would expect of such a wealthy and powerful man. There were burnished shields on the walls, and tables of rare samphur wood, but the decorations and pieces of furniture were few, with much space left for the emperor to pace. As he paced now.

I entered, escorted by bronze-armored guards, but then was left alone with the father of the woman I loved. He stopped pacing and stood for a moment staring at me. His face looked drawn and tired. Yet, beneath the exhaustion I could still see the anger that had seethed in him earlier this day.

"We are at war," he said. "Or soon will be."

"And who is our enemy?" I asked.

He shook his head, though his eyes narrowed as he glanced at me. "Would that I knew," he said harshly. His hands clenched into fists. "I would destroy them."

I did not speak.

"We must lay plans," he continued after a moment, speaking more calmly while watching my face. It felt as if I were being tested for something.

"And as my daughter's betrothed, you must be involved," he added.

"I won't be here," I said suddenly.

Perhaps I could have found a more polite way of saying it, or a better time. But then, I have never been known for my tact.

Jystral's eyes went cold.

"You would abandon Rannon and her city in its hour of need?" he growled.

I shook my head. "I'm no general. No strategist. You don't need me here except as a sword. And you have many of those. I believe that my brother—"

He snapped. "Your brother! What care I for your brother? What care I for you except that my daughter loves you? Perhaps foolishly." His voice rang with a barely contained fury that I did not fully understand.

He stalked toward me, as if he would attack me there,

and stopped inches from me. But I did not flinch, and met his gaze with mine. He had not let me finish what I'd started to say about my reasons for wanting to leave, but I would not beg him for that privilege. My muscles tensed. Heat poured into my face.

"You will remain in the city," he told me, his voice tight and harsh. "You will take up your duties as consort to my daughter. You *will* be part of our planning for the city's defense."

I looked him in the eyes, my own anger starting to break free. Barely was I able to control it.

"No," I said. "I will not." Then I turned on my heel and walked out on the Emperor of Nyshphal.

Behind me...only silence.

I was not comforted.

Chapter Six

A Thin Roll of Parchment

After the confrontation with Rannon's father, I returned in a heated anger to my apartment within the great sprawl of the palace. Kreeg awaited me there. Valyan would normally have shared the suite with us, but his wounds were being tended. Only the ex-fighting slave stood nearby to hear my curses ebb and flow.

"What do we do?" he asked during one of the ebbs.

I looked at him as I struggled for control. My thoughts needed to be clear. But another long moment passed before I trusted myself to speak.

"We leave this place," I told him finally.

"To Trazull?" he asked.

"Yes. To find Bryce. Get our gear ready. And check on some saddle birds. I have to see Rannon."

He nodded, turned to do as I had bid, and halted again as the bronze-banded door to the apartment swung open and Rannon stepped inside with Rhandh the Vlih at her shoulder.

"Ruenn," she said, running to me.

I would have taken her in my arms but she caught my wrists instead, her dark blue eyes searching my face.

"My father! You!"

"We had a disagreement," I said.

She shook her head. "More than that. He's furious. He told me...." She kept watching my face as she let a slim hand reach to touch my chest. "He told me that you were a coward. Or worse. That—" Her gaze dropped. "That you didn't love me."

Wings Over Talera, by Charles Allen Gramlich

My heart hurt itself against my ribs as she spoke. There was something very wrong here, something worse than mere anger behind Hurnan Jystral's words. It was as if he had been poisoned against me and I did not know how. Or when.

I caught Rannon's hand, held it.

"And do you think me a coward?" I asked. "Do you think that I don't love you?"

"I've seen you fight," she answered. "You are no coward." But I noted with a sickness inside that she did not respond to the more important question.

Then she glanced at Rhandh and Kreeg and her message was clear. They obeyed it and left us alone.

After the door closed, Rannon looked at me with no smile on her face and said, flatly: "My father claims to have proof that you are a traitor to Nyshphal."

A knife would have been kinder than those words from the lips of the woman I loved. I could not help but defend myself.

"Just because I wish to find my brother?" I blurted. "In finding him I will *serve* Nyshphal. He is somehow mixed up with those who are attacking us. I can—"

She stopped me with a hand to my mouth. And shook her head again.

"No. It is no longer about the search for your brother. My father knows of Bryce's involvement with our enemies. Though I did not tell him. And, he has *this*."

From the belt of golden wire that gathered her linen gown at the waist, she withdrew a thin roll of ivory parchment. I took it, unfolded it, glanced at the symbols incised on it in dark ink. There were two messages on the sheet. The second was in Nyshphalian script and I could see that it translated the other. The first message was in English, and I read it with a growing horror and sense of despair. Then I looked up at Rannon and started to speak into her saddened face.

At that moment, the doors were thrust back and guards poured quickly into the room, imperial guards in bronze breastplates and scarlet cloaks, with their hands on the hilts of bastard swords. At their head stood Kuurus Jystral, Rannon's brother.

WINGS OVER TALERA, BY CHARLES ALLEN GRAMLICH

The parchment fluttered from my hand.
"Arrest Ruenn Maclang," Kuurus shouted. "For treason against the empire and its princess."

Chapter Seven

Betrayer

"Arrest Ruenn Maclang," Kuurus had shouted.

And I stepped suddenly back from Rannon, heart speeding with shock, glancing from Kuurus to his sister—the woman I was to marry.

Where was Kreeg? Why hadn't he warned me?

Rannon's eyes met mine. And I understood where Kreeg was. I understood why Rannon had brought her Vlih bodyguard with her and why she'd sent him from the room with my friend. Rhandh's job had been to get Kreeg out of the way.

I saw it. I knew it. From Rannon's eyes. And the knowledge ripped me like a talon.

The guards started forward, in step, not yet with weapons drawn. Rannon's face grew haggard under my gaze, a dampness welling in the lush darkness of her lashes. She started to speak.

"He was supposed to—"

But I did not listen. I drew my sword, brought it out with a whickering sound. Light flashed from the mirrored steel. The guards saw, tore their own blades free of the lacquered sheaths that swung from scabbard-hooks at their belts. They socketed their shields into place on their arms.

Rannon gave a tiny despairing cry. She leaped forward to grab at my wrist.

For an instant I hesitated, wanting to fight, wanting to hurt—not Rannon but some surrogate for her. But she was there in front of me, a wild blueness in her eyes. Her hair was too soft.

I turned and ran. Toward the window. Shutters of tharspa wood covered that opening against the night's chill. I went through them, shoulder and hip taking the impact, the thin slats of wood exploding outward in a rending shatter of sound.

The guards were close. I heard them shout. I heard Rannon. But I was dropping through debris and air. A dozen feet below lay one of the many small, protected gardens that dot the inner workings of Hurnan Jystral's palace. I tucked my limbs close to my body, the blade of the sword beneath my left arm, hit a cropped sward with knees bent, and rolled before springing back to my feet.

Voices from the apartment above hurled orders at me like arrows. I ignored them. Ran. I leaped a row of sweet blooming goldenswords, dashed between bushes rich with hanris berries. A short wall welcomed me. It was barely six feet high—no need to keep people out when they already had to be in the inner court to reach this place—and I went over it easily.

Beyond lay a covered walk that sliced straight between the wall of the garden and the rising granite shoulder of the central keep. There were more apartments here—those of the royal family...and their guards.

I turned left along that brick-lined walkway, racing toward the backlit glory that marked the chapel of Sevarian, the major Nysphalian god. Behind the alabaster pile of that chapel stood the darkness of the stables, with the outer wall of the palace rising on the other side.

It was to the stables that I headed, thinking of the horses there, and of the saddle-birds. Thinking of escape. Rannon had betrayed me, had been in on the plan to have me arrested. And now I was running. As if what that piece of parchment had said concerning me was true. But I didn't care. Rannon should have believed in me. She should have....

My feet slowed. I pulled to a stop with the chapel looming over me in marble splendor. In the distance I heard the sound of the guard being rousted. Soon the grounds would teem with hunters.

I thought of the stables again, thought of moments ticking away. My fists clenched. I tasted anger, smelled it in my own sweat.

"No!" I muttered to myself.

I turned away from the path to the stables and strode up the steps of the chapel, pushed through the doors and made my way down into the nave. A monk came hurrying toward me, to inform me that the chapel was closed for the evening. He didn't yet know that I was an outlaw. I didn't tell him before I punched him in the face and knocked him cold.

I trussed and gagged him, then stuffed him in the open space beneath his altar where curtains of costly silk would hide him from casually searching eyes. I regretted having had to hit him, but he had something I needed—his clothes.

I took his robe and his hood and slipped them on. They fit tightly, but they hid my sword and face. And with his garments I donned the respect due him as an attendant upon Sevarian.

It was well that I hurried. The robes were just settling around my ankles when there came the stomp of boots on marble and the doors thrust back to reveal a dozen guards with drawn steel. Half of them started down the aisle. They didn't notice me at first, and when they did they stopped instantly.

Their leader was young, a devout man it seemed. He made no attempt to look into his monk's face. He could not have seen it anyway.

"Forgive the intrusion, honored Phrer," he said, bowing. "But we search for an outlaw. A dangerous man. Have you seen anyone?"

I placed my hands on the copper altar and inclined my head. "I have not," I said. "But only moments ago I heard running feet outside the chapel. I think it was toward the stables that they headed."

The leader nodded, eyes brightening in the candled dimness.

"Of course," he said. "Thank you, Phrer."

He turned abruptly, pushing his men ahead of him back down the aisle. In moments the chapel was empty, the air silent as the dead. I waited for the silence to enter me, waited for it to freeze my rage. And when my heart felt as cold as the copper of the altar under my fingertips, I left the chapel in my cowled robes and strode through the palace grounds toward the central keep and the dungeons beneath. By now, Kreeg was probably there in one of the cells. Diken Graye certainly was. And I didn't intend for either of them to stay behind when I left Nyshphal forever.

Chapter Eight

At Dungeon's Heart

I always imagined dungeons as cold places, with fetid water dripping on fungus-slimy walls. The dungeons of Timmuzz are not like that. The halls where I walked were of a delicate coral color, dry and warm, and well-lighted with rundal-oil lamps that cleanly scented the air. And though they were below ground, in the belly-soil of the island of Nyshphal, the corridors were wide and the cells as adequate as any cage can be.

I found Kreeg pacing his adequate room like a spear-maddened ghyre. I hadn't needed to kill anyone to find him. That didn't mean I hadn't hurt a few. The dark robes of a Sevarian monk had served me well as a disguise. I'd entered the keep unopposed, and because the monks commonly minister to the prisoners I'd been able to surprise what few guards I'd encountered on my way into the gaol. Those guards were now bound and gagged and resting uncomfortably in various hiding places. I didn't think they would soon be found, but still imagined that getting out of the dungeons would be tougher than getting in, even though I now had a set of keys dangling in one hand.

Kreeg's glare was enough to fell a stugah when I opened his cell door and stepped through.

"I need no priest," he growled. But when I pushed back my cowl and he saw my face, he rushed forward and bear-hugged me.

"I won't have to kill the Emperor after all," he crowed, squeezing me even harder.

"No you won't, I said, gasping. "Seeing as how you are killing me *for* him."

He blinked, then quickly released me and stepped back. "I am sorry, Ruenn," he murmured.

I only laughed and slapped his shoulder. Then I handed him the weapons I'd taken for him—a short-sword and the four-foot ironwood stave that is sometimes used on recalcitrant prisoners. None of the guards I'd knocked out had worn armor big enough for the massive ex-slave, though I'd found a steel cuirass for myself that I wore beneath the robes.

As we turned toward the door of the cell, Kreeg stopped me again, with a hand on my arm.

"I am also sorry...Ruenn. That I was not there when they came to arrest you. That Vlih dog. Rhandh. It was a trap."

I met his gaze. My eyes went hot. "I know," I said grimly. "But Rhandh was only doing what he was ordered. Our betrayal was not his."

Kreeg nodded. He had apologized to me—though truly there had been no need—and now his straight-furrow mind was already turning itself toward the next concern in his life.

"We get out. But how?"

"I have an idea. But first we fetch Diken Graye. And Valyan after. Graye is the best chance of finding my brother," I added.

I had wondered if even Kreeg would protest the idea of taking along Diken Graye. But he trusted me and followed without comment as we exited his cell and turned down the corridor toward the central core of the dungeons. After all, I'd led him deeper into dungeons before and gotten him out. I prayed I would again.

The underground prisons of Timmuzz are shaped vaguely like a wagon wheel; the interrogation chambers where Diken Graye would be held were at the hub. With lamps growing fewer and the smell of the corridors growing steadily more rank, we reached those chambers in a few dhorrin (minutes). In a few more we found that which we sought.

Diken Graye sat alone in a stone cell, unharmed, apparently untouched. The key to his door of iron bars hung on the wall, and I had no suspicions of it being too easy until sudden torches flared up behind us. I had just reached to take the key, but now I stopped and turned, my skin grown clammy with sweat beneath my robes.

Immediately outside of Graye's cell was a circular room about fifteen feet across. It contained a heavy, scarred table and several chairs. Three sets of steps led down to it. We had come down one set. Kuurus Jystral, brother to Rannon, had just come down another with a dozen of his personal guard before him. These wore black tunics with silver snake-and-lightning piping on the sleeves. A few carried torches; the rest bore crossbows that were locked and loaded. All of them held the bite of violence in their eyes.

I heard Diken Graye rise from his cot behind us but did not turn my gaze from Kuurus. Rannon's younger brother was slighter than I, less than six feet tall and probably weighing no more than a hundred and eighty pounds. His hair hung longer than mine—past the shoulders in artificial curls—and was as glossy dark as his sister's. His eyes were blue in a handsome face. There were those who called him "pretty," though not where he could hear.

Seldom had Kuurus and I spoken. I did not think he liked me much, though I did not know why. Now he smirked with a curve of lips that were almost too generous to be those of a human male.

"Amazing," he said. "My father is such a *brilliant* man but he did not think to look for you here. And my sister.... Well, my sister is blinded. 'Tis fortunate that I am not so easily beguiled."

"Aye," I said, smiling.

Kuurus frowned, wondering, perhaps, why I did not look afraid or angry, why I smiled. I did so because his words had told me much of interest, not least of which was that only he and his twelve men knew where we were.

I glanced at Kreeg. His sword was held in his left hand; in the right he idly spun the ironwood stave. My own blade twitched in my fist and I took a step forward and spread my arms.

"Kill me, Kuurus," I said. "That's the only way you'll stop me." I started walking toward him.

Muscles went tight in the arms of Kuurus's men. Fingers

quivered suddenly on crossbow triggers. Pupils dilated. Then Kuurus was shouting at his guards not to fire. He knew, as I knew, that it was not quite yet acceptable to shoot me down like a dog or a wurstid. He wanted to capture me. He *needed* to capture me.

"Free me!" Diken Graye was shouting from behind his bars. I had no time.

There came the putting away of crossbows, the drawing of swords. At dungeon's heart would stand thirteen men against two. But the thirteen could not come at the two all at once. Kreeg took the left side of the room, I the right. The ex-slave kept the table between himself and the guards; I stalked forward openly.

The attack came. I kicked a chair into two of my foes, sent them down in a tangle, followed that with a blazing lunge that cut a man to the bone of his shoulder. His sword clattered to the floor as he fell back. The stench of blood shocked the room.

I heard Kreeg's staff crack on flesh, heard an aborted scream. Then the mad heat took me. The anger had roiled in my belly ever since the word treason had been mentioned beside my name. I released it now.

A sword stabbed toward me. I slapped it aside with a bare hand against the flat of it, slashed my own blade down across the man's face. He vented a shriek that spumed with crimson. I ducked another sword, spun and lashed out with a foot. Nyshphalians have never invented spurs but the heels of their boots are often adorned with spiked buckles that serve much the same purpose. My buckles acted as weapons now as my swinging leg ripped one man's feet from under him in a spray of wet red. I came around with my sword whickering out to cut another man across the wrist, sending his weapon flying, making him back away in fear.

Kreeg wielded a vicious cudgel, keeping his short-sword as a defense and backup. He'd put two foes out of the fight, was engaged with two more. Others were blocked by the oaken dining board. One man jumped on top of the table near me, hoping to leap down behind us. I kicked the table's claw-footed leg, jarred the man into a fall. He landed on hands and knees and I hammered him to blackness with the hilt of my sword.

Six of Kuurus's men were out of the fight, in the space of moments, and neither Kreeg nor I had been touched. We'd killed none of them, for they were Rannon's people and I still loved her, but they were no good to their prince now. I heard Kuurus screaming at his men to take us, his voice growing shriller as I skipped about, my sword flaming, parrying, riposting. I shouted at him.

"You're next, Kuurus!"

A guard lunged at me, tripped over the body of his friend, and I cut him across the neck just deep enough to let him know how easily he could have been dead. The man dropped his weapon and grabbed for his throat. He rolled away from me and I shouted at Rannon's brother again.

"That's seven, Kuurus! How many more do you have?"

The prince panicked, forgetting that he needed to capture us, in terror now for his life. I saw it come over his face and cursed myself as a fool for pushing too hard.

"Kill them!" Kuurus shrieked. "Shoot them! Kill them!"

Two of his men backed away, reaching for their crossbows. It was my turn to enjoy fear. Kreeg was hard pressed by a massive fellow who hacked madly at his defenses. Another pair of enemies stood between me and the crossbowmen. I attacked those two, cutting left and right, driving my foes back with a sustained flurry.

It wasn't going to be enough.

Already, the two disengaged guards had drawn their crossbows. I heard the mechanisms lock as they chambered their bolts, the sound like a rusted snarl.

"Watch out!" I shouted desperately at Kreeg, as I wished for a shield and raised my sword for one slim chance at blocking a flashing quarrel.

"Tell them to hold!" a voice boomed, cutting through the murk of violence. "Tell them to hold, Prince Kuurus. Or I *will* kill you."

Everyone stilled. Fingers locked on crossbow triggers, or on the hilts of swords and staves. We all glanced up. Valyan stood there, the gleaming point of his rapier pressed against the pale throat of Kuurus Jystral.

"Do as he says," Kuurus growled, his eyes seething...and scared.

"And have them put down their weapons," I added.

Kuurus nodded, and the clack of steel on stone that followed made a pleasing music.

I met Valyan's gaze. His skin looked sallow beneath its normal emerald tint, and he wore bandages like another set of clothes. But his eyes smoked with threat and the point of his rapier did not waver.

"Thanks, old friend," I said.

"I came as soon as I heard what happened," he replied. "They overlooked me in the infirmary and I came here, knowing how unlikely it was that you'd allow anything to thwart your plans."

I only nodded as I bent and picked up a crossbow. Valyan understood me well.

Kreeg opened the cell for Diken Graye and we herded Kuurus and his dozen guards into the room as Graye left it. None of them were wounded so badly that their bleeding could not be patched with strips of torn clothing.

I slammed the cell door; Kreeg locked it. Kuurus grabbed the bars of the small window, stabbed me with blue eyes.

"You've destroyed yourself here," he sneered.

I shrugged and turned away. Diken Graye armed himself with a sword and crossbow. I well remembered his skill with the latter and did not tell him nay. We might have need of his skills. He followed Kreeg and Valyan and myself as we left the interrogation chamber and started up the steps away from the dungeon.

Behind us, I heard Kuurus ranting. "Traitor! Bastard! I'll kill you! You're finished, Maclang!"

None of it hurt except the last.

"Rannon will hate you for this!" he shouted.

Chapter Nine

A Morning of Wings

"Should we gag them, at least?" Diken Graye asked, speaking of Prince Kuurus and the men we'd left locked in Graye's cell when we'd freed him. "Do you not worry that they'll be heard?"

I said nothing as I strode on.

Graye continued with his questions. "So our escape will be swift? How? A flyer?"

"Those will be watched," I snapped.

"Saddle birds then? How far is it to the stables?"

"We're not going to the stables," I said.

There was a building on the palace grounds, of course, where both land and air mounts were normally kept. But we weren't going there.

I knew that Diken Graye must have glanced at Valyan and Kreeg then, seeking confirmation that the man they followed was mad. I didn't think he would get what he wanted. The Emerald Llurn and the ex-fighting slave only rushed to keep up with me as we fled up the stairs from the dungeons into the keep proper.

Graye grabbed my arm and dragged me around. His face was flushed.

"Then tell me where we *are* going," he demanded.

With both hands, I took him by the collar of the leather vest he wore and smashed him back against the stone wall, jarring him brutally.

"I don't like you!" I snapped. "I dragged you free of that stinking cell to help me find my brother. Perhaps another of my family who might be with him. But I *don't* like you. *Never* touch me again!"

Graye's eyes lit with inner flares and I waited for him to lash out at me. I would have welcomed it. But after a moment he looked down and the tension broke in both of us—mine more slowly than his. I released him with a half shove and turned to hurry onward, my anger fading under the flying spurs of time.

At each corner of the main keep there wound a set of narrow granite stairs that reached from the wine cellars to the roof. Few ever used those steps to move from floor to floor, preferring the magnificent bone and glass staircases in the center of the castle. It was mostly guards who took the danker stairwells, or children at play on the steps as if they were city walls to storm. Now, we followed one of those musty ways, four tough men with honed blades ready.

Diken Graye had wondered why we did not head for the stables, where saddle birds could be found that might allow us a chance at freedom. What he didn't know was that not all the Emperor's birds were kept in the stables. On the roof of the keep there were half a dozen at least—of a species known as sabrun. These are slender, thin-boned, sleek, and over short distances they can outpace any other saddle bird in the sky, even the swift and savage kryll. Their weight carrying capacity is limited, but then, critical messages from the Emperor do not generally weigh much in the physical sense.

When I had first heard of the sabrun messenger corps it put me in mind of the pony express on my own world. There were the same devil-may-care relay riders, and the way stations where exhausted mounts could be replaced with fresh. The major difference, other than the medium through which the messages were carried, was that the sabrun corps served only the purposes of the emperor.

I well recalled how, in childhood, I would wish that I had lived in the time of the pony express. It seemed I was about to have that experience after all. In a way. We were going to steal four of the sabrun. I thought they might be overlooked by the searchers who hunted us.

We reached the roof. Deep overhead, the sky was still raven-dark, though a thick mist curled around us that was tinted with the promise of morning. I had not realized how much time had passed while we were in the dungeons. In a few dhorrin the city's life would stir and our chances of escape would lessen.

We started quickly forward through the clinging fog, feeling the cool wet of it spiderweb our skins, and in a dozen paces the outbuilding that housed the sabrun loomed ghost-like from its surroundings. There were no sentries here. Not on this side of the building. We found them in front of the gridded door that faced the outside wall of the keep. There were three guards and two bird riders. The latter were marked by the variety of hooks and straps that decorated their clothing—for fastening them to their mounts amid the wild currents of the air.

All five men were armed, but they didn't look ready for a fight. Even if they *had* been told of the traitor Ruenn's escape, they clearly didn't expect him to come here. I sent Valyan and Kreeg around the back way to come up behind them, then stepped out from the corner and strolled casually in their direction. I still wore my monkish robes, and the men straightened their backs when they saw me. One dropped the rolled jitter grass that he was smoking and ground it out under a heel. Religion is a powerful thing.

I stopped a dozen feet from the men, just as they began to show agitation, and proclaimed in a loud voice: "The Lord God Sevarian's servants require the use of your mounts, good warriors."

"What?" a guard asked. They all blinked, then looked at each other in confusion.

"I want your birds," I explained.

"But—But—Phrer," one sputtered. "We cannot grant such a request."

"You don't understand," I said, drawing a crossbow from under my robes. "I'm not asking."

The five of them gaped, too stunned for the moment to even reach for a weapon. By the time they remembered steel, Valyan and Kreeg had stolen up and cocked their crossbows loudly just behind them.

"Don't," I snapped at the two who started to turn. And they all stood quietly while they were disarmed and bound against the wall.

In another few moments, with the mist pearling all around us in the coming dawn, we had opened the sabrun mews and led out the birds. They were balky about being awakened, and fluffed steel-gray feathers at us while glaring from violet eyes. But they were well trained and did not threaten to use their beaks or black talons against us.

Two of the birds were already saddled and Diken and Valyan saddled two more, moving swiftly in the vague grayness. Still, I chafed at the delay. It was barely a handful of minutes before the bell of the fourth dhaur would call the morning. Then the sun would pour over the horizon and the light would grow swiftly. The flyers of the day patrols would lift and we would certainly be seen. And even the swiftest sabrun cannot outrun a flyer.

Then the birds were ready and the last problem we had to solve was upon us; I had never ridden a saddle bird before. Graye and Valyan were experts. Even Kreeg had experience. It is something most Taleran warriors and nobles do at one time or another.

Valyan gave me three minutes of instruction. "There are four reins," he explained. "Left, right. Up, down."

I noted that the reins were attached to a black iron collar that fit snugly to the bird's neck. From there they ran to an elaborate metal bit that locked around the beak, serving not only to guide the beast but also to keep its hooked and deadly mouth closed.

"Left and right reins are the same as in a horse or tasaber," Valyan continued. "Up and down are just what you'd expect. Don't get them confused. The sharpness of a turn depends on the amount of pressure you exert. Haul back on the reins to slow and stop. Release them for speed."

I nodded.

He handed me the "wing-stick," a blunt-headed prod about two and a half feet long, with a wrist strap at the other end.

"You can use this to help guide him," the Nakscherii warrior told me. "Or at worst you can beat him about the head with it if he tries to eat you."

I glanced at him to see if he was joking. If there was a

smile, it was well hidden.

"Thanks...ever so much for the advice," I told him, as I took the prod.

The bird squatted when I touched its throat with the wing-stick and I climbed into the small saddle, which sat just forward of the massively thewed pinions. I locked my feet in the attached stirrups as Valyan showed me how to hold the reins, down and left reins in the left hand, up and right in the right hand. It was awkward to have to use the fingers of the same hand independently.

The green Llurn strapped me in and then raced for his own bird. Graye and Kreeg were already mounted. As Valyan saddled up, the morning bells pealed out and my heart caught. Now the city would begin to awaken.

"Haih Kerang," Graye shouted, and his sabrun took two steps and leaped from the roof of the keep. I heard the snap of wings and the bird rose, Graye clinging to its back, working the reins. Kreeg followed, looking distinctively ill. And then it was my turn.

"Haih Kerang," I shouted. "Let's ride."

Now my bird took its two steps and leaped. For a blink we were in free fall, my heart hammering, the earth rushing fast to meet us as I jerked the up-rein taut. Massive wings spread and snapped against the foggy air. The jolt nearly took my breath as the sabrun's fall was arrested in an instant and we were rising instead.

I saw Kreeg and Graye above me, their birds still climbing, and already the lifting sun was upon them as it burned through the night's mist. Behind and beneath me, distantly, I heard Valyan shout and knew he was coming.

A patrol flyer drifted around the far corner of the keep. Its sleek outline and slanted prow marked it as a pursuit craft. There were two men on board with the pilot. One would certainly have a signal horn.

I worked my left hand reins, bringing the sabrun around in a tight curve toward the flyer. We leveled out and I let both sets of reins trail down over the bird's neck, giving the creature the slack that signaled for speed. Its wings stroked; we leaped forward. My right hand dipped alongside the saddle and came up with one of the steel lances that are habitually sheathed there on riding birds.

The three men in the flyer looked shocked as they saw the bird coming at them with me on its back. In another moment they would have detected our small group anyway, and would have kept us in sight while calling for the pursuit that would surely overtake us. There was no way short of killing all three of them to keep a signal of our escape from going out. And I would not have their murders stain my soul. But perhaps....

The bird and I swept toward them, our shadow blotting across their sky. I saw one man darting for their ballista. The other hefted a crossbow. I half stood in my stirrups, the lance rising in my hand, poising itself for a strike, and as we passed above them, scarcely a dozen yards over their deck, I hurled that strike. The lance seemed to shiver in the air, and then it hit, tearing deep into the rotors that channeled power from the energy wands to the ship's drive. With a tortured shriek those rotors locked up.

I grabbed the sabrun's reins again, wheeled the bird to the right just as a crossbow bolt flashed past my cheek. It did no more damage than the curses that lifted from the airship's crew. They wouldn't be trailing us now, and even though they would signal an alarm we had a good chance to elude any blind pursuit that would follow.

Suddenly, Valyan was there beside me and we both put our birds into a climb. We found Kreeg and Diken Graye up above, and as the sun ascended fully over the horizon the four of us arrowed away through the gathering brightness, toward the city of Trazull on the Rosjavik Peninsula.

I glanced back, saw the rose and coral buildings of Timmuzz blushing under the morning sun, and the finality of it sledgehammered me. I was leaving. The life that I'd thought awaited me in Nyshphal was over. But that was hardly the worst.

Rannon Jystral was gone from my world.

Chapter Ten

City of Outlaws

We landed in a flurry of wings in a bustling marketplace of the city of Trazull. People and chickens scattered. Tavarels bleated. Vulls and terthins whirled up in a thrumming cloud from where they pecked and fought over garbage. We dismounted our sabruns among the gaping onlookers, not all of whom were human.

Diken Graye had argued for a quiet approach to the city, for slipping in under the cover of darkness. I'd vetoed him. We would go in boldly. If my brother were here, I wanted him to know of our arrival. And if there were enemies of Nyshphal who wanted us dead.... Well, let them try. Despite my rejection by Rannon and her family, I had determined to find out who was attacking their lands and put a stop to the plundering. If I could.

Somewhere in this city we would find news concerning the "who" and "why" of the recent raids on Nyshphal, and tangled with the answers to those questions was the fate of my brother. Because of him, the goad of impatience bit me deeply.

Handing the reins of my sabrun to Kreeg, I strode a dozen paces past stalls and carts and awnings and people, the sounds and odors a bright assault on my senses. This was only one of the bazaars of Trazull, but at this time of the day it was the most heavily trafficked. The crowd nearly filled the smallish square and spilled over into the surrounding streets. There were half a dozen races among them, but mostly I saw humans and Kaldi and Ss'Korra. They all made way for me as I reached the central fountain and stepped up on its rim.

Gray stones, worn and scuffed by years of use, seemed to welcome my boots. A mist-spray of water filmed over me, cutting through the burn of cook fires that tingled in my nostrils. Dogs yapped, circling widely around the sharp black beaks of the sabruns and the raw eyes of Kreeg, and Valyan, and Graye. The people fell silent and watched. There were hard beings among that crowd, beings with old scars and fresh bruises, beings with swords ready for callused hands. Even they watched.

"I am Ruenn Maclang of Nyshphal!" I shouted. "I seek my brother, Bryce. Or any that know of him. I will ask you all to send word."

I glanced around. Directly across from me hung the thorn-wood sign of a tavern. I pointed to it.

"Tell Bryce Maclang!" I shouted again to the crowd. "Tell Bryce to meet his brother at the sign of The Rattling Saber. Tomorrow at the tenth dhorr."

I stepped down from the fountain, strode back to the saddle birds. The four of us mounted. Broad wings spread and flattened against the air, and the sabruns took the sky with cries of "Haih Kerang" cracking across the square. A cart overturned in the buffeting wind, sending copper pots clattering like thunder in a gathering storm.

The sound seemed appropriate.

* * * * * * *

I gazed down upon the lights of Trazull. It was now near the twentieth Dhorr, the Taleran midnight, and we were encamped upon the brush-dotted ridge that curves around the sprawl of the city from the southern shore to the northern shore of the Temeri Sea.

It is said that this ridge is not natural, that it was once a wall. I believe it, for in scrounging for firewood I had nearly fallen into a narrow, stone stairwell that descended *into* the ridge. Trazull is a very old city, built long years before and settled by men unlike the pirates and outlaws who inhabit it now.

Wings Over Talera, by Charles Allen Gramlich

Diken Graye coughed and I turned toward him. Kreeg and Valyan were asleep. It was my watch. Graye had not even tried to seek his blankets. He squatted, this man who had once been a Thorn Nomad, and stared into the fire as if he searched for solace there. I strode over to him, squatted across from him and poured myself a cup of fragrant verhlis tea. He glanced up.

"Why have you not fled?" I asked him. He was, after all, a prisoner of sorts. And yet there were no bonds holding him; he even carried weapons. A dozen times he could have escaped us aboard his sabrun. I wondered why he had not.

He shrugged in answer to my query, his black eyes finding and holding mine. Then he looked away.

While I sipped my tea, the mercenary glanced down the ridge toward Trazull. Even to this distance the occasional raucous shout carried. Trazull is not a city that goes early to bed.

"I once thought I belonged with such men as those," Graye said abruptlly, jutting his chin toward Trazull's harbor where pirate brigs rubbed wooden shoulders with sloops and caravels manned by outlaws.

I did not speak, letting him find his own way through his thoughts.

"I told myself that my home was a deck or a saddle," he continued. He shook his head. "But it isn't enough."

His gaze met mine again. "Do you understand?" he asked.

"Yes," I said, and I thought of Rannon and felt a pain that I was suddenly sure Diken Graye knew something about.

He sighed, and I changed the subject. But it was for my sake rather than his. "Did you ever," I began, "hear of a man named Eric Ryall? Perhaps linked in some way with my brother?"

He frowned. "The name is not familiar. Why?"

I started to answer, but he clicked his teeth at me as it occurred to him. "The other member of your family!" he blurted. "He of whom you spoke before. Without naming him."

"Yes," I agreed. "He, too, is lost."

Wings Over Talera, by Charles Allen Gramlich

"I do not know of him," he said. "I'm sorry."

We both remained silent for a bit. It had drizzled earlier, a barely chilled drizzle that meant the coming spring was almost upon us, and the damp wood crackled in the fire as we sat there. I pulled a blanket around my shoulders, for winter still owned this night at least.

"I apologize, also," Graye added, "for my behavior in Nysphal's dungeon. I should have been grateful for the rescue. Even if it was not friendship that motivated it."

"We were both frustrated," I said. "My own anger was uncalled for."

He nodded, and after a bit: "Do you think it will be your brother who meets us tomorrow at the Rattling Saber?"

"I think it will be men trying to kill us. I'm not sure *why* I think that."

He nodded. "Your brother seemed...an important man among them. He did not...."

I waited for him to continue, and when he held his words I prodded. "He did not what?"

"He did not seem much like you."

"How so?" I asked, not sure that I truly wanted to know.

"He was cold. I judged him brutal. And thought he needed no reason to show it."

I started to protest but he rushed on.

"He resembled you greatly, though his hair was dead white and his face tattooed, like the ritual scarrings of the Thorn Nomads. But done in ink."

"Bryce's hair is nearly as dark as mine, I said. "He has no tattoos."

"Then you have a second brother on Talera," Graye retorted. "And *his* hair is white and *his* face tattooed." He frowned as if something more had occurred to him. "There was something...odd about his markings, too. Something I don't know how to name."

"Tell me," I demanded, leaning forward, fists knotted against legs. "What about his marks?"

Graye met my gaze and did not flinch. "They moved."

I shook my head. "They could not have."

"But they did," he said, and now he looked down, into the fire, and he spoke so softly I could scarcely hear. "His eyes were the worst, though. The very worst."

I reached out to grab his collar and he caught my wrist, held it as he lifted his head and the shadows and fire played on his lean face.

"His eyes were red. Like pearls. Bloody pearls. He had no pupils. It wasn't...human."

I shook off his hand. "You lie!"

His lips twisted. "I am still enough of a nomad not to lie. And you and I both know that I speak the truth now."

My shoulders slumped. The blanket and fire were suddenly not enough to warm me. "What has happened to him?" I asked to no one, and wondered if my voice sounded as hollow and empty as I felt.

Diken Graye shrugged, rose to his feet to loom over me.

"I will stay until you find your brother," he said. "Or," he paused, scuffing a furrow in the dirt with his boot, "until it is clear you will not."

Then he turned and sought his blankets, leaving me alone in an overwhelming darkness.

"Brother," I murmured. "Where are you? *What* are you?"

There was one other question that I did not voice. Even in a whisper. But I thought it.

The parchment note that Rannon had shown me in Timmuzz, the one that had done so much to discredit me in her eyes and in the eyes of her father: why had Bryce written it?

Chapter Eleven

The "Rattling Saber"

Alone on my sabrun, I landed in the market square of Trazull where yesterday I had announced the search for my brother. It was deep into the Spring Passage by now but still there were no celebrations underway here to rival the kind of city-wide festivals that would be taking place in Nyshphal and many other lands. I suppose a government is needed to plan such affairs, and there is no government in Trazull save the will of mercenaries and pirate captains.

Fewer people were in the square today than before, but it was clear that most knew who I was. Fingers pointed; I heard whispers as I led the saddle bird to the hitching rail in front of the Rattling Saber tavern and tied him off. From beneath the stirrup at the right side of the bird's saddle, I drew out a twelve foot lance of steel. My left hand gripped the scabbard of my sword, just behind the quillions where I could push the blade forward to draw it quickly if needed. At my right hip, and in a sheath sewn into my boot, there were daggers.

The door to the tavern stood open. Even in the fresh sun and the salt air I could smell stale odors from past spills of wine, and ale, and kumiss. I stepped onto the wooden walkway in front of the tavern and strode inside. Six beings sat at the tables, not all at the same table. Bryce was not among them. Nor Eric. I had not expected them to be. Finding Eric here was a fool's hope anyway.

My glance found the stairs and followed them to the second floor. A balcony and railing circled that floor but I saw no one there. I nodded to the bartender, who poured a pewter mug full of ale and passed it to me. I took a sip as I turned toward the larger part of the room.

"I'm looking for my brother," I said. "He was supposed to meet me here at the tenth dhaur." *At noon*, my mind translated.

"You are Ruenn Maclang?" a voice asked.

I glanced toward the speaker, not letting myself forget the corners of my eyes and the others who watched. The being who rose and faced me was too large for the chair that had seated him—nearly seven feet in height. He was of that race called the Nokarra, who are superb warriors, who are cat-like in appearance and grace. His eyes had a strange crimson sheen, though primarily they were blue, unlike most of his race who have gold or green eyes—or both. His fur was short and bristly and almost black. That color, too, was unusual. He smelled like cloves.

The haft of an axe protruded over the Nokarran's shoulder, and he wore twin short swords scabbarded behind a thick black belt that held up russet leathers. The Nokarra are humanoid—two arms, two legs, two eyes. The fur of this one's chest was partially shaved and bore an inked symbol consisting of a solid sphere inside another circle, with lighting bolts connecting the two at six separate points. Something about the symbol struck me as familiar, but now was not the time to worry over it.

"Aye," I said, in answer to the Nokarran's question. "I am Ruenn Maclang. Who are you?"

"Your master," he replied, drawing the axe over his shoulder and seating it firmly in both massive fists.

"Perhaps," I said, shrugging. I made no move to reach for my own blade. My left hand was filled with a mug of ale; my right still held the lance. Its tip pointed at the floor.

The Nokarran did not even glance at the other five occupants of the tables. By that I knew them all for his allies. I took a swig of ale, half felt and half saw a shifting of bodies to either side of the Nokarran. My muscles tensed and from the corner of an eye I glimpsed something that flashed toward me. I batted the wheel-dagger aside with my mug, sending the weapon spinning and clanging away in a spray of bitter ale. From the balcony above, there leaped a blurred streak of light that materialized as an arrow through the chest of the knife thrower. He went back and down, dragging a chair with him.

The Nokarran glanced up, wildly, looking for the archer. The other four assassins were on their feet as well, but held for an instant by the threat of feathered death. I silently thanked Valyan for his aim as I tossed the warped mug aside and drew my sword left handed. Two of the remaining assassins were human, one was an outlaw Klar, the fourth a burn scarred Ss'Korra.

The Ss'Korra leaped toward me, shouting: "Kill you, human!"

I put my lance through him with a savage cast and he vomited blood as he fell backward. Then I switched hands with the saber and attacked, charging the Nokarran, who I judged the most dangerous of the bunch.

The axe-wielder swung his weapon desperately to keep me off, his timing thrown by Valyan's unexpected presence. I dodged, not blocking with my sword. His axe was of the type sometimes called blade-breaker, with twin, crescent-moon heads of polished steel that curved and hooked viciously toward the haft. I slashed at him above his guard and cut one cheek to the bone, but missed the eye as he hurled himself backward, agile as a lynx.

Outside the tavern there was commotion. I heard running feet. And six men burst through the door into the room, weapons drawn, eyes on fire with the threat of violence. They were looking for me, and that meant at least twelve killers had been used to set this trap. Probably more. I didn't know how many heads Valyan had taken when he'd secured the second floor.

Another arrow flashed from the balcony and one newcomer went down kicking. I heard someone shout, "Get him!" and three of that crowd rushed the stairs after Valyan. I wished him the best and parried a sword coming in from my right. Two others among the original assassins tried to charge me. I cut them both and leaped away.

Then the Nokarran came roaring in, axe twinkling, striking down. I dodged and the heavy weapon splintered an oaken table into fragments. He was fast and the axe licked up and to the side, quick as a snake's strike. I felt the brush of it against my leather jerkin as I dodged again. Snarling, I slashed at him, felt the shock of his strength as he blocked with the axe's bone-reinforced haft. He twisted the weapon, trying to drag my blade down and break it.

"You're meat," he growled.

"Not yours," I said, and I disengaged with a spin, coming around with the spiked heel of my boot snapping high.

I was going for the beast's throat but got his shoulder and upper chest instead, tearing raw furrows through fur and skin. He howled, fell back, and I ended the spin with a drop to one knee, lunging with saber held straight and flat toward the Klar, who was coming hard from the side. He impaled himself, the tip lancing from his back in a spray of red froth. In the next instant I was back on my feet, the sword coming free of the Klar's body with a wet, grating sound.

At the bar, the two remaining newcomers prepared to rush me, to finish the fight. They never got the chance. The bartender knocked them cold from behind with the drunk-persuader that is usually to be found in such taverns. Then, Diken Graye tossed aside his club and his disguise and vaulted the bar with a laugh and a readied sword.

Of the six assassins in the Rattling Saber when I arrived, only three were left—two humans and the Nokarran axe-wielder. The men turned to face Diken. The Nokarran's eyes locked with mine, filled with a feral light. And from above on the balcony we all heard attack turn to rout, as the three men who had gone after Valyan found Kreeg slipping from a supposedly empty room to take them from behind.

With the dice rolling now in *my* favor, I stepped back and offered the Nokarran a mocking salute with my sword. He growled, and rushed. I should have leaped aside; I could have avoided him. But there are those who say that in battle I am devil-possessed, and perhaps they are right. As the being side-armed his axe toward me, whipping it across his body to split me apart, I leaped in.

The axe-head missed me; his arm struck my side. I barely felt that blow as I dropped my sword and punched with a shoulder into the beast's rib cage. He grunted and I grabbed one of his legs and a hip. And I picked him up and threw him into the wall behind us. The room shook when he hit, and again when he crashed to the floor, and before he could get to his feet I whirled and palmed a dagger and hurled it. That foot of steel buried itself to the quillions in his throat, and his axe fell from useless fingers as he died.

Valyan dropped soft-footed from the balcony to the floor, and Kreeg rushed down the stairs with a bloody axe of his own. The remaining two assassins licked dry lips and backed away from where they had been pressing their attack against Diken Graye. Outnumbered and surrounded, they tossed their swords aside. The battle was over.

* * * * * * *

"All mercenaries," Valyan said in disgust as he looked over our slain foes and the four survivors bound against the bar. Two of the latter were still unconscious from Diken Graye's clubbing.

"All except this one," I muttered, bending over the Nokarran. He no longer smelled like cloves. Already, corruption was seeping in. I pulled my dagger from his throat, wiped it clean against his fur, and sheathed it. Then I bent further to examine the odd tattoo that etched the center of his chest.

A bystander, more curious than wise, peeked into the tavern, then ducked quickly out as Kreeg glared at him. I ignored the distraction, studying the tattoo, and again that sense of familiarity struck me. Two spheres? One inside the other? And lightning bolts connecting them?

For the first time I noticed some smaller details of the symbol. Above the solid central sphere, but inside the outer one, a small...orb was inked. This was quartered in fours, each a different color—blue, green, gold, red. On the opposite side of the central sphere, placed close together, were four more orbs. These were evenly spaced, but from left to right each was bigger than the one before. They also were colored, and a chill flashed along my spine.

"Blue, green, gold, red," I murmured to myself. I bent closer. "Yes!" Two dots, no larger than freckles, straddled the third orb of the four. And I knew.

"Why don't you think that one is a mercenary?" Valyan

asked over my shoulder.

I did not answer him, but said: "Someone who covets, or who carries a grudge, is launching the attacks on Nyshphal. Who? And what do Bryce and I have to do with it?"

"The target *must* be Nyshphal," Graye said. "You and your brother are only pieces on the board."

"Likely," I agreed. "But again I ask who?"

"I think Ubai," Kreeg said.

Valyan glanced at him. "The Pangalan Empire! Why?"

"I do not like them," Kreeg replied.

Diken Graye chuckled and Kreeg frowned. I let my eyes rest on Graye's for a moment. He flushed, then looked away.

"I don't think it could be Ubai," Valyan continued. "They're too new at empiring. Got their hands full with the Thorn Nomads to their east. With Delnad and Revanor to the north. They'd be fools to attack a power like Nyshphal."

"Then who do you name?" Kreeg snapped.

Valyan shrugged.

"What if we're thinking too recently?" I asked.

The others looked at me blankly.

"Thirty, Thirty-five, years ago," I said, "most of central and eastern Nyshphal was conquered territory. Half a dozen factions were involved. Hurnan Jystral beat them all. Ran them out. What if today's attacks have old roots? Revenge. Or simply a renewal of plans deferred."

Valyan raised an eyebrow.

"Aye," Kreeg spat. "It must be!"

"Possible," Diken Graye agreed. But which faction?

"There were six," I said, speaking from the reading I'd done in Nyshphalian history. My thoughts softened and ached. It had once seemed wise to learn as much as I could about my adopted country. My *almost* adopted country.

"Delnad and Revanor were two of the six," Valyan offered.

"Yes," I agreed, pulling myself back to the moment. "And Menes-Menehse. The Demalion Alliance at Trazull and Quetta. The Northern League...."

"The Northern League," Graye mused. "Jarn Thevasa's attempt to unify the Waithian clans. But that collapsed right after Jarn's death and the clans have been killing each other ever since. They're not unified enough to pose a threat now."

"Nor is the Demalion Alliance," I said. "The pirate alliance as it was called. These raids might seem their style but it's been thirty years since that coalition self-destructed."

"Menes-Menehse was swallowed by Ubai," Valyan added. "And I don't see how Delnad or Revanor would have the wherewithal. Not with Ubai just waiting for its digestion to clear before it eats them next."

"You mentioned six factions," Diken Graye said, looking at me. "I've only heard five named."

"The sixth was different," I said. "It was a religion. The Priest-Cult of Rampuur."

"Sorcerers, weren't they?" Graye asked.

"So it was rumored. Worshippers of a goddess named Vohanna."

Valyan snarled and I glanced at him in surprise. His lips were thin; his cheek twitched. Then his eyes cooled. "Sorry. It's only that I haven't heard that name in a very long time. And I don't care for it."

Diken Graye beat me to, "why?"

Valyan considered, spoke: "Vo...hanna was one of the twelve First Gods. Those who made the world."

"The Asadhie," I blurted, my thoughts suddenly shocked with recognition. I'd heard Vohanna's name before (see *Swords of Talera*) and knew she was one of the so called "First Gods." But now.... I glanced at the dead Nokarran's tattoo, and back to Valyan.

"Yes," Valyan said, nodding. "They are sometimes named that. The...Asadhie created chosen races to serve them, the Llurns, the Koro, and others. My people, the Nakscherii, were given form by the goddess Ivrail, who was loving and kind."

From what I had heard of the Asadhie, I had my doubts about the kindness of any of them. I didn't interrupt Valyan's story, however.

"Ivrail was one of only two goddesses among the Twelve. The other, her mortal enemy, was Vohanna. Out of jealousy and spite, Vohanna attacked Ivrail. Their followers joined them in the war, and eventually all of the Twelve became involved."

WINGS OVER TALERA, BY CHARLES ALLEN GRAMLICH

He glanced at us. "I know you've all heard of the God War, the destruction from which swept three-quarters of Talera into ruins. That was thousands of years ago. Afterward, the First Gods left Talera." He motioned about, his gesture clearly indicating more than just this tavern. "I was always told that Vohanna's earthly empire covered this sector of Talera. Perhaps that is why parts of Trazull seem so ancient and so much finer than one would expect pirates and outlaws to build."

"And why, in the northern plains of Nyshphal, there is a ruined city called Vohan," I added.

"It was supposedly the capital," Valyan said.

I considered what Valyan had told us. There were, I thought, inaccuracies. But no more than one would expect of religious traditions. The Asadhie had surely existed. But they had never been gods, merely scientifically advanced beings who delighted in manipulating more primitive societies. I knew this from Jedik Ver Lha Yed, a friend who was dead now but who had, himself, been born of a scientific people.

And though there had been a "God War" as Valyan mentioned, it had been only hundreds, not thousands of years ago, and it was not clear at all that the Asadhie had left Talera. Jedik had been convinced that they still shaped this world, though with greatly diminished powers.

I glanced once more at the tattooed symbol inking the Nokarran assassin's chest. Thoughts that had been stirring coalesced. A few moments earlier I had recognized the tattoo for what it was, a perfect representation of Talera, complete with sun, moons, and atmospheric shield. Now, while not exactly a secret, the true nature of Talera as an artificially constructed world is not generally known. None of my companions knew it. And I was aware of no maps that showed the connection between the atmospheric shield and the Taleran surface. Except one. This tattoo.

So who had designed the tattoo? It had to be someone who knew the truth of Talera. Someone like an Asadhie. My mind took the leap that it wanted to take.

I walked over to our prisoners. Three of them looked up at me, fear in their eyes. The fourth was still unconscious.

"Where would a man go if he wanted to worship Vohanna?" I asked them.

Two of them quickly shook their heads to deny any knowledge. I believed them. The third man turned pale and stiffened before he, too, shook his head in denial. I squatted before that one.

"Tell me," I whispered, and Valyan later said that my voice sounded like the purr of steel shredding silk. "Tell me, and you'll live."

Chapter Twelve

Kellet's Bay

The brush around us dripped with night fog; the grass clung wet to our boots. Kreeg, Valyan, Diken Graye, and I stood at the edge of a marsh and looked out upon the small settlement named Kellet's Bay, which lies southwest of Trazull near the craggy tip of the Rosjavik Peninsula. It seemed a typical fishing village. There were no pirate ships anchored here, only skiffs and a few bigger boats. Already the lights were out or dim, though it was barely the sixteenth dhaur, when the drinking would just be starting in Trazull. But these were working people, with hands callused by fishing lines and the handles of scaling knives rather than the hilts of swords. They went to bed early, and rose before dawn.

Yet, there was also a temple to the Goddess Vohanna in this village, at least according to a would-be assassin from a tavern in Trazull. "Tell me and you'll live," I'd said to him. And he had. He'd been afraid to tell. But he had. I wondered what he was so afraid of.

We started forward, the four of us spread out slightly, hands on weapon hilts. Fog swirled around us, patting our faces with slick fingers. The long, rawhide coats—which we'd acquired in Trazull and which were habitually worn by bird riders—flapped tails around us in an occasional leaden gust of salt-tainted wind. The sabruns, we'd left in the marsh, in a small clearing where they were tied loosely enough to work their way free eventually. In case we didn't come back.

The temple seemed to crawl out of the fog toward us.

We stopped. To the left, where fish were scaled, gutted and packed, there stood a row of stalls. Even the wood of them stank, the very grain impregnated with fish oils and blood. To the right were small shacks where fishermen and their families lived. The temple sat between, on an artificial rise, and it had not always been a temple. It was low and squat, and old, built to last, of solid oak and walnut. I figured it originally for a council lodge of some sort. Nothing moved in our fields of vision, though somewhere a sail flapped.

I strode up the stone steps of the temple and pushed at the brass-banded doors, which opened quietly enough to show that the hinges were oiled regularly. The others followed, eyes warily scanning the too-empty night. I stepped inside, where cressets smoked gently. An open skylight let in mist that made a faint golden haze. The room was empty except for light and shadows, and at the far end an altar of peeled tlatel wood. I motioned with a finger and Kreeg stepped into the shadows to keep watch.

Whatever burned in the cressets had been impregnated with rundal oil. I could smell it sweetly curling in my nostrils. And though rundal oil is relatively cheap, poor people such as these fishermen would not casually waste it.

"Why keep it lighted?" Graye asked, echoing my thoughts.

"Perhaps Vohanna fears the dark," I said, shrugging as I started forward through the empty temple toward the altar. Or perhaps, I thought, someone here was expecting visitors tonight.

I considered then my reasons for being in this place. Some connection in my head had argued that the worship of Vohanna was at the heart of both the attacks on Nyshphal and the mystery of my brother's whereabouts. That connection was built out of historical oddities and strange tattoos that were more than they appeared. It linked extinct cults with the present day hiring of mercenaries, and mixed them all with a twisted feeling of dread in my own mind. And there *was* the strange way that Vohanna's name kept popping up in my experience. To free the Klar slaves we'd had to fight a cult who worshiped Vessoth, Vohanna's supposed husband among the gods.[4] Now, here was Vohanna again. I knew I could be wrong, but what else did I have to go on if I wanted to find Bryce?

I stepped behind the low altar and bent to peer at the shelves beneath. Copper bells were there, and a slender dagger, censers, an aspergillum, and other tools of the priestly trade. I shifted a pile of parchments and felt a chill flash through my chest. My hand found a reddish, horseshoe-sized oval of stone and drew it out to set on the altar. It was smooth, about four inches thick, and flat on top except for a dozen empty depressions where something rounded would fit. I recognized it as a matrix for holding toir'in-or stones, a tool of sorcery.

"What is it?" Valyan asked over my shoulder.

I started to explain, but a voice interrupted.

"What do you here?" a man called from the doorway.

He was an old man. He quavered. He quavered even more when Kreeg slipped corded arms around his neck from behind to press a dagger to his throat. A button of blood appeared on the sun-wrinkled skin and I motioned Kreeg to stillness. None of us except Kreeg had heard the door open, and Diken Graye stepped forward to close it again and drop the thick lock-board across it. He leaned there so no one else could come in. Not easily anyway.

"We don't want to hurt you," I said to the man, my voice echoing in the open space. "But we need information. Are you the priest of this temple?"

The old man shook his head slightly but stopped as Kreeg's dagger pricked. "No...no," he said. "I'm only the caretaker. I saw...movement. I thought it was...."

"Thought it was what?" I asked, stepping around the altar and walking slowly toward him.

"Thought it was them," the man said, his body shaking, his voice barely a whisper. "They would...need."

"Them who?" I asked. "And what would they need?"

The door against which Diken Graye leaned boomed loudly as something massive hit it from the other side. Brass nails squealed; hinges rattled; the wood creaked and cracked.

---

[4] See *Swords of Talera*.

Graye jumped back, eyes dark and wild. Valyan muttered an explosive oath. I half crouched, the sword leaping to my hand with a whicker. Something slithered like wet leather along the outside wall. And the wall bulged.

"Them!" the old man suddenly screamed. He tore loose from Kreeg's grip with frenzied strength and ran toward the altar. Kreeg hardly noticed, his mouth open and startled as he spun to face the door.

That door seemed to...breathe. Planks strained. A square nail popped free and clattered at my feet. A second followed, leaving holes through which spilled an intense reek of salt, and fish, and rotted seaweed. I took a step back, unable to stop myself, my heart pounding. The others were around me, faces twisted, muscles bunched like wire.

"What devils are these?" Kreeg blurted.

"Perhaps we'd better—" Graye started.

"We'll stand," I snapped, cutting him off. "Anything that can come through that door can die on the threshold."

I don't know if they believed me. But they stood. I don't know if I believed myself. But I held my sword ready.

Something...snuffled against the door. Then a series of thumps raced along the wall, each one softer than before, each one higher along the wall than a man could reach comfortably. Kreeg growled. The mist in the room swirled and eddied, as if stirred. The skin went cold beneath the hair lifting at my neck.

I turned. A gagging sound came from the direction of the altar. The old man was suspended over the polished wood, his face purpling, bloating. Something rope-like and liquid-looking had wrapped itself around his neck, reaching above his head into the shadows that hovered near the ceiling. I looked up, toward the skylight. And saw there the face of an angel. Or a demon.

The door behind me split with a gunshot crack and buckled inward off its hinges. Splinters sleeted. Something dark came through.

Chapter Thirteen

Demon-Haunted Dark

Kreeg bellowed—in anger. Valyan and Graye shouted, their voices surprised, any meaning lost in shock. Forgetting the angel/demon whose face loomed in the skylight, I spun about to see some massive thing thrusting through the door that had burst inward beneath its weight. Kreeg bellowed again—in pain—and went down beneath an axe-shaped head, scrabbling desperately to keep recurved fangs from tearing his face off.

A leg as thick as an ale barrel thrust against Valyan, knocking him sideways into me. I caught him, spun him toward safety, then lunged forward, blade sizzling in the light as it went in beneath the creature's shoulder and plunged deep.

The thing roared, like fire exploding into a dry tree. It pulled back then, for a moment, nearly twisting the blade from my hand. I hung on, jerked the sword free in a shower of red froth. The beast was a laith, though bigger than most of its ilk. Its head arched above me, snouted and fanged like a moray eel, with eyes wide set beneath a broad forehead. Those eyes were stone white with dagger-point pupils; they looked sick and maddened. And sick or maddened the beast must have been to come up from the sea's depths and attack on land.

The laith snapped at me and I slashed it across the mouth to stop it, cutting through its fleshy upper lip to leave a salmon pink arc behind. The rest of it was an iridescent black, like oil on water. From the corner of my eye, I saw

Wings Over Talera, by Charles Allen Gramlich

Graye grab at Kreeg's arm to try and pull him to safety. The laith glimpsed him, lashed out with a foot that knocked the mercenary sprawling and then smashed down to pin Kreeg like an insect beneath it.

An arrow hissed past my shoulder to sprout like a quill from the thing's right leg. Valyan had unlimbered his deadly bow. A second arrow followed the first as I leaped in, sword hacking to draw a tithe of blood. The laith backed up. One step. Two. But it dragged Kreeg with it. A third arrow fleshed itself in the same leg. The creature took another step back, venting an oddly plaintive cry, as if confused by our resistance to being eaten.

I cut at the thing's head and it reared, showing a slender neck that slanted down to a barrel chest and heavy, lizard-like shoulders that gave rise to massive front legs. Beyond those legs the body tapered twenty-five feet to tiny hind limbs and a fluked tail like a whale's.

I ran to my right, shouting long and loud, trying to draw the beast's attention and make it turn. Graye was hovering, waiting to leap in to grab for Kreeg. But my ploy failed. In horror, I saw the creature's weight come down on my injured friend. The head dipped, mouth opening almost daintily as it bent to shred him with savage fangs.

Valyan was shooting, shooting. The arrows flew and struck, seemingly without effect. And I jumped forward, bringing the sword up and over my head in a desperate gamble, spinning it and driving it down again behind the laith's left shoulder to seek the heart. The creature screeched in raw pain and...shrugged. That ripple of muscle snapped my blade off in the wound and sent me jolting backward to smash hard into the side wall.

I staggered and went down to both knees, shaking my head, my vision winking and blooming with scarlet pinpoints of light. My right fist held only a foot long stub of sword now, but I clenched it tight as I tried to get my legs under me. Pain arced along overtaxed muscles but I found my feet and swayed there. At least I had the laith's attention. It turned and humped toward me like some monstrous walrus, tail lashing against the doorway through which it had burst. Heavy logs shivered and broke away, bringing down half the wall.

I readied myself, mouth sandy dry, heart pounding like frenetic surf. As the laith shifted its bulk to attack me, Graye got hold of Kreeg's arms and dragged him free. I couldn't see whether my friend lived or not, but, if dead, he might soon have me for company. Valyan had emptied his quiver and drawn his rapier. He ran toward the laith, moving to aid me now. Then he froze. I heard a strange, almost ghostly shout, but couldn't see where it had come from or why Valyan had hesitated.

The laith struck at me and I tried to dodge, and only the buckling of its arrow-weakened right leg saved me. The thing smashed snout first into the floor in front of my boots, and for that bare instant it was vulnerable. I took the only chance I had, half leaping, half falling across its muzzle, the stub of sword rising and dropping, burying itself deep into the juncture where soft eye met harder skull—with the brain just barely beneath. Jagged steel grated and then locked as the quillions hooked on bone and held.

A convulsion rippled the length of the laith's body. It started to rear, but I was up before it could crush me against the roof, my feet slipping, then catching as I lunged forward over its fleshy head and slid-rolled down its shoulder to sprawl on the stone floor. Death bit and tore at the laith's straining muscles and I threw myself away from its shuddering agonies, then rose, drawing my dagger as I reached my feet. I saw what had pulled Valyan to a stop.

Half a dozen bony creatures skittered through the torn wall, their claws clacking like metal rain on the floor. Mist wreathed their antlered heads. Two launched themselves at Diken Graye and the unconscious Kreeg. The other four came for us, for Valyan and me. Valyan leaped to meet them, rapier weaving. I followed, my chest shuddering for breath. Sweat coated me, slicking the dagger in my hand, and I wished desperately for something more than that slender blade to guard myself. At my back the laith writhed its last and died. There was no time to rejoice.

Our new foes were Sporns, a race that I had not seen before but knew of from stories. One story had involved the Priest-Cult of Rampuur, the sorcerous worshippers of Vohanna who had been a faction in the invasion of Nyshphal some thirty-five years ago. According to legends, the Sporns had been no more than ignorant beasts before the Cult's wizards raised them to intelligence and made them their servants. I did not know the truth of those tales, but the presence of the creatures here taunted me with the sound of secrets unlocking.

The Sporns were—vaguely—insectoid, with eight limbs and eight eyes in a chitinous face that otherwise seemed full of feelers. The antlers that I had first thought to mark a helm were part of their exoskeletons, like the horns of a rhinoceros beetle on Earth.

The creatures ran on their lower four limbs, carried weapons in their upper four. One of them reached me, and attacked. A lead-weighted mace hammered down at me; a curved sword, like a yataghan, slashed across toward my side. I ducked under and around, came up to slam my dagger in beneath my attacker's mandible. The thing loomed over me by a foot but the power of the blow nearly tore its jaw off.

The being's claws clicked at my shoulder and I slapped them aside, my other hand reaching, catching the Sporn's bone-like wrist. I whirled, using my weight to tear the yataghan free of the dying thing's grip, and continued the spin, sword coming around just above its thorax, slicing through the thin neck, sending the head leaping. A jet of silver blood fountained, prickling on my skin where drops struck me, the smell like a corrosive acid in my nostrils.

All around me were clanging blades and swift movements. I knew this kind of fighting. I'd been afraid of the laith. Not now. I dropped to one knee, hacked sideways at another Sporn's lower limbs. Two of those parted beneath the blade's curved edge and the creature dropped with a high pitched squeal, its other limbs thrashing. I silenced it with a stroke that cut through its body and struck sparks from the floor.

A shadow passed over me; a sudden breeze stirred my hair. I sensed it and then it was pushed out of my mind as Diken Graye yelled in pain and I jumped to my feet. A Sporn swung at me with its mace and the weapon grazed my thigh even as I tried to dodge, the glancing blow still enough to numb flesh and bone.

The pain enraged me. My hand shot out, locked around the creature's throat. The Sporn's feelers lashed and tore at my wrist, but with a snarl I dashed its domed skull open with repeated blows of the sword hilt. I hurled its corpse away and heard the clatter of it falling. Gore dripped from my fist and sword, and ran on my face. I could taste it, like burnt milk.

My eyes sought Diken Graye then. Found him. He was wounded, bleeding streams at shoulder and leg. But he stood over the sprawled form of Kreeg, fighting off two Sporns to save my friend's life—if there were any life left to save. In that moment I forgave the mercenary for anything I'd once held against him, and I started forward, limping. But Valyan was there before me, taking out both foes from behind with quick movements of a sword that already streamed silver blood.

My gaze dropped to Kreeg. He wasn't moving.

Then, in the streets beyond the temple, through the half fallen wall, I glimpsed torches blooming as the villagers were aroused and began to gather. We had to get Kreeg out of here. Ourselves as well. But then that breeze from above caressed me again. And with it came a grating noise from the direction of the altar. I turned. The old caretaker's body was gone, but other items of interest had appeared.

Though the villagers would surely be angered at what we had done, it was clear now that the greatest threat to us lay *within* the temple. For the altar had shifted to reveal the flickering mouth of a tunnel. And a demon squatted at that mouth, lesser devils wheeling above it on membranous wings.

Worst of all, the demon had a rider, masked and gloved and clad all in yellow silk—with eyes that seemed to bleed.

Chapter Fourteen

The Rider

The winged devils had the faces of angels with horns. They had the wattled necks of vultures and thin wings in which blue veins pulsed. They had tails as long as those of kites. It was one such hybrid that I had glimpsed at the skylight when it was strangling the caretaker with its tail. Just before the laith's attack.

The greater demon squatted on all fours, with charcoal skin that had erupted with blisters. Tusks thrust up from the low slung muzzle, their lengths stained with crimson. Above that muzzle the face was bestial, savage, frighteningly intelligent. The eyes were stone black, without pupils.

Yet, I noted the monstrous chimeras only in passing. My gaze was locked to the being who sat so casually upon the squatting demon's back: the rider in yellow silk...except for black boots. He—it?—seemed...familiar, though I could not make out any features. The shape was human; the gloved right hand held an exquisite rapier. And as the being leaned forward I glimpsed again the glow of its incarnadine eyes behind the mask.

I was reminded of how Diken Graye had described my brother Bryce's eyes—as bloody pearls. Frowning with a quick thought, I spared a glance toward the winged fiends. They had the same eyes, and I recalled, also, the odd scarlet tinge to the blue orbs of the Nokarran assassin I had killed in Trazull. Only the squatting demon had eyes of a different hue, of dead black, and a tiny spurt of excitement ripped through me to mingle with fear. I sensed mysteries unraveling.

Then I jolted as a wild hope suddenly burst in me that the rider *was* Bryce. An instant later that hope was dashed. This man was shorter than my brother. Even if Bryce had changed his eyes and hair, he could not have changed his height.

I snarled and started forward then. Behind me I smelled the smoke of torches as the villagers arrived at the temple. I heard their muttered anger die away to awed murmurs as they saw the tableau spread before them. But I did not care that the odds were overwhelming against us now, and that surely we would die here. *Someone* would tell me of my brother.

The squatting demon spoke. Everything stilled.

"Kill him," it said. I did not realize who it was talking to or who it meant to die until the rider in yellow dismounted and strode toward me.

Valyan took a step forward and I held out a hand to stop him.

"Mine," I said. "See to Kreeg. Carry him if you have to."

The green Llurn glanced at me, his eyes hot. Then he nodded and stepped aside. But his offer of sacrifice cooled my own rage for the moment. It was all right to risk myself but I had no right to risk my friends if there were any hope of escape.

I raised my curved blade, readied myself. The yellow-clad swordsman kept coming. No one else moved, and even the winged devils settled to watch. If they awaited the outcome of this fight I might have long moments to think and plan an escape. Then the swordsman lunged and I found I had no time to think at all.

The man's rapier made a blazing streak of light coming in and I parried desperately. Still I took a wound, a shallow cut across the left thigh that stung like scorpion venom. The man gave me no time to riposte. He whipped his blade up, toward my face. I blocked in a shower of sparks, and he spun, coming fully around, blade level. I threw myself aside, hammering the curved length of my yataghan down. Half an inch from my rib cage, the two sword edges caught and shrieked together.

I lashed out, clumsy against the swordsman's swift grace. He ducked under that stroke, smooth as a cobra coiling, then lunged as if pointing a finger, his rapier stabbing at my throat. I leaped backward. His stroke missed. The rider straightened, held his position for a moment, the tip of his blade quivering as if in eagerness.

I took the chance to whip off my rawhide coat and whirl it about my left arm as a makeshift guard, then crouched, my own blade weaving. The swordsman's rapier was of the double-edged type, for cutting and thrusting both. It was several inches longer than my own blade, and just as strong without being as thick or heavy. I had to make adjustments; I thought I knew how.

"Come on," I growled at him.

The silken mask covering the rider's face seemed to quiver at the sound of my words. He took a step toward me, then paused, as if confused. I shifted my stance, brought the tip of my sword up a bit. Both moves would allow me to respond a sliver faster to an attack.

"Kill him," the demon-thing growled from behind the man. Its voice was like echoes.

The swordsman jerked as if struck, then came for me, drawing a short, sparring dagger into his left hand. His blade lashed back and forth, darted in the next instant toward my face. I tapped his weapon aside with mine, launched a riposte. He met it smoothly. For a moment we fenced wildly, face to face, so close I could smell his sweat. Our steel blurred, clicking and chiming, locking and coming free. He stabbed at me with his dagger and I blocked with my arm, hearing the sound of the rawhide coat tearing as it saved my flesh.

I stepped into the man then, pushing him back. He gave only a few paces of ground before launching a blazing counterattack. This time I matched his speed, and the tip of my yataghan cut a slice through the silk at his shoulder. Human skin peeked through, pale but scrawled with tattooed lines. The swordsman leaped away. Both of us were breathing hard.

I gestured at him with my sword. "Last round," I said.

WINGS OVER TALERA, BY CHARLES ALLEN GRAMLICH

Again my voice seemed to abrade him. He paused. His whole body shook, though I did not think it from fear.

Behind him the demon shrieked. "Kill...*him!*"

The swordsman gave a tortured half moan, the first sound I'd heard him make. Then he came, rapier driving at my chest. I blocked with an upstroke, knocking his sword out of attack line, then spun off my right heel, left foot curving around, snapping straight into his belly. He grunted and folded over. I planted my boot, hammered back with an elbow that exploded in his face.

The man's whole body went loose, arms flying outward. I twisted into him, dropping the coat from around my left arm as that hand dove down to catch his wrist and my other hand rose over his shoulder, the yataghan spinning up in my fist.

"The tunnel!" I shouted at Valyan, as the masked swordsman faltered into a slow collapse and I took his rapier away with one clean jerk. My right arm straightened and I hurled my own sword in a flashing bolt toward the demon that crouched before the altar.

My move was completely unexpected. The sword flew true. It took the demon right between the ebon glitter of its eyes. And the effect was just as unexpected to me. The skull of the beast split open; the whole body cracked wide. I heard an incandescent scream. Something chatoyant came out of the hollow shell of the demon, something not quite human-sized, but winged and glistening and wet. It hovered above us.

I gaped. My skin crawled with a sudden sick dread of the supernatural. I had not for a moment believed we faced a real demon. I still didn't. But....

The newborn being found me with a sharp and bitter gaze. Its liquid eyes were black upon black upon black. The head was heart shaped with a woman's face sculpted upon it, a face that was lovely and evil above a body that seemed a hybrid of human and praying mantis. The four wings were multicolored, fibrous but flexible, and translucent enough to show a webbing of strange textures inside. They didn't look real. The creature raised a human-type arm, pointed at me with an elongated finger, but its gaze swept over my shoulder now, to the awed and hushed villagers who watched at the torn open wall of the temple.

"The house of Vohanna has been profaned!" it shrieked to the crowd, and the words struck like daggers stabbing ice. "Destroy them! Destroy all who would befoul your goddess!"

The being whirled higher, wings thrumming, and the remaining fiends closed around it defensively, locking tails and bat-like hands. The whole mass of them swept toward the roof, surged through the skylight and away into the darkness. Behind us came the bull roar of the mob.

I turned, looking wildly for Graye and Valyan, found them staggering toward the altar with Kreeg lolling between them. The ex-gladiator's face was pasty, with a purple tinge beneath and blood all over him. But Valyan had listened to me about the tunnel. They were almost there.

"Get inside," I shouted at them.

Someone among the villagers threw a torch at me. I caught it and threw it back, sending the first line of the mob scattering for a moment. Then they surged forward...and hesitated. Voices were raised, bitter and afraid, young and old, male and female. Their indecisiveness would not last.

I shifted the rapier to my right hand, dipped down to grasp the unconscious form of the yellow-clad swordsman in my left. I dragged him up under my arm. His body was dead weight but fear gave me the strength. The crowd saw, and growled. They surged forward again.

"Stay back!" I shouted at them. "This is Vohanna!"

The lie held them. For an instant. And I turned and ran, lugging the swordsman with me. The crowd roared, and came like a river breaking its dam. I saw Valyan standing above the tunnel, saw him release Kreeg's arms to Diken Graye beneath. Then the Nakscherii warrior was turning, nocking an arrow he'd somehow found time to recover from the laith's corpse. He sent that wicked barb zipping past my shoulder, followed it with two more as fast as I could blink.

I heard the crowd falter behind me and screamed at Diken Graye to catch as I slung the limp swordsman into the mouth of the tunnel. My glance met Valyan's and I followed the rider's body, dropping feet first into the darkness just as the green Llurn fired his last arrow and hurled his useless bow into the mob.

I landed hard on soft loam, twisting my ankle and sprawling. Valyan hit next, fell against me. I rolled, trying to get to my feet as a grating noise tore at my ears. Diken Graye had found the lever that worked the tunnel opening and the altar was closing over it. An arm came through, scrabbled at smooth stone, tried to jerk back as the altar pressed in. A horrified shriek sounded, then was lost behind a ton of stone as the door closed and a hand and wrist dropped squirming to the ground.

Valyan gagged, and even Diken Graye, the hardened mercenary, turned away. I rushed to Kreeg where he lay sprawled on the dusty floor. The sides of the tunnel were lined with torches every ten feet or so. By their light my friend looked dead. I dropped to my knees beside him, placed an ear to his chest. At first I could find no heartbeat, but then I felt movement. Kreeg was breathing. My friend was breathing!

I rose. Above me came the distant thud of hammering as the enraged villagers worked at the altar that closed us off from them. I glanced at Valyan and Graye.

"They may know where this tunnel comes out," I said. "When they have a moment to think. Certainly those demon things know it. We better hurry."

"What of him?" Valyan asked, jerking his chin at the still unconscious swordsman.

"Bring him," I said. "But bind his hands. I'll have some questions when he wakes." I sheathed the man's beautifully wrought rapier in my own scabbard.

Valyan nodded at my words, bent to scoop the man up and toss him over a shoulder. I did the same with Kreeg, though far less easily. With a sore ankle and on trembling legs, I followed Graye and Valyan as they forged quickly ahead, the sounds of the howling mob growing faint behind us.

No pursuit had found us by the time we reached tunnel's end and discovered that it exited through the mouth of a natural cave in the side of a small hill. We went out cautiously but no foes awaited. Though still dark, the mist had cleared and three of the moons gleamed like lush fruit in the sky. With their light as a guide, we covered our tracks and it did not take long after that to reach the marshy place where our sabruns were tied.

I was grateful to lay Kreeg's heavy frame on the ground and to kneel beside him, gasping for breath. Valyan merely dumped the swordsman, who was now beginning to stir. Then he dragged the fellow to a sitting position against a rough-barked chelaquin tree and reached for the cloth covering the man's features.

"Let's just have a look under here," he said, grasping the yellow hood and stripping it away.

I was watching and wished I hadn't been. The shock of it was like knowing that a snake has struck you and might be venomous. The face I saw was different, but the same. It was my cousin from Earth. It was Eric Ryall's face that gleamed at me from beneath the disguise.

Chapter Fifteen

A Tale Spun by Night

I rushed to Eric, hands going out to grasp my cousin's shoulders, shaking him, shaking him. He groaned and his eyelids fluttered. I winced to see his hazel irises overlain with crimson. And his normally ruddy face was pallid and wet looking—except where black and blue tattoos gleamed sullenly and intricately.

I shook him again. And again his eyes fluttered, then opened fully. He gazed at me without recognition, with an inarticulate madness etched in his pupils. I slapped him.

"Eric. It's Ruenn. Eric!"

He murmured, then jolted as my slap seemed to register. Or perhaps it was just my voice. I remembered how it had affected him during our fight, how each time I'd spoken he had paused. But it wasn't enough merely to "affect" him. I needed to find a way to break through to him, to connect to the mind of the man he'd once been.

"Where's Bryce?" I demanded, trying to reach him that way. "Eric!" I shook him a third time. "Where...is...Bryce?"

Again my voice did more than any slap or shaking; his mouth twisted and he thrashed his head from side to side. Still, there was no true awareness in him. Something held him in thrall and I knew no way to free him.

I glanced helplessly at Valyan and Graye. Valyan's eyes burned with sympathy but all he could do was shrug and turn away to see to Kreeg. Graye, however, walked over to squat next to me.

"He's not as bad as your bro—" Graye started, then

paused to glance quickly at me. "As bad as...he could be," he finished.

I looked at the mercenary. I don't know if there was a question in my stare, but he went on as if there had been.

"I mean the hair and eyes," he said, motioning to the white that only streaked Eric's rust colored hair, and to the eyes through which the true color still peeked. I recalled how Graye had described Bryce's hair and eyes—dead white, blood red.

"So?" I asked, my voice bleak and rough.

Graye did not reply but leaned forward to study the tattoos on Eric's face and neck. I had already noted the resemblance of those inked lines to the tattooed map of Talera on the chest of that Nokarran assassin I had killed back in Trazull. Yet, Eric's markings were more elaborate and detailed, and were scrawled over with runes that shone like surreal glyphs.

A frown creased Graye's face and he glanced to me. But I'd already seen what he'd seen. On Eric's forehead there coiled a winged pattern of colored patches—blue, red, green, gold—rotating around a central mandala of entwined thorns. And at the mandala's center, at the point of reintegration, there glistened a small oval of whitish matter, like glass or marble. At first I thought it a speck of dust and reached to wipe it away, but it clung like a leech to Eric's skin and felt warm and oily to my finger. Then I knew what it was.

"A milkstone," Graye said needlessly.

I shivered. "Aye," I said. "And embedded in his flesh."

I wondered, then, if that Nokarran assassin in Trazull had worn such a stone amid his tattoos. I had not noticed one but had not been looking for it either.

Graye interrupted my thoughts. "That...thing may be how he's being controlled."

"Perhaps," I agreed.

And what of Bryce, my mind added. Was he, too, being controlled?

Graye reached to his hip and unsheathed his knife. I caught his wrist above the wolf's-head hilt.

"What do you?" I asked.

He stared hard at me, his eyes asking—I thought—for

trust.

"I'm going to remove the milkstone," he said after a long pause. "It might free him."

"Or kill him," I murmured.

He nodded. "There is that possibility. But...." He cocked his chin toward Eric's slowly writhing form, as if willing me to note the lost gaze and the drool-flecked lips. "...would you rather he stay like this?"

My hand tightened on the mercenary's wrist. I growled an oath, then released him abruptly.

"Take it," I said.

"Hold him down," Graye replied.

He drew a silver flask from his boot and poured a mouthful of the contents along the edge of his dagger. I smelled whisky and cinnamon, then leaned forward to grasp Eric's shoulders and neck. I held him tight, pressing his back to the tree against which Valyan had leaned him.

Even through his emptiness, Eric felt the knife. He jerked and shrieked as the cold blade touched him, and I fought him to stillness as Graye made a quick circular incision around the milkstone and yanked away the small flap of tissue in which the stone was embedded. He threw the whole of it off into the bushes as blood welled and clotted instantly in the tiny crater.

Eric stiffened, his heels drumming. Then he began to gag wildly. I rolled him onto his side just as a green bile jetted from his mouth and nostrils. There were specks of crimson in the bile but the release seemed to clean Eric of something foul. He slumped deeper into unconsciousness. Yet, I thought this new state closer to true sleep than to the emptiness he'd shown before. I pulled him away from the spreading pool of vomit and used one of our blanket rolls to pillow his head. He moaned, but his writhing had stopped.

Graye rose from his squat after wiping his dagger on a clump of marsh grass. He sighed. It seemed in relief.

"Well, he survived," he said.

I nodded, not trusting my voice, then rose as well, leaving Eric in his stillness while I strode over to Valyan where he bent over the injured Kreeg. Graye moved to check on the sabruns, to make sure they were ready if we needed them quickly.

"Tell me," I said softly to Valyan.

The Green Llurn glanced up at me. He'd bound Kreeg's chest tightly with cloth he'd found in one of the saddlebags. He'd splinted an arm. And there were other things.

"He lives but I don't know if he'll stay that way. He's got broken ribs, a broken arm and wrist. Head injuries. He may be bleeding inside. I pray Ivrail that he isn't. He needs a trained healer."

"Vriun is in Nyshphal. In Timmuzz," I said. "I know of no other we could trust."[5]

"Vriun is an old friend," Valyan agreed. "But Timmuzz is far and none of us dare show our faces there since...." He did not need to finish.

I sighed, biting at my lower lip. "I think—" I started to say, and a hoarse whisper interrupted me.

"Ruenn."

I spun about to see Eric's eyes open. And he had pulled himself to a sitting position against the chelaquin tree. I raced to him, dropped to my knees beside him.

"Eric?"

His eyes were still shot through with blood but they seemed brighter to me, more their natural color. In amazement, I noted that the small wound in his forehead had completely closed, as if his body had rejected the mark of the toir'in-or. The puckered scar that remained was a good sign, I told myself.

"I need.... Need...water," Eric struggled to whisper.

Diken Graye heard, and as I turned toward the sabruns where our water gourds hung he tossed me one that sloshed deliciously. I lifted Eric forward from behind the shoulders, uncorked the gourd and let him sip, stopping him when he would have gulped.

He drank slowly, for a long time, then leaned his head back to gasp for breath. His eyes seemed brighter still, though I feared some of it was fever.

---

[5] Vriun the Healer first appears as a slave of the Klar in *Swords of Talera*. He is of the race called Kaldi, and was freed by Ruenn. Later, he became court physician to Rannon and her family.—CAG

"Where...where are we?" he asked. A thread of water spilled down his chin.

"On the Rosjavik Peninsula," I answered. "Near the village of Kellet's Bay." Even though he nodded, I could see the names meant nothing to him.

"What do you remember, Eric?" I asked gently.

He glanced at me, and away. It seemed he was frightened. He took another sip of water, swallowing as if desperate to avoid thoughts of what had happened to him. He looked down then, and mumbled something I couldn't catch.

"Eric," I prodded. "Tell me what you remember."

"Vohanna," he said after a moment, his gaze cast to the dirt, his voice lost and ill.

Valyan heard the name he hated and walked over to stand above me. Graye listened from among the sabruns. The night held frogs that drummed the marsh with their songs; there came the plash of movement in the waters around us. But between the four of us a silence ached.

I finally broke that silence with two questions. "What is Vohanna? *Where* is Vohanna?"

"Vohanna is god," Eric answered, as if it were something he'd memorized. "She dwells in the ancient earth." Then: "Ruenn," he said. His voice seemed bruised.

"What, Eric?"

"You must save Bryce. Must...."

The muscles twisted beneath my skin. My heart banged. I leaned forward. "Where is he?"

Still, he did not look up from the ground.

"Eric!"

He winced. But his words came in a tumble. "He is with Vohanna. In the city below the city. With the ruins above."

"Vohan," Graye interjected. Then he glanced at me, rushed on. "Our attack. The day I was captured. When we...shot down your airship. I had flown in from the east but was joined by others. They came from the north. From the direction of Vohan."

I nodded. Graye was only speaking my own thoughts of that ancient and fallen citadel on Nyshphal, rumored to have once been the center of Vohanna's empire. I wondered. Was it still?

My thoughts flew to Bryce then, lingered, and circled back to Eric. The cousin I remembered had been wild and joyful, willful but brave—with his mind always focused outward on life. My eyes grew damp to see him now, shivering, terrified, sick all the way to his bones.

"What happened to you, Eric?" I asked softly. "How did this come to pass?"

He tried to straighten but fell back against the tree weakly. I gave him more water and it steadied him. He wiped his mouth with a hand that trembled only slightly.

"That night," he began. "On Earth."

I knew what night Eric meant. His last night on Earth. Mine too. After a storm at sea, we had dropped anchor at an island where Eric and others of my then crew decided to camp on shore. They had disappeared in a blaze of sorcerous fire and it had been in searching for them that Bryce and I stumbled upon the gate to Talera and were drawn through (see *Swords of Talera*).

"That night, we were taken. By beasts that thought like men. We were taken as fodder for Vohanna's armies, as she gathers her power to restore her rule in this world."

My teeth clenched. "And the others of my crew?" I ground out.

"They serve her now. Or they're already dead." He seemed to shrink in on himself. "I don't...remember much of it," he added. I knew he lied but did not have the heart to force that story from him. But....

"And what of Bryce?" I asked. "He was not stolen with the crew. How did he end up with Vohanna?"

"I don't know," Eric said. "He was brought in later. She...Vohanna...took...." He stopped for a moment, panting slightly, as if it were growing difficult for him to breathe. "She took a...liking to him."

A cold belt of fear tightened around my chest at those words, but his next ones were worse.

"He didn't...didn't fight her. Not much at least."

"And the others fought?" I asked, the pitch of my voice rising in my own ears. I lifted a hand to my mouth, began to gnaw at my thumb.

"Some did. I did." He half sobbed. "Not that it mattered.

No one fights her for long. She wins. Always wins."

I forced my hand down to grasp his shoulder. I forced my voice into a semblance of control.

"It'll be all right now, Eric," I said. "We've taken out the stone she was using to rule you."

He laughed bitterly. "Only one of them, Ruenn. Only the most obvious. There are others."

"Where?" I asked, squeezing his shoulder harder. "Tell me and we'll take those too."

His next words let me know how foolish I was.

"Inside, Ruenn. Inside my body. In my guts." His voice sagged. "In my soul."

I wanted desperately to weep.

"How long?" I asked, and he did not question my meaning.

He shrugged, hopelessly. "Hours. Minutes! As soon as she recognizes that she's lost the connection she'll move to regain control."

He grabbed my hand where it rested on his shoulder. His grip was strong but it was a desperate strength—a false one.

"Kill me, Ruenn," he begged. "Kill me."

I jerked my hand away from him as if burned, my mind and body both recoiling.

"No! Eric. I can't."

Again he grabbed my hand, his eyes raking into mine, crimson streaked and eerie as he searched my face.

"Kill me, Ruenn. For I'll surely try to kill *you* when she takes me again."

This time I did not pull away. I reached with my free hand and locked hold of his wrist; I leaned forward.

"I *will* not. We'll bind you. Keep you bound until we find some way of freeing you from Vohanna."

Eric snarled. His eyes flushed with blood. The tattoos on his face seemed to writhe as he tore free of my grip and lunged for my throat, his fingers hooked into talons. I went back and down under his weight, feeling his nails ripping at my flesh. I smashed at him with a fist, felt the jolt of the blow. It didn't stop him.

His grip tightened. I bucked wildly beneath him, trying to throw him off. My lungs spasmed for air. Firefly sparkles swept and darkened over my vision. I heard shouting.

Then I could breathe again as Diken Graye and Valyan reached us and dragged Eric up and away from my throat. I pushed to my knees, gagging, saw Eric struggling madly against the hands that tried to imprison him. He snapped his head back into Valyan's face, tore free as the Llurn's grasp weakened. Diken grabbed for his shoulder, missed his grip as Eric lunged for me a second time.

I threw myself to one side, lashed out with a booted foot at the same instant. That boot stripped Eric's feet from under him and he smashed hard to the ground. But he came back instantly to all fours, hurled himself at me with his mouth open and snarling. I saw blood flecking his lips where he'd bitten his tongue.

Graye clubbed him at the base of the neck with both fists, and Valyan tackled him from the side and rolled him, locking Eric up with legs around legs, arms around arms. Graye drew his sword and planted the tip at Eric's throat, dimpling the skin over the artery that pulsed there.

"No!" I shouted, leaping to my feet. "Don't kill him."

Eric twisted his head toward me. Only, it wasn't Eric. His face had changed. Pallid skin had turned dark as olives. The cheeks had hollowed and the lips were swollen and ripe. The eyes had altered from crimson-stained to obsidian black.

The thing that was not Eric smiled at me. Then it gave a low mirthful chuckle that was sweet as rancid honey.

"Ruenn Maclang," it said caressingly. "Brother to my darling Bryce. Come find me if you can. Bryce will be so happy to see you again. And to introduce you to his lover."

"Beast!" I snarled at it.

The curved lips twisted into a pout. "How cruel. And I had so hoped we would be friends." Then the thing giggled. "I think you should be punished."

It winked at me, and I saw how it would punish me. I saw awareness return in a flood to Eric's eyes. And at the same moment I saw him turn back toward Diken Graye and look up at the mercenary. Graye's sword still rested against Eric's throat, and with a quick thrust of his head my cousin impaled himself on that blade.

Graye jerked his weapon back with an oath, but it was

too late. I was too late as I leaped forward. Blood spurted and I reached Eric only as he slumped to one side, his gaze finding mine and shocking into me.

"Ruenn," he gasped, as his fingers scrabbled at my shoulder. I caught his hand, his blood on me, pooling in my lap, matting the hair of my arms. His eyes rolled back in his head and he convulsed his way into death.

I held him. I wept.

After a long moment, Valyan and Graye walked away to leave me alone.

Chapter Sixteen

In the Memory of Ruins

I watched as Valyan and his sabrun disappeared toward the morning, leading behind them a second bird which bore the unconscious form of Kreeg strapped over its back. The breath came heavy in my chest of a sudden. My hands shook. After one long glance toward me, Diken Graye turned away to recheck the remaining two saddle birds, leaving me alone in stillness.

In a few minutes we, too, would be mounted and on our way. We would take a different route, a wind-road that would lead us to the ruined city of Vohan, where Eric Ryall had told us we would find the goddess Vohanna. And Bryce. But for this moment my thoughts were only of Nyshphal. And Rannon.

The sky overhead was green in the dawn, a delicately jeweled shade of olive. In Nyshphal, this day would be the culmination of the spring festival, the celebration of regrowth and vigor. I knew that Rannon would have many duties at court and among her people. I wondered if her whole heart would lie in those duties, and I was selfish enough to hope that some part of her was troubled.

I had sent Valyan *back* to Rannon, and he had gone willingly even though he knew he'd be arrested. But Kreeg needed the treatment he could get only in Nyshphal, and, too, on one issue my feelings were still clear. I loved Rannon and would not see her people devastated. Valyan was to tell Rannon that the source of the attacks on her land lay below the stones of the fallen metropolis of Vohan—in Nyshphalian territory—and that the roots of this aggression traced back to the early days of her father's battle for Nyshphal, when the Cult of Rampuur had first sought to revive the rule of the "goddess" Vohanna. If I knew Hurnan Jystral, he would launch his own attacks soon after hearing that word.

Graye coughed and I turned and strode toward him. From the corner of my eye I glimpsed an earthen mound that marked a freshly dug grave. I'd cut two sticks of wood and bound them to form a cross to mark the head of that grave. Even though Talerans would not understand it as a religious image, the cross had meant a great deal to Eric Ryall.

I did take with me one thing of Eric's, the ornate-hilted sword that he'd used against me in Vohanna's temple. My own blade had been lost, broken off in the body of the laith, but this new weapon more than made up for it. It was a rapier, though of a modified style with a heavy, double-edged blade for use in both cutting and thrusting.

The steel was unlike any I'd seen before. It shimmered like water under sunlight, like moiré silk. But it was flexible and strong and incredibly sharp. The hilt fitted my hand perfectly and the guard was an elaborate swirl of linked chains and metal loops intertwined with runic symbols. It rested now in a sheath hooked at my left hip, and I was glad of something to remind me of my cousin as we mounted our sabruns and left that place. I doubted I'd ever see Eric's grave again.

The sun was upon us all the way to the coast of Nyshphal, with not a single cloud to mar the green. Though we flew high to avoid patrols, it was not cold as one might imagine. While the temperature plummets as you go higher in Earth's atmosphere, the reverse is true on Talera. The temperature climbs as you climb because, in fact, on this artificial and encapsulated world you are getting measurably closer to the sun.

The sabruns were tiring by the time we crossed the northern straits of the Temeri Sea and landed in the port town of Elul to eat and rest for the night. Elul bustled and moiled with life—farmers, cattlemen from the interior whose herds were mostly of the short horned terval, a few fishermen and traders. All were here for the spring festival, and to purchase or sell seed and supplies for winter's end.

Elul also marked the northern end of the Road of Wagons, which runs all the way to Timmuzz. Though I was not particularly worried about being recognized, having never been here before, we stayed away from the crowds as much as possible.

Graye had a local healer look at the sword cuts he'd received in the Kellet's Bay battle. I had cleaned and bound the gashes before we'd left the Rosjavik Peninsula, but the healer cleaned them again and packed them with curing herbs. With his wounds freshly tended, Graye rejoined me at the sabrun stables and we found an inn that still had a few sleeping spaces to rent on the floor of the common room. I scarcely noticed the hardness of the floorboards; exhaustion softened them.

Only one further incident of importance occurred in Elul. I had noted that Graye was silent and distant to me during our ride and during the night in the inn. I thought I understood why. It had been his blade that had taken my cousin Eric's life, and I was sure that he expected me to blame him.

"Diken," I said to him the next morning, as he moved to mount his sabrun for the continuation of our journey.

He glanced back at me, his eyes haunted and raw. Then he proved my guess correct as he suddenly blurted, "I'm sorry."

I shook my head at him. "The fault is Vohanna's," I said. "And in no way yours. You have been a good companion. I have ridden with a few as good. Not any that were better."

His eyes remained locked with mine for long moments. He smiled then, slightly, though still with a touch of sadness, and we bestrode our saddle birds and took to the air, leaving our doubts of each other behind in the dust of Elul.

* * * * * * *

Amid the thick shadows of late evening, we reached the outskirts of lost Vohan and landed along what must have been, at one time, a major thoroughfare leading into the city. It was a roadway of glimmering black, of some kind of cement, cracked and broken in many places, elsewhere buried beneath layers of fertile soil through which grass and bushes stabbed.

When I had heard of the "ruins" of Vohan I'd assumed we would see gigantic blocks of stone piled on top of each other, and shattered buildings half standing, with spider-webbed statues and dry fountains decaying around them. What we found was more the *memory* of ruins, devoured in what could only be described as a jungle.

Across the north-central plains of Nyshphal the land was mostly tall grass prairies broken by copses of trees, with here and there a stream running near full from spring rains. But where Vohan had stood there now grew a tropical forest. Only patches of the oily black stone peeked through among the verdure, and there were vague outlines within the green that were more regular than nature liked.

Lush blooms of scarlet, lavender, and saffron dripped sweetly putrid odors along narrow beast-trails in the undergrowth. Trees soared above, most of which were completely unfamiliar to me, and all the forest—from gnarled giants to fallen, half rotted logs—was woven together by vines. The only animals were tiny silver and black birds that darted about like dragonflies. There were no bigger creatures to be seen, which left me wondering what had made the trails.

It intrigued me to find such tropical growth in what should have been a temperate climate, but for the moment I pushed that curiosity aside. Eric had indicated that Vohanna's stronghold was located below the surface here. The question was how to find an entrance, and the jungle made that task more daunting than I had hoped it would be.

"Well...we can't take the sabruns with us in there," Diken Graye said, gesturing at the forest.

I nodded. "Agreed. But leaving them tied up out here would only provide food for the prairie ghyres."

"Then what?" Graye asked.

"We release them and walk," I said. "If Eric is right and the attacks on Nyshphal have been supplied from here, then somewhere below this jungle is a place big enough to hide a near army of birds and riders. We'll steal what we need when we get ready to leave again."

Graye chuckled. "I rather like that idea," he said, as he began to strip the two birds of their saddles and gear.

I glanced up at the quickly darkening sky and a new thought occurred to me.

"I believe," I said to Graye, "that the sabruns may yet serve us in another way."

"And that would be?" the mercenary asked, lifting an eyebrow.

"They're domesticated," I said. "When it comes time to go to roost they'll seek a warm mew among their own kind."

"So?"

I let him think on it for a moment. Then a smile curled his lips and the scar on his chin tightened, shining whitely through his dark stubble of beard.

"Perhaps they'll lead us to the entrance we need," he said.

"Aye. If they can sense their cousins in or below this jungle."

"Tis worth a try, at least."

"My thoughts as well," I said, turning to stride toward the nearest big trees. I called over my shoulder: "It's near the time they'd seek their roosts if they were free. Release them when I say. Shoo them off."

I did not wait to hear his answer.

The forest giant that I chose to climb was thinly barked and smooth of branches for the first twenty feet up its redwood-sized trunk. So many vines wrapped it, though, that the climbing was easy enough until I reached the lower limbs. Those limbs were massive, three feet wide or more at the base, tapering only gradually after that. But they made the work go even faster and I soon forged my way into the very top of the tree, relishing the physical action after so long in the saddle.

All above me the olive-green dome of the sky was deepening toward emerald as the night closed in. But light would linger for a while yet over the treetops.

I called a signal to Graye and heard him shout, "Haieee!" at the sabruns. With chattering cries, they whirled up. I saw them rise above me and then try to settle to ground once more. Rocks flew from Graye's position and the birds lifted again, circling wildly. I shouted at them too, from my hidden perch, and they shied and headed further away over the forest.

I watched them wheel and dip. Then one of them steadied and beat its wings off toward the northwest, toward the center of this odd jungle. The other followed. Trees grew at the center that overtopped their neighbors, and it seemed to me that they stood like a battalion of guards around some sort of building that was no more than an outline under the setting green sun. Our sabruns circled there, swinging lower and lower until I could see them no more. Though I could not be sure, I thought they had alighted.

Noting eagerly the direction and distance, I began clambering down from my eyrie. It was already full night beneath the canopy of leaves. I heard Graye moving around below, dumping equipment and supplies at the base of the tree I had climbed. We'd camp here tonight, in the forest to avoid the ghyres. Tomorrow we'd head inward toward the jungle's heart, leaving the saddles behind but carrying our food, water, and weapons.

A low, trilling whistle sounded, lingered...died.

I paused at the lowest limb on the trunk, my heart rhythm jumping from slow and steady to thud-thud-thud. The forest floor was swathed in darkness twenty feet below. I could see nothing.

"Graye?"

There was no response, though I heard movement clearly. A lot of movement.

"Graye?" I called again.

A flat, savage growl answered me.

Hair curled at my neck. I wanted to shout, to scream for Graye. But the words had fossilized in my throat and I sat very still.

More low growls rippled through the dark. There came the padding of light feet on leaf-covered ground. Then sparks of wine-red flared up all around the base of my tree, dozens of pairs of sparks.

Eyes, I realized, eyes glittering with internal heat, with no light in this dark forest to reflect from them. The bodies of the beasts could not be seen.

WINGS OVER TALERA, BY CHARLES ALLEN GRAMLICH

In the background came a gagging sound, a choking groan of physical and mental agony. In the next instant it broke off. There in the trees, the skin went tight over my knuckles and fear knotted in my chest. My mouth had been reborn a desert.

Then there was light. It flared up suddenly, a sallow, yellowish gleam from a thin pile of twigs that had been set to burning. Diken Graye bent over that fire, blowing gently on it. He looked up at me and smiled, though he should not have been able to see me among the tree limbs. His lips were a thin, hard line, and the scar at his chin seemed to pulse. Behind the sullen, bloody glow of the red eyes I could see nothing left that I could call my friend.

"Vohanna!" I cursed in a whisper, and rage began to pluck my strings.

How could this "goddess" have possessed Diken Graye? I had seen her take Eric Ryall, but she'd had a link to Eric, had been able to project her power through the milkstones embedded in his flesh. Graye bore no such stones.

Or did he? Had he been implanted somehow? If so, I could only believe that it had been done without his knowledge. I did not think he would have kept such a detail from me. Or, was Vohanna growing stronger as we neared her lair? Could she take someone without a milkstone if they were physically close? Why hadn't she tried to take me, then? Was I not more dangerous to her plans?

The questions had no answers. Not yet. Then even the questions fled my mind as the being who was *not* Diken Graye straightened and stepped forward to the foot of my tree. Around him, the red-eyed beasts opened a way, leaving of themselves only an impression of barrel-squat bodies to accompany their railroad flare eyes.

The man/being looked up at me.

"I take it that you are Vohanna," I said, not intending a question.

The man chuckled, like grating ice floes.

"What's the matter, Ruenn? Don't you recognize me? How could you forget your brother Bryce?"

Chapter Seventeen

Brother's Keeper

I heard the words that spilled from Diken Graye's lips.

And they were Bryce's words. In Bryce's voice. The shock of it was like a sluice of cold water. The tree in which I sat seemed to rock beneath me. Fear clawed in my chest. Not for myself, but for Bryce.

"No," I whispered.

"Oh, yesss," he said. "Your one and only brother. Even if I don't look much like him at the moment."

If hearing Bryce's voice issuing from Diken Graye's mouth was meant to panic me, that plan came close to success. I felt the panic rising, but underneath the horror I felt also a bitter, burning anger. And the anger was winning.

This *was* Bryce. Somehow, his spirit—his khi as the Talerans call it—had entered and possessed another being. Yet, this was also *not* my brother. Not truly. Something had been done to him, something terrible enough to warp the basic fineness of him.

"No!" I said again, more forcefully. I cleared my throat. "You are not my brother. *My* brother would never take delight in cruelty. He would never even steal a coin, much less another man's body."

Sparks whirled in Bryce's cinnabar eyes. He shifted from foot to foot, his mouth opening and closing—like a fish on a pond bank. Then the crimson began to fade around his pupils and his shoulders hunched. I heard a faint gagging sound.

My muscles tensed. Something was happening. Was

Graye fighting from inside? Was Bryce losing control? My hand locked about the hilt of my rapier. I shifted my boots on the wide branch where I squatted, lifting up onto my haunches, preparing to act.

The moment passed.

Once more it was Bryce who looked up at me, his eyes blazing brighter than ever, like flaring coals.

"Do not try to task me, Ruenn," he snarled. "I am no longer your little brother. Following you around. Wanting to be just like you." He snarled again. "I could tear you apart."

It was my turn to chuckle. Without humor. I gestured at the half circle of beasts that backed him.

"Then send away your little pets and face me."

He shivered, as if with ague. His eyes dulled again, but in the next instant rekindled. He straightened, body stiffening as a spray of scarlet light misted like smoke from his sockets. His mouth fell open and he spoke, though the lips no longer moved.

"You're gonna die now, Ruenn. Gonna die now."

A convulsion swept him. The eyes rolled back and a total collapse followed, as if he were a sail hacked free of its masts during a storm. Bryce had moved on. The body of Diken Graye dropped, thudding to earth.

From all around in the darkness there arose a howling. Then the red-eyed beasts came swarming, mouths open, distended as they voiced their wails. For the first time I saw them clearly, in the saffron light of the fire that Bryce/Graye had built. They were maybe four feet tall, over a hundred pounds each. Their baboon bodies were squat, bristle furred, with arms longer than the bowed legs and yellow talons at all four paws.

I leaped to my feet, sword flashing into my right hand with a jingle from the scabbard hooks, my left hand slapping the hilt of my belt dagger, drawing it. There were maybe thirty of the creatures, foaming now in a gray wave about the massive base of the tree. Vines shivered as the beasts grasped them, started up the trunk, moving swiftly. The howling grew louder, insistent, maddening.

I reversed the dagger in my hand, hurled it down into an open muzzle full of gleaming, saw-edged teeth. The beast shrieked, fell back into a roiling mass of its fellows. I heard it shriek again as the other howlers tore at it.

I hacked at vines with my sword. The blade sliced through, sending more furry bodies plummeting. But there were too many vines, too many beasts. One reached the limb upon which I stood. I cut that creature down. Another hurled its body at me, using its legs to drive it. I backhanded it, sent it flying. A single talon raked along my sleeve, rending the cloth, stinging through to the skin beneath.

Turning, I took two running steps along the broad back of the tree limb, leaped outward. On a second tree, a shadowy branch loomed flat and wide. My boots slapped down upon it but skidded on the smooth bark. I stumbled, caught the trunk and held on as my body swayed out over the ground.

The red-eyed howlers swamped the limb where I'd been, filled it, with muzzles turning, snuffling. They saw me. The small fire was dying below. It was growing too dark for me to see. I didn't think that would be a problem for my hunters. With such eyes as theirs they were surely nocturnal.

I shoved the rapier in my belt, grabbed a hanging vine as thick as my arm and started to drag myself up it. Behind me I heard leaping, thudding bodies—and howling, like goblin bells ringing.

Something grabbed my heel. Even through the good leather I felt the clasp of teeth. I kicked it away, climbed faster. The vine shuddered in my hands as another beast replaced the first. I kicked again, felt teeth and cartilage crunch. Hardened nails skittered on my jeans, fell away. I heard the creatures in the trees all around as they tried to out climb me. But their hypertrophied claws made it difficult for them. They must have been ground hunters, not used to the heights.

I dropped onto a foot-wide limb, raced along it, leaped into a third tree. Climbed. Now, a smattering of light filtered down through the canopy to help me. Nimeru had risen, the first and smallest Taleran moon, known as "the dreamer."

A burst of howling exploded in front of me. Three of the beasts came hurtling along the branch on which I moved. They might have had me if they'd remained silent. I whipped my sword free, spitted one creature like an overripe fruit, slung it away. A second beast leaped at my face. I ducked aside. It missed, dropped into darkness.

The third struck me in the knees, sent me teetering backward on a limb that was narrow at this height. My left hand barely snatched a hold on a thin side-branch, but in the instant it took to keep myself from falling I felt teeth and a sharp, sharp pain in my left leg.

I slashed downward with the sword, cutting completely through the muzzle of the creature. Gore sprayed. It screeched, turned tornado on the limb in front of me, whirling madly in its pain, claws lashing. I spun the rapier, locking both hands around the pommel as I dropped to one knee. The good steel stabbed deep, pinning the monster to the branch. It shuddered, went still.

I rose, jerked the blade free with a steel-on-bone rasp. My breathing came with a sandpaper rawness. My heart drummed too fast. The warmth of blood ran down my leg. But there was no time to rest. All around me I heard scurrying movements in the trees. And no howling now.

I lifted the rapier, bit down on the blade to taste the wicked copper of blood. With both hands free I leaped upward, caught a limb, pulled myself up. Then did it again. And again. Sullen red eyes glittered from a dozen limbs below me. They climbed with me.

But they didn't attack!

Bark and moss came free beneath my fingers, showered down my collar. My boots crushed scorpions, ants, phosphorescent grubs as I climbed. Sharp twigs ripped tatters in my shirt. My lungs were a bellows; the tissues of them felt torn.

Why didn't the creatures attack? Did they fear my sword?

I reached a thorn tree, turned at bay, trying to breathe. Blood squelched in my boot. My left leg was slashed with red furrows through the faded blue of the jeans I had worn all the way from Earth. That limb trembled, though I felt little pain. Yet.

To my right, the canopy of forest leaves opened a bit. I glanced out over a clearing filled with mist and the electric blue glow of Nimeru. Emperor moths flitted there, big as a man's hands held together. They looked greenish under the moon, though I knew they were crimson as the hearts of rubies in brighter light.

My glance turned upward. I heard a gasp burst from my own lips. Anchored to the tree a dozen feet over my head was a rope bridge leading off through the clearing toward the north, toward the jungle's center. I could not see its end, but as I turned my head to follow its path the corner of my eye caught a hint of deep wedges cut in the tree for steps.

Quickly I looked down, and saw across from me in another tree a dozen of the red-eyed beasts. I didn't know where the rest of them were, but these watched me, silent for the moment except for their panting breaths. My own wind was coming back. I gestured at them.

"Come on," I growled.

They growled in return, their eyes deepening in savage color. Their movements grew more animated, their claws clicking together as they shifted from side to side.

"Come *on*!" I shouted at them, brandishing my sword.

I wanted them to attack me here. Now. Masses of red-tipped black thorns would keep them from climbing up the sides of the tree where I stood. They'd have to come at me along the flat of the branch where my boots were planted firmly. And they could not come all at once.

Then come they did, chittering, leaping, howling. I fought, sword flashing, the hilt tight in both hands. The steel blade stabbed, dipped, slashed, hacked, blocked, cleaved. Gore spattered. Flattened skulls sundered. Taloned limbs went flying. There was no time for thought, no mercy to be offered.

The battle was a whirl of fetid breath, spittle, squealing mouths sharp with teeth, stinking fur crawling with vermin, of blistering red eyes, raking claws, tearing cloth and a weaving bloody sword. I saw it all in flashes, like the way night rain is stilled by lightning. I took wounds. Felt them burn. Cuts. Scrapes. Bites. I let the pain enrage me. And I killed.

The beasts went down, falling away, shrieking, tearing their own wounds, dying. I had no count of the killed before one beast slipped beneath the blade that tore out its fellow's throat and slammed savagely into my right side. It knocked my sword arm up and back, pinned it with a hundred and twenty pounds of raging madness.

At the same moment, a growling something jerked hard on my left boot. My foot slipped in gore and I fell heavily on my back, nearly rolling off the branch into the depths. It was the beasts themselves that held me on that limb. They had me down. They tore at me. I felt teeth gouging at my arm, screamed in hot agony as fangs ripped through cloth and flesh to grind down on bone.

Still screaming, I kicked out wildly with my free leg, my boot stomping into the face of the creature that gnashed at my other foot. Its teeth gave away; its mouth pulped. I kicked again and its hold on me broke and it went spinning off the limb into darkness, falling away with a shriek that cut off in a brutal thud of yielding muscle against unyielding tree.

The beast pinning my right arm stopped its savaging of my flesh for an instant. It glared at me, rosary-bead eyes flaming red, its mouth open over vicious yellow teeth that hung with shreds of shirt and skin. Madly it glared, and just as madly I glared back. And in that instant of time, my left hand reached to the tree, found a six inch thorn and tore it loose.

The beast hissed, fur standing up all over its body. My hand rose and hacked down, and I drove the spike of that thorn through its eye so deep that it grated against the back of the creature's skull and snapped off. The thing spasmed only once and collapsed half across me. I shoved it off, rolled onto my side, trying to get my legs under me.

A grunting snarl rang in my ears and I looked wildly about, then realized the sound was *in* me rather than outside me. I forced myself to silence. The night was empty. Pieces of dead howler lay scattered around but nothing lived here except for me. I'd killed all of my immediate attackers. Or driven them away.

I'd won. But at what cost? My right arm and hand would scarcely work. My left leg was mangled and smeared a blood trail behind me as I tried to move. I could hardly tell where the shreds of my left boot ended and shreds of my foot began. The only good thing was that the bone wasn't broken.

I fumbled with my good hand and found a small limb, pulled myself up onto my good knee with a convulsive effort. Floaters bloomed and multiplied in my eyes, then slowly faded as I got back my breath. By some miracle the sword was still clutched in the rigid claw of my right hand. The fingers had spasmed and would not open. I reached with the left hand and took the blade away—though I had to jerk it free—and sheathed it at my hip.

"Get up," I rasped at myself.

Somewhere in the trees around there were more howlers. I couldn't see them but knew they were there. And if they attacked now they would kill me. I had to try to get away. For myself. For Bryce. For Rannon.

I reached higher on the tree, grasped another limb, hauled myself up onto trembling legs. Thorns poked and stabbed at me but the pain of them was little enough against the larger pain with which I already lived.

Just to my left was one of the deep notches in the trunk that I had noted before, the rungs in a ladder leading up to the rope bridge overhead. I forced my left leg to move, was surprised when it obeyed. Wedging a torn boot into one of the notches, I bade the leg hold. My left hand searched higher. Fingers scraped away loose bark and locked in another of the worked grooves. Gingerly, I let the weight settle on my leg. It shook, but held.

Kicking the toe of my right boot into a notch, I used the muscles in my good leg to push myself higher up the trunk. Then I brought the left leg up alongside the right, wedged the boot into the same notch. My perch was precarious. My right arm dangled. But my left hand had the strength of fear in it.

Trying to breathe shallowly to avoid having the thrust of my chest push me off the tree, I reached up with my left hand and searched for another hold. I found it, clung for a moment before pulling my right leg up to another notch.

By such inches I moved—working toward the rope bridge that led I knew not where. At first I talked to myself, urged myself on. Then even whispering came too hard and I just climbed. My thoughts drifted. I wondered if Diken Graye was alive. Had the red-eyed beasts taken him once

Bryce had abandoned his body? I began to wonder where the rest of the beasts were. There had to have been at least a dozen more than what I had killed.

There was nothing I could do for Graye now. I could barely do anything for myself. The fear began to come back from the place where it had hidden while I fought for my life. But I couldn't climb any faster.

A vine brushed my cheek. *No!* Not a vine but a length of drooping rope. I glanced up. The bridge was right there, right overhead. Exaltation swept me. Crashing terror followed. I was so close, and so afraid—so afraid that the beasts would come take me, drag me down, tear me apart as Bryce had prophesied.

I reached up with a shaky hand, caught one of the wrist-thick ropes that anchored the bridge to the huge thorn tree. I drew myself up. Nothing came to get me.

The bridge itself was a dense webbing of finger-width ropes woven from some plant resembling hemp. Flat boards of cedar-red wood, worked fine and smooth, lined the bottom of the webbing to make a walkway. I got my right knee up on that walkway, used my left hand to pull myself onto it. My other arm thumped painfully on the boards, although at least now I could move the fingers.

Still, nothing came for me.

I rolled over, lungs gasping for the sweet air. Nimeru was setting. Above me forged Sieona, the second moon, known as the storm queen. Her turquoise face seemed to smile at me.

I began to chuckle. And even though I knew it was not wise to make a sound, I could not stop.

They didn't come for me, I thought. *They didn't come.*

I chuckled some more.

Far away to the southwest I heard the cannonade of thunder, saw the faint splash of lightning in building clouds. Here there was only the stirring of a faint breeze.

"They didn't come!" I said. I thought I shouted it.

An emperor moth landed on my belly. I startled, then burst out with laughter that came close to hysteria. A second moth settled on my left knee, huge scarlet wings opening and closing, its feathery antennae tickling over the lacerations on my lower thigh. The emperor moth is nearly as big as an Earthly pigeon, though weighing scarcely as much as a hummingbird.

A third moth landed on my right wrist. I tried to shoo it but it merely rose and settled again. Frowning now, I watched its tongue unfurl, black and long, looking...plumper than I'd ever imagined a moth's tongue could look.

More fluttering movements filled the air around me. More moths settled. Dozens of them. Black, sticky tongues slid from scarlet mouths, began to lick at my wounds. I didn't like that. I shook my left arm free of clinging bodies, began to brush the things off my belly.

Still more landed. Wherever their tongues licked a pleasant numbness began to spread, soothing, easing my pain. I stopped trying to brush them away. A lassitude gathered behind my eyes. I closed them, could not open them again.

The numbness grew. Began to burn.

I tried to scream and failed.

Chapter Eighteen

Storm Queen

There were torch-red eyes in the moonlit jungle, and the distant, bitter howling of beasts. There were the pulsations of soft, plump bodies that thudded on my cheeks, at my eyes, against my lips. And the whir of moths was as loud as thunder in the dawn, loud enough to cover my screams as I began to choke on glistening wings.

With a cry, I jerked to full awareness, brushing wildly at my face and chest, feeling the quiver of feathery legs and antennae tickling all over me.

Nothing was there.

Sweat ran. My chest heaved. I sat up.

Nothing was there! No eyes, no wings, no ribbon tongues licking at raw wounds.

But something *had* been there. I remembered well the reality from which this "dream" had sprung.

Pushing away a coverlet that seemed quilted of soft, cool moss, I rose stiffly from the kind bed of woven rushes upon which I had lain. The dream *and* the reality slipped into the background for the moment as I found myself alone and naked in a strangely cluttered room scarcely half a dozen paces across. Before me stood a table, or rather, grew a table. It lifted in one graceful piece from the living wood of the floor. Piled on top of it were candles, crucibles, wooden plates, scraps of rusted armor, weapons, ancient books half turned to dust.

Beyond the table, in an outside wall of the same wood, was a small, rounded window through which I glimpsed afternoon light and the crowns of trees below and around me in the jungle. I was *in* a tree, I realized suddenly, inside the upper trunk of some forest giant more massive than any redwood I'd ever heard of.

How had I come here?

I turned to study the room, looking for some explanation of my circumstances. I found none, but the chamber and its contents were themselves arresting in their harmony and discordance. There were more windows—enlarged knotholes in the tree I saw now—and even a cloud-dimmed sun filled the space with airy brightness. How much more lovely this room would be when the sky was clear and jeweled, or when the arc of a rainbow slashed past the tree's upper reaches.

The inside walls of the room were naturally beveled, with a hundred nooks and cubbyholes and ledges where ferns and flowers were planted in a rich humus brought up from below, or where sat tiny crystal bottles, river-smoothed stones, intricately shaped works of deadwood. Gourds and chimes hung about. Miniature figures coaxed into being from feathers, twigs, and leaves fluttered from mobiles that danced with each pant of breeze through the chamber. Everywhere there grew vines that bore delicate sunburst blooms of white.

To one side of the table, embedded in the wall, a rock basin received a steady trickle of clear water from a mossy knothole above it and lost the same amount in overflow through a second knothole beneath. Animal-thirsty, I strode over, bent and drank. The water tasted sweet and cool.

Next to the water basin, hidden behind a fall of silver and black honeywhisper, I discovered an exit. It was a vertical slit in the tree trunk barely tall enough and wide enough for a man of my size to pass through—if he ducked and turned sideways. On a rattan chair by the door lay my rapier and clothes, or at least my jeans. Sword and pants had both been cleaned of blood, and the jagged tears in the left leg of the pants had been sewn up.

Sight of the jeans brought back my dream and its triggering reality in a hissing flash: fighting the red-eyed beasts, climbing to the rope bridge, the moths. *My wounds*! My right arm had been savaged; my left leg had been a bloody mess. I should barely be able to move, but I felt little pain.

Almost fearfully, I glanced down. My wounds were bound with cloth and whoever or whatever had brought me here had applied poultices. With my awareness shifting, I felt for the first time a pleasant tingle beneath the bandages, and smelled a dozen bright, clean odors of growth and life.

I held up my right hand, clenched and relaxed a fist. It hurt, but the fingers flexed normally. And my left foot and leg supported my weight with barely a twinge. I couldn't understand it. My injuries had been serious. How could they have healed this much in less than a day?

A chill struck me then. What if it hadn't been a day? It was late afternoon now, but how many such afternoons might have passed while I slept here? What might have happened in that time—to Diken Graye, to Bryce, to the world I knew?

Quickly, I grabbed up the jeans and yanked them on, then buckled the sword about my waist. I had to get out of here, had to find my way to Diken Graye, find out if he was still alive, then pick up the trail to Bryce and Vohanna. I was bending to look under the chair in hopes of finding my boots when a voice from behind stopped me.

"How soon they flee my hospitality," the voice said. "And without even a thank you."

I spun, still in a crouch, hand dropping to my sword's hilt as I expected to see some red-eyed thing with a demonic smile. A woman stood there, clad in a simple kirtle of oat-brown. Her eyes were jade. Beautiful. Her hair was a copper-fire mane that hung tousled to the small of her back. She was barely five feet tall, slender waisted with hips flaring sweetly below. Her mouth was generous in a face of sharp cheekbones and large, almost hollowed eyes. Her chin was strong, her nose delicate. She wore her sadness so well that it almost seemed she wore none at all.

I straightened slowly from my crouch, blushing as her words registered.

"I'm sorry," I said. "I was raised better. I *do* owe you my gratitude. Thank you."

The woman's lips curled in what could have been either a smile or a smirk. She let go of the rope ladder that she'd unfurled from above to use in climbing down the hollow inside of the tree, and walked to the table carrying a bird nest in which several somethings chirruped. She placed the nest into an old, battered war-helmet and dropped in a handful of bread crumbs.

"A harsupex got their mother last eve," she murmured, not looking at me, not even seeming as if her words were meant for me.

I knew what a harsupex was—a kind of ferret-cat with the smarts and habits of a racoon—but I wasn't sure how to respond to her comment.

"And left them alone," is all I said.

She looked at me, studied me for a moment, then looked away. "I will accept your apology," she said.

She leaned down and tugged a small chest from under the table. Opening it, she drew out a long sleeved shirt of ivory linen and tossed it to me. Next, she came up with a pair of calf-high boots that did not appear to be made of leather but of some flexible steel-gray shell, like sea-turtle shell that had not yet hardened. She tossed these to me as well.

"Yours were beyond repair," she said. "Those should fit."

The shirt was button-less. I slipped it on, tucked it in my jeans, then sat in the cane chair and began to tug on the boots. The right went on easily but the left was a tight fit over my bandages. After a few moments of listening to me curse, the woman came over and knelt to help.

"Thank you again," I said when the boot was on.

She shrugged, rising. "There is no use for them here anymore. And you will need them where you are going."

I looked up at her. There was some meaning behind her words of "here anymore," but that meaning sounded personal and I did not wish to intrude.

Instead, I said: "I am Ruenn Maclang."

"Ahrethane," she said. I took that as her name, wasn't sure if it was one name or two.

"And where is it that you think I'm going, Ahrethane?" I asked, responding to her earlier comment.

"The heart of the jungle," she replied. "And below."

I blinked. "How do you know that?"

Her cheeks hollowed a bit. Some shadow of past pain flitted across her lips and was gone. "I know the forest," she said. "I know what happens in it. Who comes and who goes. And why."

She added: "Your friend is no longer under the tree where he collapsed."

I started in my chair. "Diken Graye," I said. I looked at her...hard. "Then where? What happened to him?" For a moment, I paused. "How long have I been here?"

"I do not know where...Diken Graye is. He is not in the forest, though. I imagine he was taken below. As for you, it is the afternoon of the third day since you were brought to me."

Nearly three days lost," I thought. But I said: "Who carried me to you? And," I held up my bandaged arm, "how is it that my wounds have healed so quickly?"

"There are those in the forest who aid me," she said. "They brought you here."

"And *they* healed me?"

"No," Ahrethane said.

She turned her attention back to her table. Taking up the old helmet with its cargo of bird nest and chirping occupants, she placed it on a shelf to one side. Then she began to stack swords and daggers and books to make a space that she immediately filled again with two large wooden bowls. She placed thorn-forks beside the bowls and began to shred into them greenery and bits of dried fruit.

"Who then?" I insisted. "Who healed me?"

"No *one*," she said. "It was the moths. I merely poulticed your wounds with herbs to continue what they began."

Lifting handfuls of shelled nuts from a small wooden keg, she dropped them into the bowls with the greenery and fruit.

"The moths?" I asked, incredulous.

She filled two wooden cups from the water basin and set them on the table.

"Eat." She motioned to one of the bowls.

She pulled a chair up to the other bowl and began to fork food to her mouth. I hesitated. Getting information from this woman was a little easier than plucking a scorpion-hawk's tail barb, but not much. I felt an intense urge to shake her, but was quite sure it wouldn't do me a bit of good. In fact, judging by the way she handled edged weapons it might well do me some harm.

I drew my chair up to the table. Sat. Ate. The greens were tastier than they looked; the fruit was filling; the nuts were delicious. I hadn't realized how ravenous I was.

After a bit, I chuckled.

Ahrethane stopped eating and frowned. I met her gaze, smiled innocently as I plucked out a nut and crunched it between my teeth.

She put down her fork. "The moths weave," she said. "It is what they do. To the forest." She flicked a finger toward my cloth-wrapped arm. "To those who are injured in the forest. You thought they were hurting you but they are incapable of harm."

I put down my own fork. "Some healing balm in their saliva, perhaps," I said.

"Yes, perhaps" she agreed. "And more."

"I appreciate you telling me."

She watched me. After a moment she nodded, and I felt that nod as a victory.

"What will you do when you go below?" she asked.

"Find my friend," I said.

"And?"

I did not speak at first. My hand found my water cup and I drained it. I ate another nut.

She chuckled, quite deliberately.

I looked at her in surprise, then grinned. She grinned back. Her face lost years.

I took a deep breath. There was no clear reason why I should trust his fire-tressed woman. But I did.

"My brother is below," I told her. "A witch has him."

"Vohanna," she said.

"You know her?"

The years came back to her face. "I know her. You named her witch but she is far worse. If she has your brother then...I am sorry. It is unlikely you will be able to save him."

She glanced down into her bowl, then pushed it away as if her appetite had fled. "I was never able to," she whispered.

Again her words were personal but this time I *did* ask. "Never able to what?"

She glanced up. Her lips had thinned, lost their lushness. Her eyes grew even more haunted. She said, very clearly: "I was never able to save *my* brother after Vohanna took him. Or any member of my family."

I made no murmur of sympathy. Though she deserved it, I did not think she would take it well at that moment. Instead, I asked her: "How is it that *you* remain?"

The tiny flicker of a humorless smile played over her lips.

"Vohanna leaves me alone," she said. "The jungle hides her from the prying eyes of the world, and without me the jungle would die."

She said this so matter-of-factly that I knew it was true.

"Are you efrinore?" I asked.

She seemed surprised that I knew that word—which in English might translate as something like druid-shaman—but after a moment she nodded.

"That won't matter when Vohanna reaches her full strength, though," she added. "Then she'll not need the jungle and there will be no place for me or any other who does not serve her."

I was no longer hungry. I pushed away my own bowl and rose. Time was precious. I had to go.

"But *you* Vohanna fears," Ahrethane said, watching as her words caught and held me.

I felt my eyebrows arch. "That seems unlikely."

"She has tried to discredit you. Frighten you. She tried to kill you more than once. Her failures gall her."

I didn't ask her how she knew these things that she should not know. The efrinore have their ways.

Thinking of the parchment note that had sent me fleeing from Timmuzz, and of all the things that had happened since, I said: "She discredited me with those I care most about. Killed some of them. She's hacked years off my life in worry. Failure seems a poor choice of words for what Vohanna has done to me."

Ahrethane shook her head. "That's not enough for her. She's underestimated you at each step. She won't again.

She'll have an army waiting to stop you. Monsters that make the red-eyed howlers look like children's pets. Men that are worse."

"Then I'll have to hope that I continue to be lucky."

She nodded at my need for luck, rather vigorously, I thought. "You'll need all the fortune you can muster. But also, I must help you. I cannot...go below. There is nothing but death there for an efrinore. Where no natural life can thrive."

"Then how *will* you help?" I asked, showing a faint irritation that I knew was unreasonable.

She did not notice it. Or chose to ignore it.

"I can give you cover," she said. "The worst of Vohanna's creatures will be in the forest. She will not want you to reach the underworld. But if you can. Undetected. You *might* have a chance."

Moving quickly then, she rose and pushed aside the honeywhisper that curtained the exit I had found earlier.

"Come," she called, as she slipped through the split in the trunk and I lost sight of her.

I followed, more angry now, and angry with myself for feeling that way. I wanted to tell her that, lucky or not, I had done pretty well before without her help. But that would have been both cruel and foolish. Cruel because, if anything, she had suffered worse from Vohanna than I had. And foolish because, I *did* need her help. I might very well be dead now without it. Certainly I could have been crippled.

Trying to swallow my pride and finding it hard, I joined Ahrethane outside her tree house on a broad branch to which several rope bridges were anchored. The efrinore's home tree bulked huge in the center of a clearing, with lesser giants in a circle around. Still other hempen walkways—many of them in poor repair—were moored to limbs above and below me, leading off in every direction through the forest. It was as if Ahrethane's tree had once been a traffic hub for a jungle-spanning network of trade and travel that no longer existed.

As I glanced from the rope bridges to Ahrethane, I had the sudden impression that the walkways behind me had filled with slender men and women, strolling, chatting, smiling, stopping here and there to hug—or to kiss. And for that instant I swore that I heard the sweetly languid sounds of the kalina, the seven-stringed Taleran guitar, drifting over the clearing. Then the feeling was gone and I understood finally what had been lost here in this place.

I looked away from the woman who stood beside me. I looked up into the brilliant green sky and the last of my pride went down my throat in a lump. I wanted to tell her I was sorry for my anger. She gave me no time; she pointed to a hempen bridge at my right hand.

"That is the route," she said. "At the jungle's center it is anchored to the top of a black pyramid. But do not follow it all the way. At a tree with a lighting-blasted limb you will leave the bridge. Under that limb is a door into the tree's heart. A ladder will take you down. Flat in the ground at the bottom you will find a strange, smooth stone as big around as a man's body. This lifts. If you have the strength. There, is an entrance to the underground. One that I think Vohanna may not know."

I was about to thank her one last time when she turned and silenced me with a finger to my lips. She rose on tiptoes to dab a kiss at the corner of my mouth, then pulled back, her brilliant eyes studying mine.

"I am sorry if I sounded...unkind before," she said. "Do not be angry with me. It is only that I want an end to Vohanna as badly as you do."

She stepped back, into the narrow doorway of her strange abode. "Go with the storm," she said, and disappeared inside.

For a moment, I hesitated. There was no storm except the one in my thoughts. I glanced into the sky, glanced back to the tree of Ahrethane.

Then the faces of Bryce and Diken Graye, and of Rannon, swam up before my eyes. I turned and started along the bridge that Ahrethane had indicated to me. And from the trees all around arose a vast cloud of Emperor moths, like a blizzard of scarlet snow. They gathered, so many that I could hear the thrum of their wings and feel the stir of wind currents in the air.

A crackle of static electricity discharged in the clearing around me. Lightning answered from above. I saw a drop of rain, then more, and ran for the trees at the other side of the open space. The moths peeled away in flight, diving for shelter as a tempest exploded in fury out of what had been clear air moments before.

I ran. And though the storm stomped in the forest it barely brushed my path with wet fingers. Something protected me.

I ran.

And whispered: "Coming for you, Vohanna."

Chapter Nineteen

Going Below

Moving within the storm's shroud, I reached the lightning-savaged tree that Ahrethane had told me to watch for. No one, no thing, contested my passage; I saw no sign of enemies, though I sensed something malevolent nursing at the very air through which I passed.

But if there *were* foes here, they must have had their heads bent against the flood of rain and wind. I wondered if they prayed to Vohanna as a goddess to save them. I doubted she'd be much help. This forest, at least, was still under Ahrethane's dominion.

In the distance ahead of me, shrouded in robes of rain over the tops of the trees, there lifted the matte black pyramid Ahrethane had warned me to avoid. That pyramid lay at the center of ruined Vohan, the city over which the jungle had grown, and I recalled that when Diken Graye had released our saddle birds they had flown to that building and settled. We had both suspected then that Vohanna's own bird riders held their mounts at that place, and glad I was not to have to pass through what was surely an army.

Instead, I vaulted off the bridge onto the lightning-twisted tree limb and clung for a moment to rain-slick bark before searching out the opening in the trunk that would let me bypass the enemy's front door. I found that opening, slipped inside. It was dry there. Protected. There was light—animal-made light—from insects that crawled here and there on the rough inner walls. I recognized them as tris, candlebugs, which are common to dark, enclosed places all over Nyshphal. I'd seen them in sewers before, and in wine cellars.

Tris are not like the fireflies of Earth. For one, they are smaller and flightless. For another, their glow is nearly constant. And they typical live in mats of millions. Here there were only a few handfuls, and I was sure that those had come up from the underground, from below.

The soft turquoise light of the tris revealed a ledge—almost a rind of wood—around a hollow core in the tree. I perched on that rind; a rope ladder dangled down the core. I swung out on it and went swiftly down.

The open space in the tree's center widened toward the bottom and there were more tris there, clawed feet clicking on and over each other as they moved ceaselessly. I let my boots down on a musty, friable soil, saw before me in the earth the stone Ahrethane had spoken of. It was rounded, gray and smooth, and I thought it not stone at all but some kind of metal. There were no obvious handles or grips so I drew my dagger and dug around the outside edge until I could hook my fingers beneath.

I pulled. Pain slashed through my right arm but my grip held.

The stone didn't budge.

I tried the lift again. Again nothing moved.

I stood, frowning as I studied the closed portal through which I had to pass and could not. And then Ahrethane's words came back to me. "This lifts. If you have the strength."

I had assumed she'd meant those words literally. But I *was* a strong man and clearly my muscles alone did not seem enough. I doubted even Kreeg, the strongest man I knew, could have hefted this stone by himself. I looked around for something to use as a pry bar, but all I had was my sword and it was far too flexible for this task.

Then I *heard* the words, like a whisper out of the air: "*If you have the strength.*"

An electric shiver coursed my spine as gooseflesh rose. That sound had been only the brittle shells of the candlebugs rubbing together, I told myself. I knew I lied.

My gaze turned back to the gray stone. This barrier, I had to pass. There was no other choice. The lives of those I loved depended on it. And if I could not do it with muscles alone, then I'd have to find something more inside. Was that what the softly murmuring voice had meant? That I could find something more?

Again I squatted, hooked my fingers under the stone's edge. I closed my eyes.

"You have the strength," I told myself...out loud.

I locked my arms, pushed down hard against the dirt with my legs. Muscles tensed, drew tight over bones. Tendons creaked. My healing leg ached, my right arm throbbed. I pressed harder with my boots, driving them against the soft soil, feeling them sink in half an inch. An inch. The stone grated. Dust puffed up. I grunted with the strain, feeling my spine curve. The stone fought me, and from somewhere inside a growl bubbled to my lips.

"You *will* move," I snarled.

Heat flashed through me, along every sinew, within every cell. Then I stood, slowly, every inch a war, and the stone seemed to tear itself out of the ground to reveal its true shape as a long, gray cylinder.

When my legs were fully extended, the base of the cylinder just cleared the lip of the hole in which it had rested. Dropping the heavy thing to one side, I stood with trembling limbs, sweat soaked and breathing like a bellows. Pain was alive in my body, but the way into "Below" was open. That way was not dark but bloomed with the lurid blue-green of massed tris. Even as I watched, a horde of the small insects began to pour through the hole and spread out over the ground.

Ignoring the bugs that scurried over my boots, trying to ignore the agony of my overextended body, I bent and looked through the hole. There was a fall of seven or eight feet to what looked like solid earth. I stepped through the opening and dropped, landing in a crouch with the scrunch of candle-bugs under my feet. Tris swarmed all around, their light delineating a tunnel some seven feet high by four across.

It was hot here below ground, very hot, and as my skin

grew clammy with sweat I wondered if it was this unusual heat that fed the growth of the jungle above. It didn't matter really.

The bandages on my arm began to itch horribly and, unable to stand it longer, I peeled them off to gaze at fresh, pink scars where bloody gouges had existed only a few days before. My leg was the same underneath its wrapping of cloth. I wondered how much of it was truly the moths, and how much the magic of Ahrethane the efrinore.

For the first time, then, I became aware that there had been a friendly...presence accompanying me through the forest. It was gone now, the voice in the tree above having been its last and most powerful manifestation. Ahrethane had told me, she could not go "below." Even in spirit, it seemed. But if I was on my own again now, it had been she who had gotten me here. She and her moths.

"Thank you," I whispered into the air, though I had no idea if she would ever hear or know what I had said. Then I turned back to the task at hand.

There was only one way to go along the tunnel where I stood, and within fifty paces I began to pick out the gleam of brighter lights ahead that could not have been made by *any* number of tris. For some reason that fact made my heart pound. I slowed, dropping a hand to my sword for comfort, and in another twenty steps reached a turn in the passageway and rounded it to see that the brightness did indeed provide a reason for fear.

I found myself on a ledge overlooking a cavern beneath the earth that was several hundred yards across and perhaps a third of that in height. Most of it was shadowed, with the dark mouths of tunnels leading off in every direction. Above each tunnel I saw a glyph painted in white on the stone, each different, their twisted shapes flickering in the light of torches that gleamed beside them in brackets of iron.

But it was not the glyphs or the weak glow of the torches that held my attention. In the center of the cavern, wreathed in a pale gray mist and limned by a brilliant fluorescent light that shone from some kind of hanging globes, there loomed a monstrous thing. By its design, it was clearly an airship—one unlike any that had been seen before in

Taleran skies. It was huge.

The biggest battleship in the Nyshphalian navy was about two hundred feet long. This beast added another fifty feet to that length. The great vessel's hull was armored with plate that would block any trebuchet stone, turn any ballista arrow. And there were no masts or sails, only giant screws, propellers really, jutting from the ship's aft end. Through gaps in the armor at the stern I saw what could be none other than massive steam engines, and worst of all was the row of ports along the side from which protruded the mouths of cannon.

Engines! *Cannon*!

Immediately my thoughts went to...Bryce.

Gunpowder had been unknown on Talera until recently. I was convinced of that from my readings in the planet's history. It *had been* unknown. Until Bryce and I arrived.

I remembered the gunpowder-filled crossbow quarrels that Diken Graye had used against Rannon's flyer—had it been barely a week ago? I had not thought of it before now, but Bryce knew the formula for gunpowder. So did I. You mixed three-quarters saltpetre with a bit of charcoal and sulphur. As boys we'd made our own firecrackers. And "I" hadn't shared the formula with anyone. Had Bryce? I began to think so.

As if cannon weren't bad enough, my experiences with sea vessels on earth had shown me that steam-powered ships were faster and more maneuverable than sail-powered ones. This giant craft would not only be able to outshoot any comparable airship on Talera, it would be able to outfly it as well.

Though Bryce had been no expert on steam engines, some of my old ship's crew from earth *had* been. According to Eric Ryall, Vohanna had taken members of that crew as prisoners. Below me was evidence that the would-be goddess had milked the information on steam from their minds. For a moment, I wondered just how hard Vohanna had to work to get gunpowder from Bryce. Then I forced that thought aside.[6]

---

[6]Although Ruenn didn't seem to think of it, I wondered why Vohanna, if

WINGS OVER TALERA, BY CHARLES ALLEN GRAMLICH

By now, Valyan would have reached Timmuzz with Kreeg. He would have spoken to Rannon about Vohanna and a Nyshphalian battle fleet would be on the way to the jungle of Vohan. It was what I'd hoped for. If I knew Rannon and her father, it was exactly what was happening. And when that fleet arrived I would have led them into a trap. This one ship and its cannons would be devastating enough. If there were others like it then the air fleet of my adopted homeland would be pulverized. Rannon with it, perhaps. I doubted she'd stay behind in Timmuzz.

I had to do something. But what?

Finding a way down from the ledge was easy enough, and there were outcroppings of stone and clumps of a desiccated, mesquite-like brush that offered ample concealment as I worked my way across the cavern. I had no idea how plants were growing here where no sunlight penetrated, and there was certainly nothing of green about them. But I was thankful for the cover, especially as the brilliant shine from the light globes grew stronger near the ship. Soon, I had to crawl from one hiding place to another to remain undetected. I sweated more.

At fifty yards distance, from behind a detritus pile of scrap metal, I raised my head to study the scene around the ship. The vessel seemed largely finished. Much of the scaffolding had been removed and the catwalks strung high above the decks were empty of laborers. I saw a lot of guards, which suggested that Vohanna did not trust her own workers much. I liked that idea.

I noted one officer in particular, an arrogant and strutting fellow who wore a gold-chased helm and a scarlet cloak while the others wore helmets and cloaks of simple gray. There was something about him I did not care for—perhaps it was just that he seemed too aware of his duties while his men looked lax and bored—and I waited until he had gone around the far side of the ship before acting on the vague

---

she were a product of an advanced civilization, would need to steal technological knowledge from a group of early-twentieth-century humans. Then it occurred to me that I, who live in the twenty-first century, don't have the faintest idea how to build an airplane or computer.—CAG.

plan forming in my mind.

A few yards off from my position there drifted one of the light globes. I'd assumed at first that these were some sort of hanging lantern, but had soon realized my mistake. They floated...freely, glass spheres that burned bluish-white without fire. Sorcery? Or some scientific principle that I had no name for? No matter.

I'd already noted that, twenty yards beyond the globe, a lone sentry stood relieving himself against a bush. Stacked timber hid him from any direct view from the ship, and in my creeping across the cave I'd seen others come to that place for the same purpose. As I'd gotten closer, the smell had let me know that the spot was in regular use. That regularity was why I'd chosen this particular scrap heap.

The man finished his task and turned to go. I picked up a rock, hurled it. The light globe smashed in a shower of sparks and the startled guard spun around. He'd half pulled his blade in the jolt of the moment, but now he pushed the weapon back into its sheath and muttered curses as he stalked to investigate.

I smiled grimly. The laxity I thought I'd seen in the guards was real apparently. It was as if this man couldn't conceive of a true threat to his mistress's power. I circled the debris pile as he came closer to my position, then rose behind him silently and locked an arm around his throat, the needle point of my dagger pressed to his heart.

"Be quiet or die," I whispered in his ear.

He chose quiet.

I dragged him to the far side of the scrap heap and shoved him to his belly, then bound his hands behind him with strips of his own shirt. Jerking him back to a sitting position, I took my dagger and pressed the blade crossways to his throat.

"How many ships like this does Vohanna have?" I asked him.

"I'll tell you nothing," he growled.

I slapped him. "How many?"

He set his face grimly. There was blood at the corner of his mouth. I chuckled. He looked at me. Deep from within his eyes came a red flicker, like heat lightning, and nestled amid tattooed lines on his forehead was a glittering dot that marked a piece of milkstone. He was controlled. Like Eric Ryall had been. Again I chuckled, and lifted the dagger to press the point just below his speck of toir'in-or stone.

"If I cut this thing out...," I mused.

The man's face paled.

"Yes," I continued, as if contemplating some deeply philosophical question. "I wonder how long it would be before Vohanna noticed? And what she'd do when she realized?"

The man shook his head. His eyes were wide. I leaned closer until my face was barely an inch from his. I pressed the tip of the dagger hard enough against his forehead to bring a tiny spot of blood that wicked in red lines around the border of the toir'in-or.

"Have you seen how Vohanna gives death to those she thinks have failed her?" I asked in a whisper. "Have you heard them scream? How many ships like this are there?"

"Four," the fellow blurted. "There are four. Please don't!"

I relaxed a little of the pressure that I held on the dagger.

"What other forces does she have?" I demanded.

There was no resistance left in the man now. Thoughts of his goddess's punishments terrified him. He licked dry lips as he answered.

"A few smaller flyers. Mostly she has bird riders, though. Thousands of them."

"And the new weapons?" He knew what I meant.

"Only the big ships carry the cannon," he said. "The blast quarrels are common. Many warriors will have them when the time comes."

I sighed. By using the English terms "cannon" and "blast" the man had proven to me where the secret of gunpowder had come from.

Then something else he'd said registered. "*Will* have them?" I asked. "Where are the quarrels now?"

His gaze flicked down from mine. His shoulders slumped. "Stored in the ships," he said. "With the loads for the cannon."

"All right," I said. "Now, I'm assuming the white glyphs that mark the exits from this cavern are some kind of map grid. Which ones will take me to the other ships? And which will take me to Vohanna?"

He described the pictographs I wanted and I drew them in the dirt for him to verify. Then I committed them to memory. I stripped off his helmet and placed it on my own head, and took his cloak and slung it about me. I tied him by his wrists to a block of rusted metal behind him. Before I gagged him I asked him one last question.

"Have you seen a man who travels with Vohanna? With white hair and a false hand? His name is Bryce Maclang."

The man shuddered. His voice cracked as he answered.

"Yes. All have seen him. None have wished to. He is always with the goddess. 'Tis said he is a demon that she conjured to aid her."

I growled. "He is only a man," I said. "Just a man."

The fellow started to protest and angrily I stuffed a gag made from the remnants of his shirt into his mouth and tied it off. I rose then, pulling his helmet down to shadow my face and drawing his cloak about me. Turning, I strode toward the airship where it crouched like a metallic dragon ready to leap into the sky.

Only once did I glance back, to see the bound guard's eyes wide and glistening above his gag. One thing was clear. He did not believe my brother to be, "just a man."

Chapter Twenty

When Battle Is Joined

Wearing the helmet and cloak of a guard, I strode without a challenge through the slack defenses around the massive airship. Only once did I even have to pause, when the scarlet-cloaked officer that I'd seen before made his rounds past me. I stood at attention, as I'd seen others do before, and he gave me scarcely a glance as he stalked on his way. I then turned and entered the ship through the stern where the steam engines were located. It was almost frighteningly easy.

A few light globes floated lazily within the ship, throwing rococo shadows off the multi-faceted surfaces of the engines onto the inside wall of the hull. The engines themselves looked powerful enough to drive a mountain into the air. They were spanking new, all polished-bright steel and black iron. But they had been tested. Fresh oil—which I judged from the odor and color to have been made from a source other than petroleum—gleamed on exposed surfaces and turned the wooden floors beneath into iridescent landscapes. There were no guards here, no workers.

An oaken bulkhead separated the engine room from the rest of the ship, and centered in it was an open portal that beckoned me. I stepped through, silently, into a broad corridor with half a dozen closed doors to either side. There were light globes fixed to the ceiling here. An engineer—at least I judged him so by the sheaf of papers that he studied as he walked—came toward me, head down and oblivious.

"Greetings," I said.

The man jumped, nearly dropping his papers, and

looked up at me with eyes wide. Then he sputtered:

"See here! What are you doing in here? You are not—"

I punched him in the forehead and he wilted like a lily under the sun. Dragging his unconscious form back through the door I'd just passed, I stuffed him and his papers behind an engine where he wouldn't be seen. I left him unbound. I had my reasons. For one, he had not been "controlled," had worn no speck of toir'in-or stone. I wondered if, by necessity, most of Vohanna's machinists were given the same relative freedom.

Returning to the corridor, I padded swiftly along it, moving always toward the center of the ship. I met no guards, but from the attitude of the engineer I knew that being seen would mean a fight now. Some part of me rather *hoped* to be seen. I wasn't. Not yet. Then I reached the heart of the ship and stood gazing up a tightly spiraled stairwell into the belly of the beast.

Most Taleran airships have large open holds between, at most, two or three layers of decks. This one was different. Above me I counted six decks, and there were many more bulkheads and it looked like enough cabins to comfortably house a large crew. Perhaps because steam can push heavier weights than sails can pull, Vohanna's shipwrights had built with metal and heavy woods that would take an incredible pounding just to dent. But I wasn't here to admire the thing. I started up the stairwell, moving on quiet feet.

On deck three I found what I was seeking.

Here at last was an open space that could be called a hold. And in it there were cannon—twenty-five guns to a side—with ugly iron mouths that jutted through portholes in the hull. In the center of the room, stacked high within frames constructed for that purpose, were rows of shot—stone and lead balls, short lengths of chain, nails. Neither the cannon nor the shot were pretty, but I was sure they would be effective. If the powder worked.

It was the powder I hunted, and beyond the ranked piles of shot I found the room where it was kept. That room made a square within the greater rectangle of the hold, and its walls were plated with metal as defense against projectiles and fire. There was a single entrance, a brass-banded door of oak, and in front of it stood two guards wearing swords, with leaf-bladed spears leaning close to hand.

The guards had already seen me. There was no going around them, no turning back. Over the door, where torches could not be used because of the black powder, a glow globe was fastened. I stalked into its light from out of the shadows. For a moment the guards were confused by my helmet and cloak. Wasn't I one of theirs? Had I come early to relieve them? Did I bear a message? I smiled at that last thought. Surely, I did have a message for them.

Both guards were human, both male. One frowned, put his hand on his sword. He called a question. I ignored it, kept walking. More words came—a quiet order to halt and then a command, ringing. I drew my sword, left handed. They drew theirs.

One of the two had red hair. It was he who turned to sound a warning bell beside the door, and I hurled the dagger that I'd palmed in my right hand. The straight, flat, stiletto blade took the red head between the second and third knuckles of his fingers and pinned his hand to the wall.

It took a moment for the wounded man's scream to gather, and in that moment I leaped forward, sword winking as I shifted it from left hand to right. The red head's mouth opened and I cut him across the throat so that his cry was born dead in a foaming of blood.

The other guard lunged at me. I twisted to one side, heard the whiff of his blade driving past me, felt it scrape a sharp line of burn down my left side. I snapped my wrist hard across at my waist, my own blade humming as it cut through air to meet his. Steel raked on steel, knocking his sword well out of line with my body. He tried to recover. I didn't let him.

My left hand flashed out, fingers locking about his throat, shutting off any chance he had of calling for help. Then I stepped into him and drove my blade up into his chest cavity. His eyes met mine, widened for an instant, shuttered closed the next as his legs went limp and I let him fall. He hit the deck with a soft thud, pulling away from my blade so that it slipped free and hung there at my side—dripping.

"Bravo," a voice said from behind me.

WINGS OVER TALERA, BY CHARLES ALLEN GRAMLICH

I turned. Slowly. Standing there was the scarlet-cloaked officer of guards that I had seen before. Now, he unclasped the amber broaches that pinned his cloak at the shoulders and flung the garment away. By that act he showed himself to be a man proud and arrogant, convinced of his own superiority. A more cautious warrior would have saved the cloak for defense, to wrap around an arm to foil a stabbing sword.

Overconfidence was a weakness I could exploit.

I turned to face the man fully, took off my own cloak and tossed it aside. Then I removed my helm and let it drop. The man frowned. I gave him back a thin smile. He removed *his* helmet and set it down on a stack of cannon balls.

I did not know how this man had found me out. Nor did I truly care. I could see from the red-ember glow in his eyes, and from the swirl of his tattoos, that he was Vohanna's minion. And for that I would kill him. But first, it occurred to me that I should make him pay—for Bryce, for Eric, for Diken Graye...for Rannon. Vohanna was the reason they were all lost to me. Perhaps it was time I took something of hers.

The man saluted me with a flick of his blade, then took a fencing stance. I did not bother to return his gesture. That irritated him. He was one who would demand respect, a proud man.

"I find little interest in hacking up more of Vohanna's mind-controlled slaves," I said offhandedly, lowering the point of my sword to the wooden planks and giving every appearance of leaning casually upon it. That appearance was a lie, but he did not know that.

He snarled. "My mind is my own. And I am no slave."

"A lap dog, then," I said, in an agreeable tone.

The man's face flushed. "You will die for that."

"Not today," I replied, smirking at him.

Again he snarled, and lunged with his sword extended in a perfect line for my heart. His speed was incredible but his emotion had telegraphed his movement and my own blade flicked up, slapping his aside. I stepped right, letting his momentum carry him past me, and I cut him across the upper chest, leaving a long, thin furrow that bubbled red.

He pulled up, free hand rising to touch his wound, fingertips coming away sticky. I smelled the blood, sharp in my nostrils. The man met my gaze, incredulity written like Braille across his features. It was in his thoughts that I could have killed him with that stroke and had cut him instead as a deliberate insult. He was wrong, but I didn't need to let him know that. Again I offered my thin smile. And now I raised my blade and saluted *him*, mockingly.

His face went livid; his pupils dilated wildly, black on red. He launched a blistering attack, driving me back as he hurled himself recklessly upon me. I fended myself but could do little to take advantage of his rashness. He was too quick, too powerful. But he was also tiring.

Anger is a heavy emotion to carry.

The man's attack fizzled in a flurry of striking, clanging swords. He came to a halt, gasping for breath and trying to hide it, with sweat glistening on his ruddy face and beading in his hair. His eyes blazed, and were fearful at the same time—like a wolf finding that his easy prey has fangs. I affected a bored pose, letting the tip of my sword drop again to the floor-planks.

"Perhaps some lessons," I said to the man, keeping my voice mild and idly waving my left hand toward his sword.

He vented an absolute shriek at my insult, and lunged again, wildly. I spun off my left heel, dropping to one knee with my back to him, my left hand slapping across, catching my sword's hilt behind the right hand to add power to a driving thrust over my shoulder. The blade seemed to leap upward in a shining arc.

The guard officer's upper body was too far forward. His balance was ruined and his sword was well out of defensive line over my head where my heart had been moments before. He had no chance to block my thrust as it razored in from his right side. His body seemed to draw the blade in, seemed to suck it in deep beneath the ribs until the hilt met the flesh of his belly with a wicked smacking sound.

I jerked the weapon free and, continuing my turn as I pushed up off my knee, rose to a standing position behind him. He was perfectly still, leaning so far forward that I thought he would fall. But then his head started to turn toward me. I saw the glistening of his eyes, and I swung my blade around and down, chopping through his neck right where his helmet would have protected if he hadn't removed it. The head spun free, thunked wetly against the wall, and fell to roll quietly to a stop.

I was already plucking up the man's scarlet cloak and wiping my sword clean. Then I slung my own cloak, the soldier-gray one, around me. Walking over to the door of the gunpowder room, I reached up and grasped the hilt of my dagger where it had buried itself deep in the wood. I jerked it free, and the corpse of the guard whose hand it still pinned slumped the rest of the way to the floor with what sounded like a sigh.

Sheathing the dagger, I bent and picked up my helmet from the floor. For a moment, in the polished gleam of that helm, I saw my face. It was cold and bitter, the eyes like chips from a jade glacier.

I glanced toward the three dead men that I shared the room with. For the first time I realized that I'd felt nothing during those killings. I'd taken their lives remorselessly. All except for the last, the officer's. I'd felt something when I taunted him, before I took his head. It had been something like...glee.

Looking back at my face in the mirror of the helm, I thought I saw for a moment, deep within the oil-dark pupils, a blooming and shimmering of crimson.

I hurled the helmet savagely away from me.

Chapter Twenty-One

The Black Pyramid

A gleam of red. Deep in my eyes.

It was a lie. What I'd seen reflected in the helmet *had* to have been a lie. I had not become that which I fought against. I had not! Vohanna must be stopped. Bryce *must* be saved. And if that meant meeting violence with more violence, so be it.

I turned, kicked open the door to the room that I knew must house the black powder for the cannons. I was right. Kegs of the stuff stood like parade-ground soldiers in the small space. And piled high in one corner were thousands of swollen-headed blast quarrels like the one Diken Graye had used days ago to bring down Rannon's airship. All around me I smelled the hellish stench of sulphur and charcoal.

Stepping over the threshold, I sheathed my sword. A fire axe hung on one wall. I took it down. I had to work quickly. It seemed unlikely that Vohanna would keep each of her minions under constant mental surveillance, but how long would it be before she checked in and found some of her servants missing in action? Somehow, I doubted it would be very long.

A glow globe hung from the ceiling in the black powder room, and by its light I overturned several kegs of the grainy material and used the axe to smash them open. Powder spilled in dry rivers over the floor. The air began to fill with an ashy dust.

I picked up another keg and carried it to the door, then punched open the top and began pouring a thick trail of gunpowder out into the hold where the cannons were located. The keg was empty by the time the trail reached an outside wall of the ship. I tossed the barrel aside, then turned to drag one cannon away from its porthole, which was big enough to provide me an exit if the drop wasn't too far. I glanced out, saw the ground some twenty-five feet below. It was a long way but I had little choice.

Drawing my dagger and holding up the axe, I struck one blade against the other, sending a wave of sparks sleeting onto the line of gunpowder at my feet. Light flared up, yellow and ugly. An odor of burning reeked in my nostrils. I turned and slipped through the porthole to dangle for a moment by my hands. Inside I could hear the scorpion hiss of fire running swiftly over black powder, and I let go, slid along the curved hull, dropped to land in a roll and come up running.

I heard the shouts of guards, saw startled faces with wide eyes. I yelled at all of them to run. As I was running. One tried to get in my way, tried to grab at me. I shoved him aside and ran.

Then something huge lifted me. I felt heat, heard a massive *whumpf* that seemed to envelop me. And I was thrown forward like a doll as the bomb of the ship went up behind me. I rolled over, protecting my face with my hands. A crescendo of flame pillared high in the smoking crater where the airship had been, licking and coiling even against the ceiling far overhead. Acrid fumes twined in the air; debris pounded to earth around me.

I brushed off flaming splinters and ash and stumbled to my feet. The twisted iron of what had once been a cannon lay a few steps to my left, and even as I rose a jagged chunk of steam engine clanged to earth ahead of me, hissing like bacon on a griddle. I staggered around it, stumbled on away from the explosion. Around me, others were rising too. But they were far too dazed to pay attention to me.

Reaching the cavern's far wall, I glanced up with smoke-stung eyes to scan the painted glyphs that marked the many exits. The prisoner I'd interrogated had told me which glyph identified the tunnel that would lead me to the other cannon-armed airships and, eventually, to Vohanna. That symbol was an eye pierced with four thorns, and when I found it I entered the dark mouth beneath.

To destroy the second ship I came from above. This vessel was not as close to being finished as the first had been, and the scaffolding over the decks was still in place. More elaborate catwalks ran from cavern wall to cavern wall, and there were boxes and bales of supplies stacked upon them. I climbed up the rock wall to one of the walks and then followed it down to the ship.

The chaos I had created helped me. Apparently, all work on this second ship had ceased as rumbles from the destruction of the first reached here. Even as I slipped into the cavern I noted laborers leaving the catwalks and going down to reinforce the guards for defense. They were all alert, but they weren't watching behind them and they went down like ranked rows of pawns slapped by a hand when the blast wave of a new explosion struck them.

At the third ship I made use of my gray cloak—a guard's cloak—and of sheer audacity. I raced across the cavern floor, shouting in apparent panic, my helmet seemingly lost, scratches on my face, the stink of smoke heavy upon me. The officer of the guard rushed to meet me. He grabbed my shoulders, shook me. His men gathered around, tension and dawning fear writ large on their faces, especially of those not "controlled" by Vohanna. When the crowd was big enough I suddenly discovered my tongue again, and babbled wildly of armies and demons and strange new weapons that brought fire from the sky through the very ground.

I babbled so madly the officer slapped my face and commanded me to control myself. With apparent difficulty I obeyed him—with true difficulty I avoided breaking his neck for the blow—and as the officer moved to snap out orders for defense of his ship, I slipped to the rear of the crowd, entered the vessel, found the black powder room, slaughtered the guards, blew up the ship and slipped away.

Where an army is expected, one man walks through.

Though I'd been told that there were four of the cannon-armed ships, I'd not yet found the last when I exited into a truly enormous cavern lit brightly by thousands of basketball-sized glow globes. Behind me in other caverns I'd left chaos and fire. Ahead it was peaceful and cool, as calm as a lagoon's surface during the still of midday.

From where I stood, a road of crystal as clear and fine as glass ran down into the bowl of the cavern. That road ended at a black stone pyramid so immense that it reached all the way from the ground to the roof two hundred tahng[7] overhead. Here, I realized, lay the underground portion of the pyramid that I'd seen in the jungle above. And I was instantly sure that inside those bleak, black walls I would find Vohanna's lair, and that of my brother Bryce.

The valley of the cavern was as quiet as moonlight, but that quiet was a deception, of course—a trap. I walked willingly into it. There was nothing else to do; I would not stop now.

The broiling, oven heat of the other caverns was mitigated here. My sweat began to dry as my shell boots clicked on the crystal highway. To either side of me grew leathery-barked trees in perfectly spaced plots, black-leafed ones to the right, silver-leafed to the left. They were vaguely similar in species to the brush I'd seen in other places here below, though much, much bigger. Each limb of each tree drooped beneath the weight of luscious scarlet fruit.

About a third of the way along the road to the pyramid I noticed that company had joined me. Between every column of trees, in shadowy light, stood a guard. There were hundreds of them. I saw Nokarra, Kaldi, Vhichang, Llurns, Ss'Korra, Humans, even Klar. Each was a massive example of his race, armed with black axes in perfect tattooed stillness, with shimmering webs of scarlet light in their eyes. Their heads did not move to follow me, but I had no doubt they were attentive to my passing.

Fifty tahng short of the pyramid, both trees and guards ended. And I saw finally how the plants here lived without sunlight. They were fed.

A moat ran around the base of the pyramid. It bubbled and roiled and was as scarlet as enemy eyes or the fruit of black and silver trees. Huge cables, hoses really, ran from the moat up to the trees, and where the thin covering of topsoil

---

[7] One tahng equals 1.02 yards.

had worn away I saw the pulse of fluid being pumped, or sucked, uphill toward the roots that it would nurture. Some mixture of blood and other substances that fluid was—the death of flesh to give life to root and bark and fruit.

Spitting the taste of such foulness from my mouth, I strode the bridge across the moat and stopped to stare up at the pyramid as it loomed in awful splendor above me. The black walls did not gleam but were dull and lusterless, worked with bas-reliefs, raised glyphs, and friezes. Most of the symbols were completely alien to me, twisted and ill-looking in some fashion I could not name. Or did not wish to.

Along the wall overhead were ledges and portholes and closed doors of rust-tarnished metal, with glimmering, slate colored steps connecting them all. But directly in front of me was the only door I cared about, the entrance to this benighted place. It was barely as wide as one man, made of black steel bars, and it yawned wide open. I did not find that openness inviting.

Glancing over my shoulder, I saw that the axe warriors had come out from their places amid the trees and stood like a barrier of flesh and iron on the road. It seemed they did not want me to retreat. As if I would have come this far only to turn back.

Shrugging, I stepped through the doorway into the pyramid, into a corridor that had been kept narrow for defense. Glow globes drifted lazily here, above my head. And above them, on the featureless walls to either side, there were shadow-mouthed holes through which, I imagined, burning oil or some nastier liquid could be poured down on attackers. I was glad not to be an army trying to conquer this place.

The corridor took several sharp turns—also for defensive purposes—and after the second turn I began to see darkened stairwells leading up into the interior of the building. I stayed with the main hallway and soon came out into a small, circular guardroom where at last I was met.

"Greetings, Ruenn Maclang," Diken Graye said, his voice without inflection, almost mechanical. At his back I tallied a dozen dark-feathered Vhichang with loaded and locked crossbows aimed at my chest.

The Vhichang are avian but they have human-type hands and arms instead of wings. The tips of the quarrels that nestled in their crossbows were discolored red and I doubted that it was rust. Thoughts of poison made my stomach clench.

I nodded to Graye. "Greetings," I replied.

My recent confederate's eyes alternately surged and ebbed with crimson, and a speck of toir'in-or stone had been inserted into his forehead so recently that the wound was bruised and angry around it. He was "controlled" more fully than any of Vohanna's servants I'd seen before, and I knew he was here for only one reason, to taunt me with the fact that the "goddess" had taken from me my last companion.

"I am sorry," I said to him. "I should have realized the witch would try to seize you. I should have warned you."

Graye's mouth opened and closed, as if he couldn't get enough air. His body stood atremble. His face twisted then; the crimson of his eyes waned.

"You...could not have known that...."

The words died away, leaving the mouth to hang slackly open, and a chill wave of gooseflesh swept my body as Diken Graye's features wavered and...changed. Eyes went dead black; lips seemed to swell, to ripen. Skin that had been ashen with pain turned as dusky as buffed and burnished gold. The mouth pursed around a tongue that dabbed at white teeth.

I had seen such a display before, but still it shocked. I wasn't going to admit it, though.

"What could I not have known...Vohanna?" I asked calmly.

And from inside Diken Graye's occupied form, Vohanna chuckled with a voice as sweet and sick as rotted honey.

"Why, you could not have known that anyone who has toyed with the discipline of the toir'in-or is susceptible to me. Well, *particularly* susceptible to me."

I considered, then remembered. Diken Graye had flown Rannon's airship on the day we crashed into the river above Timmuzz. That proved he had some training as a pilot and some knowledge of milkstones.

"Ah," I said, smiling briefly at her then, as if it did not overly concern me.

Vohanna/Graye turned her head to one side, like a hungry bird studying a cricket. I met her gaze, keeping my face neutral.

She looked me up and down, then waved a languid hand as if in dismissal of what she'd seen.

"But *do* tell me, darling Ruenn," she said. "Before I have you killed. What possessed you so foolishly to invade my home? To destroy my lovely ships? To kill my servants?"

"'Tis simple," I said, bowing my head slightly. "I had to prove to you that you need better servants."

She frowned, and for the first time I saw her look confused.

"What do you mean?" she asked.

"You *need* better servants," I repeated. "Someone like myself, for example. You see, I've come to swear fealty to you."

Chapter Twenty-Two

Oath of Fealty

"I've come to swear fealty to you," I had said.

Vohanna's eyes, so inky black within Diken Graye's face, did not blink. But I saw a flush of copper creep up from under the dusky-gold tinge that painted Graye's skin.

"You think me a fool?" she spat. "I should have you buried alive to rot among my trees. I should see you fat and bloated with krutt larvae as they feed on your insides. I should—"

"But you won't," I interrupted sharply. "Because it makes perfect sense that I'd offer my allegiance to you. My woman betrayed me. My friends died or ran. Or they are yours." I nodded toward the body she possessed.

"My own brother serves you," I continued. "And besides. I *don't* like to lose. Those who go against you...lose. But." I lifted my left hand, raised the index finger. "I'll not wear a milkstone for you. Had your servants been less controlled I could never have penetrated this far or blown up your ships. That was a mistake on your part."

Deliberately, I'd made my tone harsh; I imagined Vohanna had seldom—or never—been spoken to in that way. I figured my chances were about eighty out of a 100 that I'd be slaughtered immediately for insolence, but there was a possibility she'd be intrigued enough to let me live a bit. My hand rested on the ornate hilt of my sword. If death was my sentence, at least I'd go out with a weapon in hand.

Diken Graye's body stiffened, and drew itself up in a way that the man I'd known never would have done. Sweat slicked my palm as the witch's black eyes flashed at me. The moment was here; now I lived or died.

Vohanna...left Diken Graye. I saw the man's muscles sag as she abandoned him, saw the brightness of his eyes dull and the red return. In the room for a moment there hovered a presence. It had a sound, like telegraph wires humming. It had an image, like smoke and golden light swirling in a sunbeam.

It had a voice.

"Bring him to my throne," it said.

Then the presence passed from the room, and I was alone with Diken Graye and the Vhichang guards with their crossbows. Graye's body twitched. He lifted his head, the face and eyes inflamed, as if he'd been running a fever. From a corner of his mouth there dribbled a thin stream of dark spittle where he'd bitten at his own mouth.

With no words, but with agony in his red eyes, my one-time companion stepped aside and motioned me past him toward a stone hall leading deeper into the pyramid. Half the crossbowmen went ahead, half followed behind; and as we pressed on, other guards, of many races, stepped from dusty, silent stairwells and joined us. I was left my sword, though it would hardly be of use against such numbers.

Gradually the hall widened around us, until we came out into a large area lit by glow lights of a soft butter-gold rather than the harsher blue-white that I'd become accustomed to. The room was built in the shape of a half moon, with—at the heart of the crescent—twelve steps of white marble leading up to doors of argent.

The floor where I stood was tiled in cinnabar and ebon, with the tiles intertwined so as to draw the eye into interpretations, like seeing faces in clouds or in the leaves of a summer tree. I did not like what I saw there—temples built from burning bodies, rose-eyed skulls with black, pointed tongues—and I forced myself to look away, to look up toward the silver doors where four guards awaited.

The guards were Klar, of that reptilian race who are pirates, slavers, and savage fighters. Their nearly naked bodies were scaled in dark grey, tattooed and gleaming, with the flat, opalescent sheen of milkstone shards flashing from their foreheads. Each held a warhammer of black iron that was as long and thick as a stallion's leg. I walked toward them, Diken Graye beside me, and two of them turned and pushed back the twin doors for us to pass within.

At the threshold, Graye drew to a halt. I glanced at him, and his disconcerting eyes met mine and held. For a moment I thought he would speak, but he did not—or was not allowed. He stepped back, his gaze dropping to the floor, and I bit at the inside of my lip to keep from screaming in anger at what had been done to him. Then I turned and entered the throne room of Vohanna.

Despite an aura of veiled decay, it was instantly clear that this was a throne room made to stand *above* throne rooms, a place to impress enemies and allies alike. Undoubtedly it had been built when this ancient city was young, when Vohanna had been a "goddess" on Talera.

The walls of the room lifted in vaulted black marble thirty feet into the air, and oriflammes of scarlet silk were unfurled from ceiling to floor, billowing softly in a zephyr breeze that blew from some unseen source. On that breeze there also carried incense, aromatic and overly sweet. And from above me there arose a light of palest sapphire, not from glow globes, but from living beings captured and held between tall, fluted columns by razor-thin silver wires.

Those beings were Phylari. I had thought them mythological, for I'd seen them only in Taleran paintings where they were often used in the same way that angels are used by Earth's artists. But these were real and beautiful, suspended as if in flight by the wires piercing their ankles and wings.

The Phylaris' wings were covered with elongated scales that resembled vein-less feathers. As in the paintings, they had no fore-limbs and their hind-limbs were long and slender, delicately clawed for perching on the high rocky ledges where they are supposed to make their homes. The nearly translucent bodies radiated light in all the pale shades of blue, and even the large, tear-drop eyes were agleam.

I wondered. Had some earthlings once seen a Phylari? Had they drawn it for their fellows and thus given rise to tales of angels? It seemed to me at that moment, very likely.

Then a thousand tiny bells sounded, as if from the air itself, and my attention was drawn toward the front of the throne room. A raised walkway of braided copper wire, intricately looped, led from the door where I stood up through the center of the chamber to disappear within a curtain of fountaining water. But now, that shimmering spray began to still as, one after another, the fountains failed.

I saw the final guards then, beyond the dying veil of water, standing or squatting, on black and red squares that resembled those of a Kyrellian game board. Those guards numbered about forty and they were not human—nor any other natural race of Talera—but twisted hybrids of beasts and beings combined. Those that had hands carried curved swords of ivory-white steel; the others were armed with tentacles or claws. Yet, all of them were alike in the soulless crimson that filled their pupil-less eyes.

I started toward them, striding, and they opened the way for me. Above me in the air the Phylari were silent, and I knew that their silence was a sign of their profound suffering, for it is said of those angels that they sing constantly in melodies more fine than the finest kalina ever strung.

And then I saw the throne. Amethyst and jade it was, onyx and gypsum and lapis lazuli, quartz and opal and olivine, topaz and tiger's-eye. It sat on a dais of black marble veined with gold, with a fragrant dark wine purling down pale steps before it that were made of skulls. Above it circled more of the winged devils that I'd seen in the temple at Kellet's Bay when Graye, Valyan, and Kreeg had stood with me against many. And beneath the winged ones, on the throne, there was Vohanna.

Vohanna!

Source of all my pain.

Lodestone for my rage.

She looked no more than eighteen in Earth years. Her skin had the hue of rose petals dusted with amber-gold and blushed from beneath with health. Her moonlit silver hair was feathered with curls of pure snowy white and foamed down over her slender shoulders, down over the simple ebon shift against which her body thrust. All the way to her ankles those tresses coiled, and in no wind that I could feel they moved and danced as if alive.

Wings Over Talera, by Charles Allen Gramlich

There were no adornments anywhere upon Vohanna—no web of black pearls in her silken flag of hair, no bright jewels at her finely sculpted ears, no copper brassards clasping her upper arms. She wore no kohl to darken her sable lashes, no paint upon lips that were already riper than the rising sun.

In her form, she looked guileless and fragile. In her face, she looked...innocent. But her gaze was ancient and black upon mine, with firefly runes twining and beating in the depths of her glance. I felt that glance like a bruise.

Then her eyelids closed in a slow blink, sweeping from left *and* right like curtains over her pupils. And still I could see the blackness beneath the flax-thin membranes of those lids. She turned her head to the side, a mannerism I'd seen her employ before. And in a mocking tone she said:

"So. Dear, dear, Ruenn. Go down on your knees and show me how much you wish to serve me. Swear to me this fealty that you promise so well."

I chuckled, and Vohanna's lips curled with a feral flash of white teeth. It seemed she doubted my stated wish to serve her. Yet, something about me appeared to intrigue her. Was it the same something that intrigued her about Bryce? That we were from another world, perhaps? Surely she'd seen men from other worlds. She'd had them kidnapped after all. No, there had to be another reason why—when she finally held me firm within her grasp—she'd not had me immediately killed. I began to wonder what that reason might be.

"Well?" Vohanna asked.

Only seconds had passed since she'd first spoken, but already her glittering ivory nails were tapping on the incised stone arms of her throne. It seemed the goddess Vohanna had no more patience than a spoiled child. I wasn't surprised.

Smiling, I offered her an incline of the head. "Forgive me, Vohanna. It was only that your mention of 'serving' you made me think of Bryce. How...is my brother anyway?"

The woman smirked.

"Oh I assure you, Ruenn. He is employed at this very moment in carrying out critical duties for his...queen."

I felt my jaws grind but fought to maintain my smile. Then Vohanna leaned forward, her fingernails tinkling over the rubies and opals and diamonds embedded like pebbles in her chair.

"But tell me. Ruenn! Where is the other who was with you?"

I frowned. "The other?" I asked.

"Yes. When I saw you at Kellet's Bay you had the one called Diken Graye with you. And now he serves me. You had Eric Ryall and we all know that he is dead."

Again she smirked, but by now my smile was firmly etched.

"You had a savage who was dying," she continued. I knew she meant Kreeg. "And a warrior with green skin. A Llurn. Where is that one? That...Nakscherii?"

She almost hissed the final noun, the name that Valyan's people used for themselves. I remembered a similar reaction by Valyan when he'd first heard the name Vohanna in my presence. I remembered what he'd said: that the Asadhie goddess Ivrail had birthed his people, and that Ivrail's foulest enemy had been Vohanna. During the time known as the "God-War," Ivrail's and Vohanna's followers had burned hecatombs of the battle-dead in their names. It seemed old enmities still had potency for both Valyan and Vohanna.

But there was something more important here. If Vohanna was asking where Valyan was, then it meant she didn't know that I'd sent him to Nyshphal for help. It meant she wasn't aware of the fleet that was almost certainly on its way to attack her. For a moment, then, doubt whispered to my ear. What if Valyan had *not* reached Nyshphal? What if Rannon and her father had refused to listen and no fleet was on its way?

I shook my head and let Vohanna think it was only in response to her question. I whispered, "they'll come," to myself—for I had to believe I did not stand completely alone—but the words I let Vohanna hear were: "As I told you, my friends either died or fled. Valyan fled."

"Ah," Vohanna said, nodding. "Adequate servants are so hard to find and maintain. And the Nakscherii were always...fickle."

I glanced toward the scarlet-eyed guards that surrounded us, and up toward the membranous-winged devils that circled above with horns glittering and long tails lashing.

"Finding servants does not seem a problem for you," I said, looking back at the woman. "But then, I guess it helps if you make your own."

She chuckled. "Are you jealous, Ruenn?"

"I'm curious." I nodded to the twisted, bizarre creatures around us. "If you can make such hybrids, then why send slavers to raid other worlds for men? I know now it was *you* who sent the sorcerer who abducted my old ship's crew from Earth. Why? And why would you need Bryce, and Diken Graye, and so many others?"

Vohanna was still leaning toward me in her seat, and now she let her elbows drop to her knees and steepled her hands before her, letting her sharp little chin rest atop her index fingers. Beneath a drift of niveous hair, her brow furrowed.

"There are so many reasons, Ruenn. So many answers that I could give to your questions. I could tell you I draw slaves from other worlds because their families do not come hunting for them." She smiled and something darkly humorous danced in her eyes as she gazed at me. "At least until now," she added.

Then she lifted her chin from her fingers and nodded toward the hybrid servants that stood all around in perfect stillness. Her voice became a bell, ringing.

"Or I could tell you that such...synthetics, are costly to make. Natural slaves come cheap. And while the synthetics are deadly, they lack a certain level of initiative. Which is, I believe, something you pointed out as a weakness of my army."

She rose slowly to her feet then, and the silk of her shift grew taut across her slender frame, moving against her skin with a whisper of friction that suddenly thundered in *my* ears. She smiled, and spoke as softly as a caress, so softly that I could scarcely hear her over the beat of my blood.

"I could tell you such things. Ruenn Maclang. And they would be facts. They would be accurate. But they would not be...true."

She took a step toward me on her dais. The breeze blowing from somewhere within the room shifted and freshened.

Vohanna's scent closed around me, enveloped me in cinnamon and laurel, in saffron-cloves and smoke, in wormwood.

"The truth is," she said. Her eyes were huge. "I take slaves because I can. Because I like it." Her lips curved in a pout. "Does that make me bad...Ruenn?"

Her scent was like silken mud clogging my nostrils. My muscles trembled. The back of my mouth, the inside of my throat, grew dry and thick. My mind roiled.

Vohanna took another step toward me. And a third. Down the skull steps from her throne she came, and it seemed her sandals spurned the dusky wine that cascaded beneath her feet. Her eyes teemed with scarlet embers and with...other things.

"Kneel to me, Ruenn," she said.

My legs ached. My shoulders rounded. I dropped slowly to one knee, fighting to keep my head up. Only the salt wetness in my mouth told me that I'd bitten my tongue bloody.

"Bryce," I rasped. "What of Bryce? How...did...you take him? Was it like...this?"

Somehow, Vohanna was standing above me. Her hand reached and her fingers brushed a fallen lock of hair back from my forehead. Her knuckles were cool and dry, smooth as stream-worn pebbles.

"Do not fight me, Ruenn." Her voice held a gentleness that I wanted to believe in. "Your brother did not fight me. There is a world gate here. In this pyramid. You were right. It was I who sent the sorcerer to steal your Earth crew. Your crew, or any crew. I sent him from here. But Bryce shot him in the sphere gate on your side, and the resulting explosion dragged you both through to Talera. Only one could come back through *this* gate. It was Bryce, who went before you. And you were hurled far away across the planet."

My head was bowed, though I did not remember lowering it, and Vohanna's fingers played in my hair, her nails curving over my scalp. Her words took on a new intimacy, as if there could be no secrets between us.

"Your brother was badly hurt, Ruenn. Bleeding at his sheered wrist from the explosion that stole his hand. I healed him. Saved him. And yes, I took him. His mind was powerful. I knew then what an ally he would make. But you could be greater. By my side."

I felt myself drowning in the cool water of Vohanna's words, felt my mind letting go, giving up. But still, from somewhere inside, some part of me flailed for a hold, for something to keep my head above that water.

"Rannon," I whispered to myself.

And yet, Rannon had betrayed me. That last night in Timmuzz, she had seen to it that Kreeg was out of the way so that I could be arrested without hindrance.

Or had she? Could there have been some explanation that I'd been too angry at the time to seek? And there *had* been the parchment note, which I realized now must have been planted by Vohanna's agents. Its scribblings were engraved behind my eyes:

> Ruenn,
>
> Find an excuse and meet me. You know where. Soon, my brother. Nyshphal will be ours. Then you can have your princess-wench and a hundred others.
>
> Bryce

Who knew what else Vohanna's operatives had done to sew confusion in the land they planned to conquer? There had been reasons for Rannon to doubt me.

Yet, she had come alone to my room. She had believed in me that far, despite the hurt the note must have caused her. And whatever she had done, I knew it had been out of concern for the people of Nyshphal, whom she truly loved.

I thought then of Rannon's eyes, brilliant perse blue against the wicked black of Vohanna's, of Rannon's satin mane against the oiled, dancing tendrils of Vohanna's living tresses, and of Rannon's scent, clean and good while Vohanna's lingered like an erotic musk. I thought such things and trembled, and whispered again, louder.

"Rannon."

Vohanna's hand stopped its slow stroke through my hair.

WINGS OVER TALERA, BY CHARLES ALLEN GRAMLICH

"What?" she asked, her tone sharpening slightly.

My right hand drifted to my thigh, toward my sword's hilt. Vohanna was so close and for a moment I thought of killing her to stop her deadly ambitions. But even as I realized that I could not murder Vohanna in cold blood, her appeal came, and I sensed now the calculated drama of her act—everything for an effect.

"And still you fight, Ruenn. Why do you fight?"

I forced my head up, looked into her oblivion-gaze.

"Rannon," I said, out loud.

Vohanna's eyes went utterly and bitterly cold, and her mouth sneered in a way that robbed her of all beauty. She stepped back, her hands lifting, nails curved like talons.

"You are such a fool, Ruenn. And you will die for it."

"Then let it be by my hand," a masculine voice said. And I turned my head to see at last my brother.

Chapter Twenty-Three

Blood for Blood

"Bryce," I said, nodding slightly as I rose to face him.

It didn't worry me to turn my back on Vohanna. She'd enjoy this confrontation too much to interfere.

"Ruenn," Bryce replied, his voice mocking as he smiled with inked-black lips.

I glanced my brother over. He looked sick...and dangerous. His eyes were the rust-red of burned earth, with savage embers of bright ruby working in the depths where his pupils should have been. His hair hung lank over his shoulders to the waist, and it was white upon white where once it had been nearly as dark brown as mine. At least his features were the same, though whip-lean and with every inch of skin covered by snarling tattoos in red, green, blue, and gold.

My gaze dropped down to his right fist where it rested on the baroque hilt of a scabbarded saber. I had wondered what Bryce's "false" hand might be. Now I saw. It was a thing of spiderweb and bone, of articulated metal wired with jeweled copper. Over it moved a translucent latex skin through which waves of scarlet pulsed. There were only three fingers to go with the thumb.

I glanced back into my brother's eyes.

Bryce's smirk grew as he walked past me then and leaned in to dab a kiss at the corner of Vohanna's mouth. His eyes never left mine; nor did Vohanna's as she reached up and stroked long, thin fingers through his hair as if petting a cat.

"You two look sweet together," I said dryly.

Vohanna seemed to have regained the composure she'd lost when I rejected her bid to control me. Now she laughed, the sound bright and clear and as stinging as glacial ice.

"Poor Ruenn," she said, her lips pouting. "He misses his lady. Oh, I'm sorry. He has no lady anymore. She appears to have betrayed him."

"Appearances can lie, Vohanna," I said. I waved a finger toward her. "For example, you *look* lovely."

Bryce's eyes flashed scarlet. A growl erupted from his throat and he half drew his sword before Vohanna's hand clutched his weapon-arm, her nails biting into his skin.

"Above," she snapped with tight drawn lips. "You'll make him pay."

My brother's rage subsided instantly, as if he were a tamed ghyre on a leash. And Vohanna's words must also have been a signal because the floor gave a little jerk and began to move. Startled, I glanced down, then realized that we all—Vohanna, Bryce, the hybrid guards and myself—stood on a long, wide platform that was rising slowly, through the roof of the throne-room into the upper portion of the pyramid.

The movement was smooth, with scarcely a whisper of friction from the walls around, and in moments we reached the destination Vohanna had chosen for us. I turned, seeing that we'd come to rest at the border of a small, rectangular amphitheater whose floor was dusted with fine sand. There were tiers of seats to my left and right, with a tightly woven fence of wickedly barbed wire between those seats and the sand.

Directly across some two hundred feet of open space from me was a black wall in which a circular gray door was centered. That door stood closed but I suspected that beyond it would lie pens where prisoners could be held for this arena.

I looked toward Vohanna. She ignored the stands, returned to her throne and seated herself upon it with a flourish. Her winged guardians found roosts among the thick, dark rafters above; her other minions gathered around her protectively. Except for Bryce.

My brother walked past me onto the sand, his gaze still

locked upon me. He unfastened his sword sheath from the scabbard hooks on his belt, drew the blade and tossed the lacquered sheath aside. Breeks of black leather encased him from the hips down, and he wore a high-collared shirt of crimson silk that he stripped off and let fall like so much litter beside his silver-studded boots.

The blade in my brother's metallic fist glimmered evilly in the smoky light of overhead glow globes, but it was not the weapon that held my attention. In Bryce's throat, just where the left and right carotid arteries slipped beneath the clavicle of his collarbone, twin milkstones pulsed in obscene harmony. They'd been hidden behind his shirt collar and were the largest implanted stones I'd yet seen. Most of Vohanna's servants bore only specks of the toir'in-or but these were the size of hummingbird eggs.

Beneath the milkstones, down his chest, over his torso, the tattoos that marked my brother's face and neck continued. I saw...things there: will-o'-the-wisp images of scorpions and nightshade moths, and of reeths, those jaguar-sleek predators which Talerans sometimes call harlequin-wolves for their mocking smiles. And I saw what Diken Graye had once told me I would see. The tattoos moved. They crawled. Like a living canvas of scars.

I snarled at myself then, shoved away the cloying dread that threatened to overwhelm me. Bryce and Vohanna would not beat me so cheaply. I drew my own sword, the one that I'd taken from Eric Ryall at Kellet's Bay. Its blade winked as sharp in the light as Bryce's did. I, too, threw aside my scabbard.

Bryce motioned to me with his left hand, his fingers urging me to come. I offered him a cold smile and started toward him; but my thoughts burned. I could not kill my brother. I could not let him kill me. I'd carried some passing fancy of delay, of holding Vohanna's attention rapt until Hurnan Jystral and Rannon arrived with the Nyshphalian air fleet.

Foolishness. It was all foolishness.

But Bryce did not let me wallow in self-recrimination.

"Are you thinking about dying, Ruenn?" he called.

I stopped walking, and looked across a dozen feet of

sand into the crimson hellishness of my brother's eyes.

"Why, Bryce?" I shook my head. "Surely you know this hate you feel for me is Vohanna's doing."

He snarled but I kept on talking—while the milkstones in his throat pulsed opalescent.

"You and I were friends, Bryce. Not just brothers. Don't you remember?"

And now *he* started toward me. I took a step backward.

"Our parents raised us to *watch* each other's backs. Not to fight among ourselves. Blood for blood. You *have* to remember that! They loved—"

Bryce was too far away for an attack but he lunged at me anyway, his sword held straight in front of him, the muscles of his legs uncoiling like springs. I saw his blade coming in like blued lightning, whipped my own blade across to knock his aside. I leaped to my left and he turned off his left heel, a low growl bubbling from his throat as he rushed upon me again.

Nearly, he had me. I'd expected a moment of respite; he gave me none. His sword drove in, tip winking with light. I parried desperately. Once. Twice. My third blocking move was too high. I felt the jar as our blades struck together, heard the keen of steel on steel as his edge slid down mine in a wrath of sparks and came free. I missed the stroke that followed, felt the burn of a wicked razor slicing in across the outside of my left shoulder. Blood spattered my cheek.

I jumped back, startled. Seldom had I been so easily cut one on one in a sword fight. I backed farther away. Bryce chuckled, and followed.

I spared a quick glance at my shoulder. Too much blood ran to judge the depth of the slash, though the limb seemed to work all right. For now. Unless the wound clotted soon, though, it would *bleed* me to weakness.

"You're quick, brother," Bryce called. "But nowhere near quick enough."

As if to prove his words, he came charging, boots slapping lightly on the sand as he ran. I half crouched, sword ready. He hacked his blade down. I blocked; I was meant to. He spun right off that parry and slashed across toward me at the midline. I blocked again, and he spun left. I caught his edge on the back of my blade. Metal shrieked as our arms strained, as our muscles bulged.

Bryce slammed a shoulder into my chest, staggering me. He followed immediately with a swordsman's lunge, his body extended, his blade stabbed like a lance at my heart. I parried. Barely. He kept coming.

Damn, he was fast.

We fenced wildly, an electric flurry of light splintering from the swords. I matched him for a moment—parried, parried, riposted. And I missed as my blade whispered past his cheek and his own blade licked down across my thigh, slicing through the tough jeans as if they were linen and flaying fire across my skin.

I bit my tongue against the pain and stumbled back. Bryce held up for a moment, grinning at me insanely with black lips, his tattoos writhing like a nest of adders. At his throat the milkstones beat and beat, like pigeon hearts. From behind me came the chill tinkle of Vohanna's laughter, and the sound of her delighted clapping.

"Excellent, my love," she called to Bryce. "Excellent!"

Bryce sketched a short bow in his mistress's direction. Then he lifted his sword, brought its tip up close to his nostrils where they flared to catch the scent of my blood upon the steel. His gaze found mine over the blade, and he grinned at me again as his vermillion eyes churned with black runes that bloomed and burst in their depths.

"I am *so* enjoying this, brother," he taunted, as he lowered his saber and let the tip inscribe small curlicues in the air.

I was breathing hard, with blood running down my arm and down the leg of my jeans.

"Mom and dad loved us, Bryce," I gasped out. "It would kill them to see us now. If...." I looked directly into my brother's face. "If they could be killed. But they're already dead, Bryce. Did you know that? Our sisters too. Did you know? Did Vohanna tell you?"

It was a last bid on my part to reach through the witch's control and to touch the Bryce that I hoped still lived inside this vicious shell. But I knew that my emotional thrust had failed as surely as any by steel when he said in response to my comment:

"I didn't know, but I'm glad."

He chuckled, and slashed his sword through the air to send ruby droplets of my blood splattering from the blade. He twirled in place, arms up, head back, his voice growing into laughter.

Then he turned to face me and asked: "Ready for the end now?"

"Yes," I replied. "*Now* I am."

He smirked and stalked forward, the tip of his blade weaving. Again came his sudden lunge, faster than a striking cobra with his sword ablur. But I caught his weapon on mine, slapped it aside. He spun, saber coming around. I blocked that one too, and he dropped the line of his thrust. I met it, and the one that followed. Our swords locked for an instant at the hilts and Bryce looked surprised that I'd parried.

I punched him in the jaw with my free fist.

Now it was Bryce who staggered back, blood at the corner of his mouth. He spat to clear it, not truly hurt but incensed beyond thought. He snarled savagely and attacked. His blade arced down. I met it with my own. He disengaged, leaped to his left, slashed across his body at my belly. I blocked the blow an inch from my unprotected flesh, then riposted and the tip of my sword whiffed close enough to his chin to fan him with a breeze.

My brother hurled himself forward instead of back and I had no time to meet his hacking steel with my own. My left hand caught the wrist of his sword arm, stayed it. I tried to punch him again with the hilt of my blade but he snared my wrist as well and we stood chest to chest, straining. He growled at me like a beast, his face contorted, every muscle in his body strung tense as wire. But I was a little taller than he, a little heavier. He could not move me.

I butted him in the face with my forehead, felt and heard the cartilage crunch in his nose. He cried out in pain, blood spraying from his face. His legs quivered and threatened to drop from under him. Releasing his sword arm, I slapped him, open palmed, ringing his ears. And while his head snapped to the side I pushed him away from me, spun off my left heel and lashed a kick to his chest that knocked him on his backside in the sand.

Behind me I could hear Vohanna hurling curses now. I ignored them, waited for Bryce to rise. He got up slowly, shaking his head, but there was no fear in him. It seemed to me that the color of his eyes had changed, that they had lost some of their crimson luster, but his face was set and he lifted his sword and stalked toward me. I met him.

We did not circle to look for openings now. There were no fancy fencing moves, no feints. Toe to toe we came together, and our blades slammed, locked, broke away, linked again in a wild clanging frenzy of scraping metal. He cut me once on the arm. I cut his cheek. And still we fought face to face, on sand that was clotted with blood from both of us now.

Faintly to my ears came the sound of Vohanna screaming at Bryce to kill me. And then the screaming stopped. In that lull of sound, as if it were a signal, Bryce and I stepped apart. Our chests heaved; our bodies were raked with sweat. I could smell the stench of it, could taste the salt of blood on my tongue.

Bryce was looking toward Vohanna. I followed his gaze to see that she had risen from her throne. Her face was pale under the rose petal blush that marked her natural color. Around her, the hybrid guards milled in agitation. Bryce reacted instinctively. He took a step toward her but her hand lifted to halt him. She pointed. At me. Her voice hissed like scorpions on a griddle.

"They're here. You lied to *me*, Ruenn Maclang. You said your friend the Green Llurn had fled, but it seems you sent him for help. The fleet of Nyshphal is here. Soon the battle will be joined to decide the fate of this world."

Vohanna lowered her hand, and even as a fierce exultation tingled every hair of my body at word of the fleet's arrival, the witch gestured peremptorily to her guards.

"No time now for pleasure" she said. "Kill Ruenn Maclang. All of you."

Jubilation died as my mouth went dry, as the guards turned with one mind and marched upon me. Overhead, I heard the whir of wings as the flying hybrids released from their rafter perches and began to circle.

"No!" Bryce shouted. "He's mine!"

Vohanna's only response was an order: "Obey!"

Bryce glanced from Vohanna to me. His face was a rictus, his hand locked in bloodless rigor upon his saber's hilt. Over his shoulder I saw Vohanna spread her arms, hands turned up, and in her palms appeared twin milkstones of heart-of-night black. They seemed to emerge, like stigmata, out of her flesh.

A column of light, golden with shimmering motes, stabbed down upon the witch from overhead. An answering flame burst from her stones. Then I saw the reality of what I had only suspected. The thing that was *truly* Vohanna discarded its human form and swept straight up into the air in a glittering weave of rainbow-spun wings and crystalline jet eyes. It was the same being that I'd seen at Kellet's Bay.

A door rasped open in the roof and with a tiny thunderclap Vohanna went through it and was gone. The abandoned human body dropped to the sand like a discarded suit of wet clothes. No doubt, the witch herself was even now preparing her defenses against the Nyshphalian fleet.

And as for me, I had no defenses but a sword against the death that came on feet and wings against me.

Chapter Twenty-Four

At the Point of Death

There were three dozen or more of Vohanna's hybrid guards, unholy mixtures of man and horse and ape, of ghyre and reeth and half a hundred other Taleran monsters. There were the winged ones, shrieking like banshees as they whirled above me. And there was Bryce, with foam flecking his lips in rage at being thwarted by his mistress. He'd wanted to take my life himself; it seemed he would have to share.

I gripped my sword in clenched fingers, wishing suddenly at the point of death that I could at least say goodbye to Rannon. But still my body wanted to live. I began to inch away, seeking instinctively for something to put my back against.

For a moment, Bryce turned and snarled upon the others. "I told you he was mine!" he shouted.

And for a bare fraction of time the hybrids slowed.

I pivoted and ran.

There was a door, I remembered suddenly, almost certainly leading to a holding area for those who would fight or train in this arena. But was it an exit? Or a dead end? Either way, it was my only hope. To reach it. To get through. To flee.

Behind me I heard the bull-throated roar of the hybrid guards as they saw me run. I heard the shrieks of the winged ones as they saw the same, and heard the pitch of those shrieks alter as leather wings folded and they dived upon me. It was the change in pitch that saved me.

Wings Over Talera, by Charles Allen Gramlich

My boots pounded the sand. Dust rose. I heard the winged ones coming, felt them coming. At the last instant I threw myself to the ground. The umbral shadows of wings swept over me; a talon raked a gash across my scalp but *didn't* tear my head off.

I rolled and came up running. The door was right there. In front of me. I prayed it wasn't locked.

It was.

But it was made of wood and not metal.

I spun. Two of the winged devils launched themselves upon me. I slashed off a leg whose talons would have removed my face. The wounded monster screamed, swerved, crashed into its fellow. Together they pinwheeled to the ground. The others circled, looking for their opening. It wouldn't take them long to find it.

The first of the hybrid guards reached me. Most were huge, slow enough to give me time, but this one was some sleek mixture of tiger, reeth, and man. With nothing but teeth and claws, it hurtled at me on all fours. I swayed aside, hooked one arm over its back and one under its front legs to add my own weight and momentum as I rammed it head first into the locked door. I was practically riding it as it hit and we crashed through the wooden panels in a shout of splintering wood and the cracking sound of the tiger-reeth's skull.

I tumbled over the creature's body, staggered up again. A thrown dagger whipped by close enough to fan my hair, and the shock of that galvanized my legs. The holding area was not a dead end. I ran.

Down a long, dimly lit corridor I raced, with the impression of wooden pens crowding close on either side of me. The roof was low enough to prevent the winged hybrids from following, and when I glanced back I could not see Bryce either. But I saw and heard the stalking, slithering, thudding of the others in pursuit.

I ran faster, then stumbled suddenly as from somewhere deep under my feet in the pyramid there came a shuddering rumble. Dust puffed from the stone walls; hanging glow globes swayed. I fired another glance over my shoulder to see that the hybrid guards were still coming, two abreast, but they themselves were slowing as the pyramid's shaking continued.

Then the rumble intensified. The world seemed to rock. I grabbed at the wall to steady myself but a sudden jolting lurch threw me from my feet. Some of the hybrids were down too; others milled about, staggering, giving voice to plaintive cries and mewls of terror and surprise.

A stairway loomed to my left. I shoved my sword into my belt, pushed to my feet and grasped the stone railing to drag myself up the steps. I had no idea what was happening. Was it the fleet attacking? It was going on too long to be an earthquake.

Again there came a lurch that threw my boots from under me. My knee cracked on a step. A wall frieze crumbled, dropping blocks of engraved marble around me. I flung my arms over my head for protection. Dust exploded in my face, carrying the dry, worn smell of age.

Something slapped wetly around my leg and I rolled onto my side to see that one of hybrids had—somehow—managed to reach me. It had tentacles instead of arms, and the head of a woman on the body of a human male. Hag-eyes of crimson flared hate at me as its rubbery tentacles wrapped my thigh. I felt them rippling, squeezing as it tried to drag me downward.

Bile burst ripe into my mouth and I lashed out frantically with a foot, kicking, kicking. The heel of my boot pulped half the thing's face and it released me with a shriek as it tumbled backward down the steps.

Other screaming rang now. I thought it was mine until I heard the pitch of it rise inhumanly high and realized it was the building screaming, that it was stone scraping and sliding rawly on stone. On the landing above me, a hulking obscenity of a statue rocked and fell, went bounding metallically over me down the steps. I heard the tentacled hybrid squeal as the heavy bronze crashed upon it, pinning it beneath half a ton of weight.

Then I was on my feet, hurling myself up the steps despite the shaking. At the landing there branched off corridors to left and right while the stairs unwound forever above me. I took the right corridor, hoping my enemies would follow the stairs, hoping this tunnel would lead to an outside wall—and a door away from this place before it shuddered itself into pieces.

But even as I thought of the pyramid coming apart, and even as I sighted a door at the end of the corridor that I followed, the lurching tremors died away to leave no more than an eerie whisper, as if of silk sliding on callused skin. In the quiet, I knew Vohanna's guards would be after me again. And soon, if not already, the Nyshphalian fleet would be engaged in desperate battle outside this stone prison.

I had to escape; I hoped the door in front of me was the way. It was shaped like an oval, like a ship's hatch, and closed off with overlapping panels of steel. I feared it was locked and knew I could not break through it, but it irised open as I slapped the latch across its center.

Beyond, I saw an emerald flash of the spring Taleran sky. With an exultant shout, I leaped through the door—and found myself teetering on the lip of a narrow ledge, with the sharp incline of the black wall beneath me and a thousand foot drop between me and the green-brown earth.

The pyramid was airborne.

Chapter Twenty-Five

Heart of War

Vertigo gripped me as I balanced on the wafer-thin edge of a fatal fall. Wind beat at my clothes. A wild open sky screamed all around. Below lay the receding jungle, a blast of green among dry, brown plains. And pouring up from among the trees were long dark lines of saddle bird riders—Vohanna's army.

I ripped myself loose from the edge, threw myself at the open frame of the hatch through which I'd come, and grabbed hold. My heart sped like a loom-shuttle in my chest. The black pyramid was an airship, a dreadnought of the skies.

Abruptly our speed slackened. We drifted to a hovering halt. From below, the birds and their riders began to catch up, began to form phalanxes whose spears and crossbows spattered the emerald sunlight. Beyond the farthest such grouping, above the jungle, I glimpsed the forging air-fleet of Nyshphal, its flanks protected by squadrons of its own saddle bird cavalry.

Between the columns of out-fliers came the big ships, dark hulled against the bright sky, with maroon sails straining at the wind. Even at this distance I could detect the activity that beehived the decks of those ships. I could see the flags whipping and knew they bore the symbols of the Nyshphalian state and the crest of the house of Jystral—Rannon's house. I knew that upon those flags, too, were sewn the emblems of honor gained in hard battle by the great galleons.

Wings Over Talera, by Charles Allen Gramlich

A fierce pride swept me. I shouted out, though the wind tore the words from my mouth and I know not what I said. These were *my* people. Whether or not they wanted me, I had chosen them. And I would fight for them now.

In the next instant, I was made to realize how desperate that fight would be, and how all the glory and honor of the ships and their crews would not hold them safe from harm. Above and below me in the pyramid walls, portals slammed open and the evil black snouts of cannon poked through.

With a start, I remembered. There were supposed to be four cannon-armed airships in Vohanna's armada. Three I'd blown up; I'd not found the fourth. Until now. What devastation this one massive gun-ship could wreak among a packed Nyshphalian fleet armed with catapults and ballista I could only guess. And there was no one to stop that destruction but me.

A wheel-dagger caromed off the doorframe above my head, spalling off chips of stone that bit blood at my cheeks. It had been thrown from behind, from the corridor I had just exited.

I spun, dropping into a crouch, my sword seeming to jump into my hand. Three of Vohanna's hybrids had found me. Only three. The others must have split off to follow other corridors. I was lucky the wheel-dagger had missed, though it must have been an awkward throw from within the narrow hallway.

I leaped into the corridor to meet the three within it, where they could come at me only one at a time. The first looked human except for the clacking mandibles that would have been more at home on a mantis. It was he who had thrown the dagger, and only now did he reach for his sword. I repaid that little stupidity with a foot of steel through his insect mouth.

The second..."man" had three arms on one side of his body, four tentacles on the other. He hacked at me with a saber and I blocked it on the forte of my sword. We strained there, with no room to free our blades. But his tentacles were lashing, striking like hooded cobras. I felt the burn of suckers across my face and shoulder, felt my left arm wrapped in rubbery flesh and nearly jerked from its socket as he tried to pull me forward within reach of the knife held in his third fist.

I threw myself against him. Our long blades unlocked. I butted him savagely in the face with my forehead as he started to swing his dagger. He groaned with the stunning shock of that blow, lost control of the dagger. It cut a gash through my jeans and through the thin flesh over my hip, scraped on bone and then spun free of nerveless fingers to clatter against the wall. The grip of his tentacles went momentarily loose; I tore myself away.

He knew what was coming. Even with his face bloodied and his mind surely a kaleidoscope of bright pain behind his pupils, he tried to lift his saber. It didn't help. I stabbed him twice in the gut with my sword, then stepped back, my anger cold at being cut yet again.

The man's body spasmed; the red in his eyes faded. He suddenly looked...scared. Then he was smashed casually aside from behind and a bellow shook dust from the corridor walls as my third foe charged upon me.

There was nothing human in the creature that came against me now. He was massive as a bull—part reptilian Klar, part leonine Nokarran, part something that I could not name. He stank. His eyes were hell-kites of vermillion. In broad hands he carried a war-hammer with a head of black iron as big as my skull.

I slashed at him, cut him shallowly across the shoulder. He shrugged it off. Those shoulders were scaled thickly enough to turn his own flesh into viridescent armor.

There was little room for the beast to swing his hammer, but the head of it was crowned with a long, wicked spike that he thrust at me like a lance. I leaped back, and he stabbed at me again. Again I retreated, leaving blood in my boot prints as it ran down my leg under my jeans. The hip wound I'd taken was not deep, had not severed any muscles or arteries. But it bled and I was already weak from previous wounds and from days of nearly constant physical and mental strain.

The door to the outside loomed behind me. I'd wanted to hold my enemies in the corridor but I couldn't stop this one. My breathing was an echoing rasp in the narrow area. I gave ground; the beast followed in short rushes, thrusting his war-hammer ahead of him.

I parried with my sword to keep him off, then half turned and leaped through the doorway onto the ledge. He charged after and I slashed hard at him as I twisted on the narrow walkway under the open sky. He blocked with the bone-reinforced haft of his hammer, then spun the heavy weapon and drove it across his waist at me. I leaped back and the iron head of the thing slammed into the pyramid's wall, racking away cover stone to reveal the softer rock beneath. He'd almost had me.

The creature drew his hammer up, stalked after me as I backed down the ledge. The wind was cold on my clammy skin. I spared a quick glance behind me. Just a few feet away the flat stretch of walkway ended in steps that angled up the side of the pyramid. Beyond that was another flat stretch, and then more steps in a zigzag all the way to the top.

I'd looked away too long. The hybrid launched an attack. Somehow I dodged it, struck back with my sword quickly enough to carve a narrow groove over the inside of his forearm. There was no blood, but he roared in anger and smashed his hammer sideways at me in a tremendous blow. I ducked beneath it, slashed him viciously across the belly. There, too, he was scaled, and the armored hide turned the stroke, leaving no more than a deep scratch.

In the next instant the beast snapped the haft of his war-hammer up into my left shoulder. It was like getting hit with a sledge. My arm went numb. I staggered back. My boots caught on the first step behind me and I crashed down on my hip and side. Bright pain lanced through me as the hybrid raised the hammer and brought it shocking down.

Desperately, I kicked out, met the shaft of the descending hammer with the heel of my boot and deflected it just enough to make it miss me. His blow struck the stairs instead, with a clang that seemed to jar the whole pyramid. A piece of step cracked away and went spinning off into the sky.

I got my boots and hands under me and scrambled up the steps to another flat stretch of ledge. I rose there, turning to face the beast with my sword ready. For a moment we paused. Sweat ran and stung on my body. My heart slammed. There was no time for this. Already I could hear the roar coming up from the throats of Vohanna's bird riders as the first arrows were exchanged with the advancing Nyshphalian fleet. I dared not spare a glance.

I backed two more steps along the ledge; the hybrid started toward me, his boots stamping on the stairs. He moved in quick bursts, the war-hammer counting time like a pendulum in front of him. He was too strong. His hide was like chainmail. I'd cut him and cut him but the wounds seemed only shaving nicks on his massive frame.

The pyramid stirred, began to drift toward the approaching fleet, and the sloping face of the stone brushed my shoulder as my legs found their balance. The beast halted on the steps to catch his own equilibrium. He gloated up at me, as if sensing the growth of my fear.

But for now he was below me.

I exploded forward from my position but did not make my lunge directly at him. Two quick steps I took—up the slanting wall of the pyramid. And just as my momentum failed, I pushed off from the side, spun and lashed a kick into the hybrid's face. The blow did not hurt him, but even as my spine crashed against the pyramid and I slid down onto the steps at his mercy, the beast took a step back to counter the imbalance caused by my kick.

Only, there was nothing to step back on.

I saw the creature's facial expression change, saw the pupils and nostrils flare. He gave a cry that was half angry bellow, half plaintive mewl. He thrust out the hammer for balance, but it wasn't enough. And I watched as he toppled backward into the brightly lit void of the air. I rose to my knees, chest heaving, and saw my enemy spin into a black top until finally, far below, he joined with the jungle.

But there was no time to relax. The speed of this...ship began to increase beneath me. In moments her cannon would be brought to bear on the Nyshphalian armada. I forced myself to my feet, glanced up to the apex of the pyramid. Somewhere up there, I assumed, Vohanna would have her control room—in a place with an unobstructed view.

If I were wrong.... I shook my head. If I were wrong then all would be lost. There'd be no second chance.

Wings Over Talera, by Charles Allen Gramlich

The path to the top twined between cannon ports and no one could pass among them unseen. Yet, it would take too long to return inside and try to find an interior route. Besides, the rest of Vohanna's hybrids would still be hunting me there.

Maybe there was another way.

The wall of the pyramid was sloped and not completely smooth. Here and there were incised symbols of moons, milkstones, and monsters. Elsewhere stood out bas-reliefs depicting scenes of conflict and carnage. Sorry now that I'd thrown my sword sheath away in a show of bravado when I'd faced Bryce below, I slid my blade into my belt and snapped one of the scabbard-hooks through the ornate guard. Then I wedged a boot among stone carvings of Bacchanalia and pushed myself up to lie flat against the wall.

From there my fingers found holds and I began to work my way up the side, moving as quickly as I dared with a mile-long fall behind me. With my back to the sky, I expected at any moment to feel the thud of crossbow quarrels striking me. It would take only one glance from one being among Vohanna's bird riders to make me a target. Somehow that did not happen. I suppose their attention was focused outward on those who were coming to kill them.

Fifty feet from the pyramid's apex I reached a ledge wider than any I'd seen before, with a balustrade of shaped and polished iron. I leaned far out from the wall where my body wanted to cling, and let the fingers of my right hand curl over the top of the ledge. The stone felt dusty and slick there. I bit at my lip, closed my eyes with my heart pounding, and tried to convince myself I could let go with my left hand and pull myself up to safety.

My feet slipped, came free of the knob of worked stone upon which they had perched. I didn't *let* go with my left hand; that grip was torn free as my legs swung out over naked, hungry sky. That sky seemed to grab at me. My right hand slid, clenched, slid. I flailed upward with my other hand, clawed at the railing there. My feet dangled, my boots dragging at me.

Then my left hand caught an iron bar and locked in a death grip. My right hand followed. I pulled myself up and over the rail, collapsed to all fours on the ledge. Sweat iced my body. My lungs seemed torn as I gulped for air.

A broad metal door stood before me, sculpted basilisks to either side and a porthole just above filled with beveled glass through which pulses of light strobed. It was toir'in-or light, milkstone light...Vohanna's kind of light. There were no more openings above. This had to be the way to reach the witch.

I forced myself up, staggered toward the closed door hoping I could get it open, and the pyramid shudder-jumped beneath me. Grabbing desperately at one of the stone dragon heads, I hung on as a hammer of sound slammed into me like a physical blow. It was the bull-roar of the cannons being turned loose.

With a wild glance into the sky I saw the looming galleons of Nyshphal, their prows parting the massed ranks of Vohanna's bird army like sharp rocks parting river rapids. All around them were melees of saddle birds and their riders, struggling in black knots against the emerald sun.

But smoke was rising, from the mouths of cannon beneath me, and from the first battleship in the Nyshphalian line. Even as I watched, I saw that ship list and begin to slide sideways and down. Its masts crashed to the decks, the great canvas sails torn and blackened. I saw the flames lick up, ugly and orange as the hull caught fire. And there, at the heart of war, I saw men go spinning over the dying ship's rails, screaming to their deaths.

From behind, I was struck and knocked flat on the ledge with someone on top of me. It was Bryce, snarling.

Chapter Twenty-Six

Wrath

I'd not heard the door to the pyramid open behind me, but Bryce had come through, had knocked me down. And now he grabbed my head from above, smashed me chin first into the gritty stone of the ledge. My lips tore; a tooth chipped.

"I'll kill you," he growled. "Kill you with my hands!"

A hard knee pressed like a brick into the small of my back. My head was slammed forward again and I just managed to turn my face to save my nose, feeling instead a brilliant lance of pain that exploded in my cheek as it split over the bone. I tasted blood from my mangled lips.

The pyramid's cannons boomed a second time—in a wall of thunder. The ledge shook but I couldn't see, didn't know if another Nyshphalian galleon had been hit.

Blind fury rolled over me. I shoved myself up by my hands, lifting Bryce off the ground as I thrust to my knees. His boots rang on stone as he caught his weight on his legs. He snapped an arm around my neck, noosed it tight. I locked hands together in front of me and smashed them like a mallet back into his face. Twice I hit him. Heavy blows. He only snarled, lowered his head, wrapped his other arm about my throat in a stranglehold.

Choking for breath, I got my feet under me, stood. I was taller than he. He tried to hang on but I threw myself backward into the iron balustrade that curved the outside length of the ledge. The blow jarred us both. I felt Bryce's arms loosen and reached up, grabbing his wrists. I tore him free as

I jackknifed forward and flung him over my head. He crashed heavily down upon the ledge.

Rushing forward, I tried to stomp him, but he spun on his back and lashed a kick into my thigh. His face was a rictus with blood, the lips drawn back in a feral snarl. His kick slowed me and he rolled away to come to his feet in a crouch.

Again I rushed. He didn't wait for it but launched himself into me, head low. I was ready and swayed aside, like a matador with a bull, then smashed downward with the heel of my hand to catch him on the jaw. He went down and I kicked at his side. He caught my boot at the ankle and shoved me away, then flipped backward to his hands and from there to his feet.

He dropped to a fighting stance, the milkstones pulsing in his throat and his hellish eyes casting red shadows on his pale cheeks. But I charged into him again, too enraged to fence with fists and feet, wanting to get my hands on him. He was as full of wrath as I.

We came together, swinging, fighting in primal silence except for grunts of effort. Bryce slashed a fist into my side, above a place where I'd been cut. The wound opened but I felt no pain, only the blood running. I swung at his chin but the blow bounced off his shoulder. He was ducking, weaving as he worked his fists against me. I tried to head-butt him and could find no opening. He hit me again in the same side. Again and again. Triphammer blows. Now it did hurt.

I shoved him off me. He spun off his left heel and snapped a kick at my face. I blocked with an elbow, chopped down with my other hand into the muscle of his thigh. That muscle spasmed and when I pushed him away, he fell.

I kicked him brutally in the ribs and heard him grunt, but his reaction time was phenomenal. He twisted like an eel onto his side, bringing his legs up and around to sweep my feet from under me. I hit hard on my back, gasping for a moment at breath, and he swarmed over me, punching, slamming blows at my head that rattled my brain like a pea in a tin cup. I shifted my weight under his, snapped up with my knees, and flipped him over my head. He came down on the metal railing hard enough to wring a long groan from his

Wings Over Talera, by Charles Allen Gramlich

lips.

We staggered up at the same time, both of us groggy and worn. My brother, too, was breathing hard now. And sweat was on him. Even the tattoos that had writhed across his chest were still, as if they were as exhausted as the rest of him.

"Bryce," I started. And he charged me.

I grabbed his shoulder and arm, used his momentum against him, and threw him over my hip. He landed in a jarring tangle of limbs, but as I came after him he snapped a kick up over his head and caught me flush in the mouth with the toe of his boot. I staggered back, fresh blood at my lips and running down my chin, and with teeth loose in my gums.

The cannons boomed from beneath us in the pyramid. Smoke wafted up, stinking of sulphur. Bryce climbed to his feet like an old man. My own movements were no better. On earth we'd been trained by the same teachers. Our physical differences in size, speed, strength were minimal; we were well matched. But now we were both tired and hurt. And angry.

Yet, my rage was different from Bryce's. His was false, grafted onto him like a limb that didn't belong by the witchery of Vohanna. *My* anger was true, though not directed truly at my brother. I had reasons for my feelings, reasons that extended into my heart rather than lying on the surface of my mind. In the end, I thought my wrath would give me strength where his would not.

I spat a mouthful of blood over the railing as the cannons roared again like a voice from Hade's throat. The sound brought a thought to me, a possibility. The Nyshphalian fleet's catapults had not yet responded to the cannon that tasked them. They were still too far away.

I grinned, wolfishly I knew. Perhaps aboard the slave ships and in the lava mines of the Klar I had learned to bank my anger until it was *time* to stoke it. Perhaps I'd learned to temper fury with cunning.

I began to circle Bryce, bringing up my hands, my weight held forward over the balls of my feet. Bryce turned with me, cocking his own fists, until his back was to the railing and I saw over his shoulder that two more of the

Wings Over Talera, by Charles Allen Gramlich

Nyshphalian ships were aflame.

Saddle birds swept by with flashing wings. I glimpsed the pale faces of their riders, both friend and foe, and the flights of crossbow quarrels that leaped between them like dark rain. Many birds carried dead men still strapped on their backs, and though there were those among the living who saw us, none had time from their own battles to interfere between Bryce and myself.

Then I saw what I'd hoped to see. The fleet of Nyshphal had been battered but the catapults of the forward ships were finally within range of the pyramid. Galleon decks shuddered as those catapults released; I saw the dark boulders whipped skyward. The ships of the fleet could never pound through the stone-sheathed walls of the pyramid fast enough to keep the cannon from tearing them up, but that wasn't what I was hoping for now.

I waited; Bryce took a step toward me. It was only seconds but it seemed longer. The missiles of the catapults arced up...came down...toward the top of the pyramid...where we stood. Bryce did not know they were coming.

I tensed. And the boulders hit, raining down like giant hail cast from an ogre's fist. A sixty pound stone slammed into the rail of our ledge with a mad shriek of tortured iron. Others hit below us, and above, and to either side. The world rang with loudness.

Bryce's pupils dilated wide in surprise. He half spun to face the noise behind him. I loosed my rage, let it flame up behind my eyes, and I hurled myself forward, at his feet, rolling into his knees as he heard me coming and tried to turn back.

I swept his legs from under him. He twisted in mid-air, like a cat, but still hit jarringly hard on his side. From the ground I lashed a kick into his jaw, snapping his head back, then turned off of one elbow to drive the other down into his solar plexus. He lost his air explosively, eyes goggling as he jackknifed in reflex.

I got up, wrapped my fists in Bryce's dead-white hair and hauled him to his feet. He slapped at me weakly as he choked desperately for oxygen, and I chopped him across the throat with the blade of my hand. Then I ran him forward and threw him head first into one of the stone basilisks that guarded the doorway into the pyramid. He struck it with a thud and went down.

Still I was seething, standing over him with my mind gone wild and my fists closed so tight the nails bit into my palms. Wrath is hard to collar again once it's unleashed. It wants to prey. But my brother did not get up to provide a quarry.

The cannons fired. More catapult boulders crashed around us. Part of our ledge broke off and went avalanching down the steep side of the pyramid. But Bryce was not getting up.

In sudden anguished fear, I dropped to my knees beside him. Blood ran from his split-open scalp. "Bryce," I muttered, calling to him. He was my brother! And if I had killed him...."

My hand went out, grasped his shoulder, rolled him over. He did not stir, but in his throat fluttered a weak pulse. He lived! I breathed again.

More boulders hit around us. Another piece of our ledge cracked away. I glanced up from Bryce, saw the sky alive with flame and smoke and the wheeling specter shapes of vullwings and half a dozen other species of saddle bird, from the big hespern transports to the predatory kryll. The great galleons of Nyshphal forged on, trying now to encircle the pyramid and hammer it down. But the cannons bit at them ravenously, smashing one after another into tangled, drifting wreckage.

I got my feet beneath me and stood, dragged Bryce up and over my shoulder. I could not leave him here to be crushed by the Nyshphalian catapults. Between the carven basilisks, the gate into the pyramid stood open. The corridor beyond beckoned. Somewhere within this stone pile would be Vohanna, and there was little time to find her before the fleet was crushed.

Just inside the mouth of the corridor lay the sword Bryce had discarded when he'd chosen to take me with his hands. I plucked it up, sheathed it in my belt beside my own, then hurried forward along the polished and narrow hall. Light globes of dark purple made the air look bruised. Those globes shook, from the pulse of cannon fire within, from the pound of catapults without.

At corridor's end was a second door, also ajar, and I burst through it onto another ledge within the heart of the pyramid. A railing bordered this ledge also, and only the iron weave of that balustrade kept me from falling, for the core of the pyramid was an open well that seemed to drop forever beneath me.

My heart tripped, and slowly recovered its beat. Then a deep, low thrumming caught my attention. I looked up. The apex of the pyramid was scarcely forty feet above my head. But below that roof, suspended in the center of the well by a web of barbed cables, there hung a huge, black crystal sphere shot through with veins of pewter and bright brass. Shadows flickered like hunting bats around that sphere, and from within came flashes of intense violet-white light.

"Vohanna," I muttered.

Glancing wildly around, I searched for some way to reach the witch's crystalline lair. Then to one side I glimpsed a set of wide, bronzed steps that anchored that lair to the ledge upon which I stood. Bryce was getting heavy. I switched him from my right shoulder to my left, then raced around to the steps and up them. They ended at a silver door in the wall of the black sphere. I tried it. It was locked.

In raised metal relief in the door's center there loomed a tusked and horned skull of what is called among Talerans, a bane—which is supposedly the offspring of a demon and a human ghost. The mouth of the skull was open, the tongue extruded like a finger-less palm. On impulse, I pressed down on that tongue.

There came a quiet snick and four holes irised open in the metal forehead. I leaped back, but nothing issued from those openings and I cursed myself for a fool to not have considered a trap. I'd been lucky. But perhaps few enemies penetrated this far into Vohanna's sanctum.

I tried the door again. It was still locked. The holes were of different sizes, set in a tantalizingly familiar arc above the bane's eyes. I frowned. A thought occurred to me and was gone just as quickly. I couldn't grasp it. A key of some kind was what I needed. Or four keys maybe.

Wings Over Talera, by Charles Allen Gramlich

I sat Bryce down, leaning him back against the door. His breathing was steady but his head lolled. Already, he had been unconscious longer than I would have expected. It was almost as if his mind were in hiding, as if he were in some kind of coma. But there were other things I *had* to worry about at the moment.

It seemed likely that my brother had possessed something to unlock the outer door where he'd ambushed me. Perhaps it was the same thing I needed here. I checked his belt and around his neck, felt in his pockets and took off his boots to shake them out. There was nothing remotely like a key anywhere. I straightened, my mind sliding toward despair.

Bryce's hands rested on the floor beside his thighs. The false one twitched, chinking like metal against the stone. I felt my eyes go wide. Four holes! The thought that had tickled my mind a moment ago returned now to hammer me. Bryce had only four digits on his mechanical hand—three fingers and a thumb.

Grabbing my brother's shoulder, I dragged him unconscious to his knees and held him there, then grasped the fingers of his right hand and thrust them at the holes in the door. They fit! A rapid series of clicks sounded within the sphere's walls and I jerked Bryce's hand back just as the portal folded inward.

Through that opening I glimpsed multicolored lights that bloomed and flitted and burst. The very air throbbed in that place, and my heart and mind throbbed with it. Before me rose ten black steps that glittered with mica, with dark, metallic rails on both sides. I couldn't see Vohanna but knew she was there beyond those steps. I smelled the acrid tang of her sorcery, heard the sickly sensuous murmur of what was still, recognizably, her voice. And in the shivering air I could feel how drunk she was on the power of the milkstones.

The hair curled and leaped on my body.

I had seen what intoxication with the toir'in-or could do to a being. In the underworld mines of the Klar slavers I had seen it—when the Thye Vessoth priest known as Nethcormundis had tried to slaughter Rannon and myself. Steel had stopped that sorcerer, but I didn't think steel alone would be

197

enough this time.

There *was* one other weapon I could use. Possibly.

I laid Bryce on the floor and drew from his boot the antler-hilted dagger that was sheathed there. What I contemplated now might kill my brother. But it seemed to me that death was even more assured, for both of us, if I did not act. Nestled against each of the carotid arteries of Bryce's throat, just above where the bone of the clavicle ran, there lay embedded a milkstone. I touched one. It felt warm and oily.

Milkstones are power. Though I do not understand the laws governing that power, I know that the crystalline structure of the stones can be used to amplify and direct thought just as a properly constructed amphitheater can channel and enhance sound. The results can be—in the hands of an adept—sorcery. And yet, to use the stones is a matter of carefully attuned rhythms and harmonies. Breaking those harmonies is...dangerous.

Pinching one of Bryce's milkstones between my thumb and fingers, I pressed the sharp tip of the dagger to the flesh just underneath it—and hesitated. I recalled what had happened at Kellet's Bay when Diken Gray had cut a fleck of toir'in-or from Eric Ryall's brow. The blood had clotted almost instantly and the wound had sealed over as if the human body were rejecting the alien taint of the stone. But would that happen here? And what if I sliced too deep and nicked an artery? Would Bryce bleed to death? If the wound did not clot would I be able to save him?

From beyond the black steps came the high-pitched cackle of Vohanna's inhuman laughter. And as sure as if I could see it, I knew that another Nyshphalian ship had been torn from the sky.

My face burned with a sudden anger that was mixed with fear for both my brother and my adopted country; my teeth ground together from the need to act. With an oath and one quick cut, I passed the dagger through the skin beneath the toir'in-or and plucked the milky jewel from the left side of Bryce's throat.

I had cut shallowly but still the blood spurted. A scarlet jet of it pulsed across my leg and boot. My heart thudded and I almost screamed as I grabbed for the wound with my hand.

But then the hole was closing, sucking itself shut as a burst of some residual heat from the milkstone cauterized it.

Bryce jerked and heaved in apparent agony, but—like Eric Ryall before him—he did not awaken and seemed to slump deeper into unconsciousness as the toir'in-or was removed. Quickly, then, I cut the second stone free. Again, red fluid sprayed, and again the wound sealed.

I closed my right fist over the two stones. Crimson dripped from my hand. I picked up Bryce with both arms—he did not seem heavy—and straightened to stalk up the steps before me. At the top I halted, incarnadined with my brother's blood, and stood looking down into a small, hollowed area within the heart of the witch's sphere.

I saw Vohanna, and knew: death has wings and black eyes.

Chapter Twenty-Seven

Vohanna

Vohanna's sanctum was lined with niches in which bodies stood. There were dozens of the still forms, behind glass panels in rectangular recesses within the sphere's ebon walls. Human and inhuman waited there, the mythical and the extinct standing next to the common. Some of the bodies seemed more machine than flesh; others mimicked the cephalopod or the arachnid.

As strange as was that parliament of bodies, however, it was Vohanna who held the stage. I had time to *see* her here, as I had not that night in the temple at Kellet's Bay or in the arena below where I'd fought Bryce. She hovered above the floor, over a table of scintillant gold. Her four lower limbs were thin as sticks and seemingly useless. It was her wings that held her, and they were not feathered like those of birds, not membranous like those of bats, not brittle and diaphanous like insect wings. There were four of them—blue, red, black, yellow—and they were moist and translucent as they beat. Through the skin I could see a webbing of platinum bones and what resembled razor-thin wire.

Vohanna's fragile, insectile legs dangled beneath an abdomen that looked like an elongated human torso. Her upper body was sexless and glinted dully, as if made of chitin or some glazed ceramic armor. But her hands were beautifully human, with four delicate fingers that danced a ballet over a matrix of a dozen milkstones loosely embedded in the surface of the golden table. From those stones her moving fingers wrung sprays of light and a whispering, haunted melody that I knew must provide power to this ship's engines and guns. And to its mistress.

The table over which Vohanna labored was near the far wall, across the floor of the sphere from me, but though the witch faced in my direction she did not see me. Her gaze was held by the display that swirled and eddied in the air before her eyes. It was, I suddenly realized, a simulacrum—a replica—of the war outside.

Struck to stillness by such sorcery, I watched as the scene roiled with miniature war-birds from the armies of Vohanna and of Nyshphal, all of them wheeling and dipping in wild disarray. The galleons of the Nyshphalian fleet were there as well, like fist-sized clots within the tapestry of battle. Though concentrated fire from the big ships had torn gaping holes in the hordes of Vohanna's bird riders, nearly half the Nyshphalian vessels were aflame. Cannons had pounded them, and some in Vohanna's army still carried— and had used—the exploding crossbow quarrels. I had not, apparently, blown up *all* the quarrels when I destroyed Vohanna's three other cannon-armed ships.

Vohanna seemed to have a few small manned flyers as well, and they had entered the fray to worry the wounded galleons like wolves at an elk. With their masts and catapults wrecked, the damaged Nyshphalian vessels were easy prey. I saw one such ship, tiny in replica though it would have been huge in reality, being cut to shreds by coordinated arbalest fire from a group of five enemy flyers.

Then, from out of the sun's glare swept a dark-hulled warship with maroon sails straining at the bright sky. It came down upon the five flyers from above, veering close into the wind in a feat of sailing worthy of heroic sagas. A bronze ram that I knew to be the length of two men gleamed like a splinter at the warship's prow. But it was magnificent. And the black clusters along the ship's rails had to be soldiers massed and ready with weapons.

The enemy flyers saw the bigger ship coming. I watched their bows start to turn. But there was no time. The warship was on top of them, coming down at a hard angle. Its oaken hull rode straight across the upper-structures of two flyers, smashing masts aside, splintering wooden cabins, turning crowds of fleeing men into red smears against the decks.

Then the heavy ram took a third flyer straight through the heart and sheered its way out the other side. The flyer's wooden hulls exploded with the impact. Knots of struggling figures were thrown free of the dying ship to pinwheel like dark dots toward the earth.

My heart surged; I almost cheered, for even in diminutive I could see the flag snapping at the mast of the rescuing warship. It was gray and maroon, bordered with gold and with the image of a trenkil, the Taleran eagle, charged in its center. I knew that flag; I knew that ship. It was the personal war-craft of Hurnan Jystral, emperor, father of Rannon—and Rannon was aboard it. The woman I loved could have been nowhere else.

Below me on the floor of the dark sphere, Vohanna laughed. My exaltation fled as my throat choked in sudden panic. My glance found the witch, saw her attention focused upon Jystral's vessel, saw her lift one delicate finger and stroke it over a milkstone that vibrated rapidly in its small hollow of metal. That single stone flickered from opal to scarlet, and even as I screamed out, "No!" it was too late.

From deep within the pyramid came the shuddering thrust of the cannon firing. I saw the Nyshphalian flagship hit, saw flames erupt as the masts and proud banner fell. And then I saw only Vohanna as her gaze rose to mine and locked. Bodies burned in the depths of her eyes. Lovers entwined their silken limbs. Visions of horror and beauty followed one upon another, beating against my awareness.

Somewhere in my mind I knew that Hurnan Jystral's ship was torn, though not how badly. Perhaps Rannon was hurt. Or dead. Yet, I could not rip myself away from Vohanna's soul-less orbs. Her pupils were black rubies within black ovals—scorpion eyes in a face that was inhumanly lovely. She chuckled, though how that sound arose from such an alien throat I did not know.

The unconscious Bryce slid from my arms and thumped to the floor. Trapped by the witch's mental compulsion, I *could not* care. Before, when I'd faced Vohanna in human guise, she had tried to conquer my mind with hers and almost succeeded. Only my use of Rannon's name as a mantra had saved me. This time, in the winged body I'd begun to think of as her natural form, the Asadhie's power was much greater, her hunger much worse. My spine curved; my knees trembled; I bit my tongue on a scream that could not escape my constricted lungs.

"Mine," Vohanna said. "Bent to *my* will."

I tried to shake my head in negation but found myself shackled by Vohanna's eyes. There was nothing else in my universe.

Then there came one other thing. There came heat. *Heat*!

A searing lance of pain leaped up my right arm. My right fist burned! I lifted it, amazed that I could move it under my own volition when the rest of my limbs belonged to Vohanna. From within the clasp of my fist, light poured, shining *through* flesh and bone with the incandescence of a tiny sun. Or, two tiny suns. It was the milkstones that I had removed from Bryce which flamed.

In that instant, Vohanna lost control of me. She gasped, her coal-colored eyes flickering with a sudden lambent yellow. She drew back slightly from her table, wings snapping in the air. The battle simulacrum froze in mid-movement, and my lips twisted in a savage smirk as my self-mastery flooded back and I whispered into the sudden stillness.

"Greetings, Vohanna! Shall we chat again about killing me?"

The toir'in-or stones still kindled in my palm but the pain was bearable and I was not about to release them when they had just saved me from Vohanna's mental chains. Instead, I used my left hand to pluck Bryce's sword from my belt where I had thrust it in beside my own.

With the tip of the blade, I pointed at the small replica of Hurnan Jystral's crippled warship where it sat stilled within the frozen weave of the simulacrum.

"If the woman I love is not dead aboard that ship, Vohanna," I said, "then I might suffer you to live. But you *will* stop this attack immediately."

Vohanna did not speak. All the taunting sensuousness of her manner was gone, and it seemed that what she had left was only the hard kernel of hate that filled her heart. I'd not even been alive when first that hate coalesced, but now I was the lightning rod to which it leaped.

The witch closed her eyes, and when she opened them again an instant later her sockets had emptied of flesh and filled with stone—with twin toir'in-or of perfect black. On the table before her, the other milkstones rattled in their matrix like dried acorns in their gilded metal cups.

Vohanna reached one hand toward me, to swat me like a fly. Her fingertips gathered light, pulled it in from the air like streamers of bright ribbon. The matrix table jiggled; the whole room went hot with a surge of static electricity that played over the walls like knots of St. Elmo's fire. The black toir'in-or in the witch's eye-sockets flushed with sick scarlet, darkened, then flushed again like the beating of a rotten heart.

To use milkstones is a matter of carefully attuned rhythms and harmonies. To break those harmonies is to beg disaster.

In the moment before Vohanna unleashed her power upon me, I tossed the milkstones from my right fist into the air, dropped my right hand to join my left upon the sword, and slashed the blade across with all my strength. The steel tip caught one stone; the edge caught the other. A backlash of molten energy slagged my blade to the quillions in an instant, but the two damaged gems whipped toward Vohanna at incredible speed.

The Witch tried to dodge—didn't quite succeed. One stone smashed her in the chest; the other hit the wall of the sphere behind her head. The world went white.

The sword-hilt cooked in my palms, but before my reflexes could react to *that* pain the ruined weapon was torn from my grip as a shock wave rippled the air like water. The nexus of power that Vohanna had planned to release outward at me went off in all directions around her instead. A crescendo of sound and bright flame churned the matrix table into gravel, shattered most of the glass doors over the niches where the bodies stood, and exploded outward through the wall behind Vohanna. I was thrown down as that surging wave of power hammered me in the chest.

Where the witch had stood, there brewed a volcano of

fire and light. Wolves of flickering red heat ate at the marble floor; the roof of the sphere vaporized and the top of the pyramid blew off as a radiant column of sparks sliced through it like a giant lance. The pyramid staggered as if its engines had stalled.

With my senses stunned, I scrabbled for Bryce and threw myself across his prone form as chunks of burning rock fell around us. No being made of flesh could have lived through that inferno, but in the next instant Vohanna came shrieking out of the chaos, her lucent wings on fire in patterns like moiré silk. She hurtled wildly at me, her voice keening, and whipped past close enough to singe my hair. Then madly around the room she whirled, smashing into walls and floor and ceiling.

Blinded, I thought. I hoped it was permanent.

But I wasn't going to trust in Vohanna's blindness. I staggered to my feet, teetering for a moment on legs that felt like spindles. The flames from the explosion of the milkstones were spattering away like the dying embers of fireworks. The cannons had fallen silent, or else my ears were deaf to them. But the pyramid itself was still moving, adrift on vagrant currents of wind. How long would its engines keep it aloft before the last erg of toir'in-or energy drained away?

The same burst of power that had ripped out the wall of the sphere behind Vohanna had also torn a gaping hole in the basaltic outer skin of the pyramid. That rent was big enough to drive a team of horses through, and on the other side of it winked the emerald sky of Talera. Lifting Bryce in my arms, I stumbled toward the open air, wanting it, hoping for something, hoping at least that the fresh, clean breeze would start to revive my brother, who only seemed to be slipping deeper into coma.

Behind me, I heard more glass shatter and glanced over my shoulder. Somehow, Vohanna had put out the flames eating at her and was now smashing the crystal panel that covered one of the wall niches. A body stood there, one of the few left undamaged after the destruction of the matrix. It was a hybrid—gargoyle and Amazon. Nearly eight feet tall it stood, with blazing red hair that flowed to its waist, with two arms and two legs that were hideously corded with muscle. Its skin was dusky gray. Its face was pocked with scars and knobbed with the bony protrusions of short horns. Yet, its lips were female and full, its breasts cupped in gold beneath the silver links of chainmail.

I had almost reached the opening in the wall, limping with Bryce cradled across my chest, but now I froze as a new horror blasted my already dazed mind. I saw Vohanna move against the gargoyle's body, saw her wings beating at its ribs. Then the suddenly stilled form of the witch fluttered to the ground as the other body stiffened and stirred. Sable eyes opened. A fanged mouth bellowed rage as one massive hand grasped a battle-axe and used it to bash a way out of the coffin/box that now seemed far too small for its owner's bulk.

I'd just discovered the secret of all Vohanna's forms. Here in this place she kept the bodies that she inhabited at will, the bodies that lived only because her mind told them to live. The sight galvanized me as few others could have at that moment.

I whirled and rushed toward the opening in the outer wall. Better to fling Bryce out of the pyramid, to let him shatter on the earth below, than to give Vohanna a second chance to own him. From behind me came a series of bestial growls and one quick glance showed that the gargoyled Vohanna had leapt to the floor of the sphere and was coming fast, the axe like a sharp cross of black light in her fists.

Then there was nowhere else to run and the torn wall was before me, its edges ragged with broken masonry. Through it I saw groups of bird riders whipping by above and below, some of them nearly close enough to touch.

I pivoted to face the witch of Talera in her savage new form. She was almost upon me when the mass of the pyramid stuttered and I thought we were going down. But Vohanna went rigid in mid-stride and in the next moment the huge ship caught itself and plowed on. Was it luck, or some heroic mental effort of the sorceress? Either way, I didn't think it mattered. Luck or sorcery, time was leaching away. How much longer could the pyramid stay aloft? And if I fought Vohanna here the battle would be long. I doubted we'd live to see who'd win.

WINGS OVER TALERA, BY CHARLES ALLEN GRAMLICH

Bryce and I had thrown away our sword scabbards before our fight below. But the scabbard-hooks were still on our belts. I snapped the empty hooks on Bryce's belt through my own, binding us together before I stepped to the very edge of the wall and counted for a heartbeat. Then I threw us both out of the pyramid.

Chapter Twenty-Eight

Wings Over the Jungle

Outward I leaped, from the pyramid into the sky, with Bryce held like a child in my arms. Downward we hurtled—five feet, ten feet—with the wind shrilling cold around us. But I had timed my jump, had tried to time it, to the movement of the saddle birds racing by in formations.

Beneath us swept a troop of hesperns, those massive birds which are primarily used as transports and which compare in size to a vullwing or a sabrun like a Clydesdale compares to a Shetland pony. From inside the pyramid I'd seen them coming, a dozen of them. We struck one.

The hespern's rider had not heard or seen us, did not know what was about to happen as I drew my legs up and hit him in the shoulders with my knees. He was snapped forward brutally over the neck of the bird. Bryce smashed down across the man's back as I grabbed desperately for a hold on something.

The impact of our falling bodies seemed to collapse the hespern for a moment. It dropped sickeningly beneath us. Bryce slid down the rider's back, slammed into my chest and knocked me further along the bird's broad, piebald flanks. My right foot slid out over the void; my hands scrabbled, clawed, caught one of the tough leather straps of the saddle. That strap stretched. But held.

Bryce's unconscious body slipped past me, nearly jolting my hands loose from the saddle strap as he tumbled off the side of the bird and was jerked up hard by the scabbard-hooks linking our belts. The bird *had* nearly recovered itself, but now its right side took a sudden dip. It gave a terrified squawk as its left wing beat wildly at the air to balance the weight differential. I was jerked further out to the right side of the bird's body, the tendons straining like living wires in my arms. Bryce hung from my waist, dangling over emptiness.

The hespern's rider groaned. I'd thought the impact of Bryce and I crashing down upon him must have snapped his spine, but it seemed we'd only stunned him. If he saw us now.... One quick slice of his knife through the strap that I held and all would be over but our fall.

I lurched forward, on my belly along the back of the bird. Other saddle birds swept past us, their riders gawking at what had appeared suddenly in their midst. I ignored them, got both my hands over the saddle's extended rear cantle, pulled myself up to my knees by main strength. With quivering arms, I dragged Bryce up beside me.

The hespern had lost some altitude but had fought its way back to level flight and was starting to circle, venting a plaintive call as it sought to locate its formation. So far, everyone was leaving us alone, too startled to know how to react. That couldn't last. In moments we'd be recognized for enemies and crossbows would be turned loose to raven us.

Then the hespern's rider sat up, coming suddenly back to full awareness. As he started to turn, still not realizing exactly what had happened, I snapped one arm around his neck from behind. He jerked in shock and grabbed with both hands at my elbow. That left my other hand free to snake down and whip his belt dagger from its sheath.

The rider had his head half turned toward me within the lock of my choke hold. The whites of his eyes glistened. He saw me lift the dagger and flailed for my wrist with one hand to keep the blade from his throat. But it wasn't his throat I wanted.

I slashed down with the blade alongside his hips, slicing through the ties that all bird riders use to keep them in their seats. The man gasped, realizing too late what I planned as I twisted hard with my other arm and threw him off the side of his own mount. The sky took him. I didn't hear him scream.

I thrust myself down into the bird's saddle, dragged

WINGS OVER TALERA, BY CHARLES ALLEN GRAMLICH

Bryce up and unhooked his belt from mine to loop it tight over the pommel horn. I reached for the cut ties to knot them around me, but the shadows of two vullwings raced past and when I glanced up I saw they were circling, coming back toward me with emerald sunlight lancing from their javelins and bows.

Forgetting about tying myself in, I grabbed the hespern's reins and worked the ones to take us to the right and down. In that direction lay Hurnan Jystral's galleon. I could see it, and the smoke that rose over its cannon-shattered upper structure.

Glancing back for pursuit, I saw that the two vullwings had paused, for reasons obscure to me. Silhouetted in the light behind them hung the great pyramid of Vohanna. And, even as I watched, that huge black dreadnought lost its last ounce of toir'in-or power and plummeted like the stone it was toward the earth.

A grim smile curved my lips before I turned my attention back to the hespern. The wing-stick had been lost on the arm of the previous rider, but the beast responded to its reins beautifully as I began to guide it swiftly down through the flotsam of war. All around us were riderless birds and birds with dead men in their saddles, birds with blood rusting on their grey or black or brown plumage. It seemed to me that those among the enemy who were still living were starting to pull back, to withdraw—as if the loss of the pyramid had suddenly chilled their ardor for battle.

A shadow warned me too late that my own battle was not over. I was struck savagely in the shoulder, knocked forward over the neck of the hespern with my right arm numbed halfway down my side. A kryll sliced past within inches of us. Its talons had struck me a glancing blow but failed to grip. On its back rode Vohanna in her gargoyle-Amazon form.

Where Vohanna had gotten a saddle bird from I did not know. Perhaps she'd taken it the way I'd taken mine. Perhaps she had conjured it. Either way she had the advantage in the air. The kryll is a raptor, green-eyed, bold yellow in coloring, with spurred claws for holding prey and a curved beak for tearing it. The hespern is no match for it in either speed or viciousness.

I jerked the down-rein taut, then loosed it to give my bird its head. Immediately, the hespern went into a dive. Vohanna was just below us and I tried to ram her smaller bird with my bigger one. But the kryll was too quick and slipped to one side, then turned almost upon its own length to come after us with a snap of wings. I heard a doubled cry, Vohanna's and the kryll's, as they launched their pursuit.

Though agony shot through my right arm, I forced movement from that limb as I grasped the hespern's reins. I didn't know if the shoulder was fractured or merely badly bruised, but I had to use it anyway as I sensed the kryll nearly upon us and tried to haul my bird to one side and out of the way. I almost made it. The kryll missed *me* with its talons but hooked the hespern along one broad flank, ripping out feathers and bits of flesh.

The big transport bird shrieked in pain and went into a steeper dive. I hung on, Bryce bouncing unconscious across the saddle in front of me. Off to one side and below us, I could see Jystral's flagship and fought to turn the hespern's head toward it.

Again, Vohanna dove her bird upon us. Though Bryce's sword had been melted into slag back in the pyramid, I still carried my own blade thrust through my belt. I drew it now, tried to slash up and over my head at the reaching talons of the kryll. I hit something.

The raptor veered away with an angry squawk, then came back hard under the goading of Vohanna. I swung at it again, had the sword jerked from my hand as a three-inch claw raked across my wrist. For the second time, then, the kryll struck at my mount, tearing away gobbets of meat.

The hespern faltered. Just beneath us but still off to the left loomed the wounded battleship of Hurnan Jystral. It was close, but maybe still too far. I sawed on the reins, trying to force the bird's head up. It fought me, then seemed to give in. With a low moan that could almost have been human, it quickened the beat of its wings. We rose, drifted over the ship.

With a scream of rage, Vohanna drove her bird directly into mine. The kryll's talons stabbed down, shearing through the hespern's wing; its beak struck, tearing a chunk from my bird's neck that left arterial blood spurting.

The hespern folded, plunged downward toward the ship's deck fifty feet below. I hauled back on the reins, screaming at the bird to respond one more time. Above me I heard Vohanna shriek in triumph, or perhaps it was my imagination giving voice to the wind that rushed past us.

The deck loomed, polished oak blackened by fire, coils of rope twining between fallen masts and bloodied flags. I saw lost helmets and splinters of white wood torn from the hearts of the masts. My throat was raw in the wind from shouting; I stood in the stirrups, hauling back so hard on the saddle bird's reins that one of them snapped in my fist.

Men on the ship were gaping up at us, gore-branded and soot-charred, with their grim hands clutching grimmer weapons. There seemed so few of them. I saw their eyes widen; many turned to run. They thought we were going to hit the deck at the speed of free fall. I thought so too.

But just as I was about to release the reins and drop down into the saddle to cover Bryce, the hespern found courage from somewhere and brought its beak up. Its wings grabbed at the air as the legs shot down in an attempt to find a perch.

The torn wing threw the hespern off balance. Its right leg snapped as we landed badly and I was hurled from the saddle. The bird squealed in pain and fear; I hit the deck hard on my back, losing my breath as the holystoned planks slammed me in the shoulders and spine. It would have been much worse if the hespern had not made its attempt to land.

Gasping for air, I tried to roll over amid the litter of spent weapons and the wreckage of a once proud ship. My muscles felt bruised all the way to the bone. My vision wavered, full of spicules of dark and light.

Bryce! my thoughts screamed. Did he live? I couldn't see him, hidden as he was behind the bulk of the crippled and dying bird.

Boots thudded on the deck, men running toward me. I heard a babble of voices. My vision started to clear of floaters; my lungs began to suck in oxygen again. I pushed onto my hands and knees, lifted my head to find myself ringed round with spears. I knew no faces among the gathered crowd.

"I'm a friend," I said quickly. "I'm Ruenn Maclang."

Startled recognition flared in many eyes. Some of the men lowered their weapons and stepped back. Others did not.

Then there came a savage shriek filled with pure, poison fury. Everyone's head turned. Vohanna's kryll had landed at the prow. The gargoyle-witch dropped from its back with the black axe in her hands, its edge cutting at the light. I could not tell which of the two, bird or being, had vented their anger in a screech. Perhaps it had been both.

Three of the men who stood over me, hard-bitten warriors carrying stained steel, raced forward to defend their ship. The kryll struck at one and took a lance-cast through the eye that put it down. But no weapon's edge came close to Vohanna. She thrust a palm toward her attackers and a blast of dark fire smashed them to the deck.

"Ruenn Maclang!" she shouted, ignoring the fallen men who writhed at her feet in agony. "I want Ruenn Maclang."

As the rest of those around me drew back slightly, I started to call out, to tell the witch where I was. But a third figure stepped between the two of us. This one I knew. He was of that race known as the Vlih, with skin dark as oiled jet and equally dark hair hanging in a coarse mane down his back. His fists were empty of swords for the moment. No blades were strapped to the two muscled tentacles beneath his arms. But Rhandh, bodyguard of Rannon Jystral, was never unarmed.

"Don't!" I shouted. "Rhandh! It's Vohanna."

But my warning came too late as the Vlih weaponmaster dropped his hands to the daggers at his belt and lashed them up and at Vohanna in one lightning move. By now the whole fleet must have known of the "goddess" Vohanna and her power. Valyan would have told them as he led them here. And Rhandh had seen what happened to those who hurled their bodies at the witch. Perhaps he thought steel alone would be faster, and it was. Just not fast enough.

One of Vohanna's hands flashed white and the thrown knives spattered into molten metal that rained sizzling to the deck. With her other hand, the witch almost casually tossed a ball of flame at Rhandh. The Vlih tried to dodge, nearly succeeded, but the whirling corona of the ball brushed his shoulder and the whole thing exploded, hurling him to one side like a discarded bit of rag.

Others started forward then. Half a dozen. Then a few more. I thought it must have been nearly all that was left of the ship's crew, but I knew the character of the Nyshphalians and knew they would not quit until Vohanna was stopped...or they were dead.

The latter seemed the stronger possibility at the moment.

"Wait!" I shouted as I pushed to my knees.

Vohanna's gaze fell upon me and the men halted their advance in confusion.

I looked at the witch. "Here I am," I said.

She smiled with a terrible curve of her lips, showing yellow teeth that had been filed into miniature skulls tipped with tiny dagger points. Her hand lifted and a finger pointed toward me that dripped rainbow embers.

"Time, Ruenn," she said. Her voice was almost soft.

I smirked, started to get up. If she were going to kill me, it wouldn't be on my knees. But a new voice, strong and vibrant, melodic, cut through the tableau, stilling us both.

"Ruenn Maclang is mine," Rannon Jystral said. "You can't have him."

I could not help but look toward the one who spoke, though Vohanna held my death in her hand. And what I saw snagged the breath in my throat. Rannon stood near the rail of the ship in a chainmail shirt and leather breeks. Her greaves and helm were of silver alloy, her buckler of bronze. She held a crossbow and a rapier whose blade was soiled with blood. There were others near her but she was the only one I noted. She was...exquisite.

Vohanna did not seem impressed. She chuckled as her glance explored Rannon's weapons and dismissed them.

"I'll leave you his husk after I eat his soul," she said.

I drew one knee up, placed my foot flat to the plank floor in order to stand and be ready if Vohanna threatened Rannon. For the first time I noticed a coil of rope nearby, maybe thirty, thirty-five feet long. One end had been cut but the other snaked through the debris to loop firmly around the stump of a shattered mast. On impulse, I reached for the sheared end where it curled near my boot.

"No," Rannon was saying in answer to Vohanna's comment. "I'll have Ruenn safe and sound. As my husband." She sounded absolutely sure of herself, and her words were like a cool kiss on my fevered heart. Rannon loved me still. As I loved her.

"But you," Rannon added to the witch, her voice growing harsher, "will *get...off...my...ship!*"

Pride swelled in me. But my hands were working as I knotted the free end of the rope around my ankle. Vohanna's attention was locked on Rannon, whose words had enraged her.

"I'll crush your ship like a rotten grape," she raved. "And all its crew will serve me as—"

I exploded from my crouch and hurled myself at Vohanna. She heard me coming, jerked her head around to face me, her palms lifting, fire smoking from her fingers. I felt the electric heat of that charge as it coalesced, but she had no time to release it.

I hit her in the stomach with my shoulder, wrapped both arms around her steel-muscled thighs as I drove her backward. The ship's rail was right there and we splintered through in a shriek of tearing wood.

Vohanna's sharp-nailed hands clawed at my shoulders, at my hair. Her mouth was open, shouting curses. The wind tore past us. Pieces of shattered wood rained down alongside us. The rope dragged around my ankle as it uncoiled like a whip across the ship's broken railing.

Ten feet we fell. Fifteen.

I let go of the witch with my arms, tried to shove her away from me. Her rage mutated into fear, into terror. Her curses choked in her throat as her eyes went wild. She clutched tightly at my shirt.

At twenty feet we hit the end of the rope and I screamed as it snapped taut, nearly wrenching my leg from its socket. The woven cord held. For a moment, so did Vohanna. Then my shirt tore and the witch dropped suddenly away from me, flailing at the air like a poor swimmer as she tried to reach across that expanding distance to find me again.

Directly beneath us was a second Nyshphalian galleon, rising toward us to come to our aid. It was still a hundred yards down when Vohanna hit on her back directly upon the spear-shaped head of the vessel's flagpole. That bolt of metal ripped through her spine and erupted a foot out of her chest in a spray of blood and tissue.

She hung there. Impaled. Her body jerked. Blood welled like dark lava out of her mouth and spilled down her chin. Her hands that had grasped at empire grasped now at air and found it just as impossible to hold.

A last spasm wracked her; her arms dropped to spread out wide from her sides. Vohanna was dead. And over the curve of the rescue ship I saw the massive cloud of dust that had spiraled slowly up from the jungle below where her pyramid had met its own end.

The war was over.

Then a fresh scream was wrung from my lips as the rope was jerked from above and I was hauled upward like a bait on a fishhook. The world spun crazily beneath my head before a dozen sets of strong hands grasped my legs, my hips, my shoulders, and dragged me backward over the rail of the ship.

I saw faces that I recognized—Valyan, Rannon's father, and her brother. There was only one face I wanted to see. And then I did see it as Rannon Jystral dropped to her knees beside me and rained kisses on my face that scalded hot with tears.

Chapter Twenty-Nine

Afterwar

It was hushed in the hallway where Rannon and I walked. Outside these palace walls, the heart of Timmuzz beat with the sounds of manufacturing and trade, the sounds of a country once more at peace. But here, where our feet spurned soft rugs of golden weave, a late afternoon stillness held sway. And things were not *quite* at peace.

After the fall of Vohanna and her black pyramid, the witch's saddle bird army had melted away rather than face the hammering of the Nyshphalian war-fleet. Then, troops had landed to clean out the caverns beneath the jungle. The remaining gunpowder and the notes on the making of the powder and the steam engines had been confiscated. Even now, Nyshphalian scientists toiled to build a new generation of weapons and airships. The technological genie was out of its bottle on Talera, and I regretted it. Who knew what changes would be wrought on this world that I loved in the next ten or twenty years.

But, in truth, I was thinking little of possible futures at the moment. Rannon Jystral walked beside me. The cedar and rose scent of her hair and skin was a living thing in my nostrils. Her breathing was as clear and sweet as a carillon's ring.

She stopped at hall's end, her fingers resting on the brass handles of a set of thorn-wood doors. I halted with her, dressed at least partly in bandages and limping a little on my right leg, which had been dislocated only a few days before in that final fight with Vohanna. My gaze sought Rannon's and lingered. She smiled, a bit wanly I thought.

"Don't tell me," I said jokingly, waving a hand toward the closed doors. "You've planned a surprise party for me."

I wanted to hear her laugh, but she didn't. She shook her head, then said: "There's been no time for us to speak since Vohanna's death. Too many duties. Too many worries over whether Bryce and Rhandh would live."

She was right. After our flurry of shared kisses on the deck of her father's ship, we'd been forced in different directions by the needs of those we cared about. Soon, days had passed with little more than kind smiles, stolen hugs, and a few words of concern that only scratched the surface of what we needed to say to each other.

"That talk can't be put off any longer," Rannon continued. "But first there's something I want you to see."

She pushed open the doors and stepped inside. I followed, stopping just beyond the threshold. Rannon walked to the center of the room and turned to face me. She wore a long-sleeved gown of white velvet, belted with silver. Her eyes were as blue as I'd ever seen them, richer still than the richest blue of the clearest sky my old Earth had ever known. Her face was pale around ripe lips, with silken hair cascading like a dark waterfall past her cheeks and over her shoulders.

"While you were away from me," she said. "On Earth. I had these rooms built. I never got a chance to show them to you...before...." She trailed off, then just stood there watching me.

I glanced about. The room where we stood was broad and open and airy. Afternoon light slanted through crystal windows where the shutters were thrown back, and in winter I knew the sun would warm this space through the glass.

Though the palace was built of dark granite, planks of yellow pine had been laid over the stone here. And over the planks were tossed thick rugs rich in sunset colors. To either side of the main entrance loomed a massive fireplace, cold now in the glory of spring, and the scattered pieces of furniture were carpentered from sturdy oak and bansul and teak, with only the inlays of rare samphur wood to indicate their costliness. The effect was neither feminine nor masculine, but warm...comforting. I liked it.

Wings Over Talera, by Charles Allen Gramlich

To left and right were other doorways leading to other rooms. The left side was a sleeping area; I could see the bed standing huge on legs of winter-dark wood, piled high on top with furs and quilts. The door to the right was nearly closed and I walked over to push it wide. I knew immediately what the room beyond was meant to be, in months or years to come. The ceiling and walls were frescoed with scenes of brightly colored kites and balls, and of animals dressed like people. Children were to be raised and loved in *this* place.

I turned to look at Rannon, my mind seething with questions. But she had moved away to open a set of casement doors that led, I suspected, onto a balcony. I was wrong. When I followed her through those doors I found that we were on the roof of one wing of the palace. And it had been transformed—into a rooftop garden where ahmbr trees drooped with blossoms of white, vying with apple and pear to shade narrow pathways of pearl-colored stone.

Alongside those paths, spring's early flowers were in riot—goldenswords and black lilies, silver nyxe, yellow angel-hair and crimson hysis. Honeywhisper moss hung in the trees, dewed with cool mist from twin fountains of jade and garnet.

Between the fountains stood a gazebo whose latticed sides were twined with roses and pepper ivy. Rannon had paused there and was looking back at me. Tears stained the clearness of her azure eyes.

I started toward her, to try an offer of comfort, but she held up a hand to stop me. I halted, hovering while she fought for control. Only when she regained it did I feel the strain in my chest from not breathing, and the tension that ached in my jaws where they had been clenched.

"I want you to *listen* to me," Rannon said.

My palms slicked with sweat; my heart began to thud—out of fear that her words would not be the ones I wished to hear. But mutely, I nodded.

"After you...left," she continued. "I hated myself."

I opened my mouth to deny her statement, but shut it again just as quickly. She'd asked me to listen and I would give her that no matter what.

"Yes," she continued. "It didn't matter that I'd intended

for you to surrender yourself to me, that I'd never planned for my brother to come barging in with soldiers to arrest you. I doubted you. And for that I hated myself."

Her eyes searched mine and she did not look away as she said, "I'm sorry."

"But I ran," I said into the pause that followed her last words. "Surely that cemented my guilt in everyone's mind."

She shook her head, leaving strands of fine hair caught like wisps of dark silk over her cheeks.

"For my father and brother, it did. And for many among the nobles who were jealous of you. But not for me. I knew why you fled. I saw your eyes. You ran because the one who claimed to love you, doubted you. Hurt you. For that I won't forgive myself. For that," she did look down then, "I release you from all pledges you have made to me."

I froze. It didn't seem as if I'd be able to breathe again. "You...." I almost choked on the words. "You do not wish to marry me any longer?"

Rannon looked back at me again, and there was in her face a look of genuine surprise.

"Did you not see the rooms?" she asked. "Built for us? And the nursery where I hoped our children would be raised? Did you not understand what they meant?"

I stared at her, then looked down myself.

"I hoped," I said.

She stepped forward and cupped my chin, lifted my head slightly to let her gaze explore my face. There was a question in her eyes, and to it I replied:

"If you cannot forgive yourself, then I cannot forgive *myself* either. If I had been stronger. If I had not doubted too. I would have let myself be arrested, knowing you would set me free."

She smiled, a little. "I would have," she said. "I know I would have."

"Then forgive," I said. "And let me forgive. And we'll not talk of such things again because there will be no need."

It seemed a long time before she spoke.

"Spirit and skin," she said. "I will always be yours."

To that there was no reply I could make.

At least not in words.

Epilogue

"What About Their Eyes?"

Hand in hand and smiling, Rannon and I went to check on those we cared about. The burns that Rhandh the Vlih had taken from Vohanna's sorcery were healing. Rhandh himself was muttering and angry over being confined in bandages. I thought that a good sign.

Kreeg was improving as well, though still weak and pale from nearly having the life crushed out of him at Kellet's Bay by that laith. His constant companion was Valyan, healthy himself, of course. Even Heril had returned from his journey and was a welcome face to see. He'd been my friend the longest of anyone upon Talera.

I regretted only two things. First, I regretted that Diken Graye had not been found. He had *become* a friend and I would have seen him pardoned for his unwitting and unwilling service to Vohanna. But not even his body had turned up. Second, I wished I'd been able personally to thank the Druidess, Ahrethane, who had aided me in the jungle. In a quick return to her leafy bower, I had searched for her and found nothing. On her table I'd left the boots I'd borrowed, and a note of thanks telling her to ask for me in Timmuzz if she ever needed anything.

One other thing had happened that caused me no regret but gave me pleasure instead. In searching for Diken Graye among the ruins of Vohanna's pyramid I had found the very rapier that my cousin Eric Ryall had carried and which I had taken for myself after his death. That weapon had been torn from my hand by Vohanna's saddle bird while I'd fought for my life against her Amazon form. Its blade was the sharpest and strongest I'd ever held, and I had learned since that it was forged from what is called Tyzinn steel, the secret of which is lost to the modern age.

Now, though, I was far more concerned with Bryce than with any sword. His room was open when Rannon and I arrived, but there were guards at his door and bars on his windows. He was sitting propped up on pillows in bed when we entered, his disconcerting silver hair coiled down across his shoulders. He turned to look at me with eyes in which the pupils were starting to show again through the rusted red. That red was itself fading gradually, leaving behind the natural grey irises with which he'd been born.

"Bryce," I said, approaching him.

"Ruenn," he replied, his voice steady but...hollow. I noted that my brother's artificial hand was hidden beneath the covers and was grateful for that. I started to take his other hand, reconsidered. Rannon stood patiently behind me. Bryce had not acknowledged her.

It seemed I hardly knew the man before me.

I could think of nothing else to say, at first. Then my gaze caught in the luminous lines of ink that had been worked into nearly every inch of Bryce's exposed skin. The brilliant colors were fading a bit, I thought, and hoped it was not just a wish.

"The physicians found specks of milkstone in your tattoos," I said at last, gesturing at the scrawled runes on his body. "But they said they got them all."

Bryce nodded, no change in the flatness of his gaze, then settled back against his pillows until he was looking up at the ceiling. I saw the puckered scars at the sides of his throat where I'd cut out two toir'in-or myself, but I was thinking of what our cousin Eric Ryall had told me when I'd asked him about where *his* other milkstones were implanted.

"Inside," he'd said. "In my guts."

"What of Vohanna?" Bryce asked suddenly, and I felt a little chill, as if a tiny, snow-laden wind had slipped its fingers along my back. "When I first woke up, you said she was dead."

After Vohanna's death, as if triggered by that death,

WINGS OVER TALERA, BY CHARLES ALLEN GRAMLICH

Bryce had awakened from his mysterious coma on the deck of Hurnan Jystral's flagship. He had said nothing, done nothing at first but lie still and stare into the sky. I'd told him that Vohanna was finished and that we'd erase every sign of her and her evil.

He had smiled then. Or smirked.

Now he smiled again, in the same way.

"Dead. Yes," I said against his smile. "She died impaled and torn open. And we took her down to the jungle and burned her on a pyre made from the ruins of her ancient city."

Bryce chuckled when I finished, and turned a face toward me that was as pallid as dying moonlight.

"I know what you're thinking," I said defensively. "That Vohanna can change bodies. I saw her do it myself. But none of the bodies from her lair were close enough for her to enter. Besides, we burned *them* too, or what was left of them after the crash of the pyramid."

My brother's stare did not go away; it began to anger me.

"*And*," I continued, "if she'd possessed someone we would have found it out. Those black eyes of hers would have given it away. I watched for them. I checked everyone on both ships that were involved. Vohanna is dead!"

Bryce drew his strange right hand out from under the blankets and reached up to idly stroke the scars in his throat where I'd taken his milkstones. Then he turned his head until he was staring once more at the ceiling.

"Of course, Ruenn. Surely you are right. But...."

"But what?" I snarled.

My brother gave that little half smile again. His voice was distant when it came.

"But what of the saddle birds, Ruenn? What about *their* eyes?"